CHILD'S PLAY

British Library Cataloguing in Publication Data. A catalogue record for this book is available from the British Library.

Revenge Ink
Unit 13 Newby Road, Hazel Grove, Stockport Cheshire, SK7 5DA, UK
www.revengeink.com

ISBN 978-0-9558078-5-5

Copyright © Kia Abdullah 2009

Typeset in Paris by Patrick Lederfain

Printed in the EU by Pulsio

CHILD'S PLAY

Kia Abdullah

Revenge Ink

For my sisters, five of the strongest, most beautiful women I know.

CHAPTER ONE

Everything about him reeked of perfection. From his precision Alexandre haircut to his polished Armani brogues. He sat, moodily nursing a Scotch, green eyes scanning the room once, twice, three times.

Allegra saw him first, eyes alighting on his solitary shape. She stood, watching the way he ran his fingers through his hair, the way he traced them along the serrated edge of his knife, the way he rested them on the dark wood of the grand Georgian table.

Every waitress had her eyes on him, lured by his film star face, dark hair, and athletic body in his expensive suit with his expensive smell. Allegra smoothed her long chestnut hair and strode towards him.

He stood, tall and confident, and offered his hand. She shook it firmly, the instant attraction jerking through her body. Taking a seat, she adjusted her posture so to appear sophisticated, elegant, nonchalant.

"Ms Ashe, thank you for joining me at such late

notice." His smooth, rich voice was comforting; familiar somehow.

She shook her head. "Not at all. It's my pleasure, sir."

He held back an amused smile. "Please – call me Michael."

She nodded, skin aflame under his gaze. She relaxed her shoulders and lifted her chin, exuding indifference.

A waitress flitted over, coyly glancing at Michael before turning to Allegra. "May I get you a drink?"

Allegra drew her eyes from his. "I'll have a glass of white wine please."

Deep lines creased across the waitress's forehead, cracking her thick makeup. "A white wine?" she faltered. She glanced at Michael and then leaned in towards Allegra. "I'm sorry, Miss," she said quietly, "but may I see some ID? We would lose our licence if we were to serve alcohol to an underage person."

Allegra felt the blush spread across her cheeks, shattering her veneer of sophistication. Eyes downcast, she reached for her bag and pulled out her driver's licence. The picture depicted her smooth olive skin, large hazel eyes and bee-stung lips – features frequently mistaken for those of a teen's.

Satisfied, the waitress jovially announced, "One white wine coming up," and sauntered off.

Allegra watched amusement dance in his eyes. She held his gaze and asked, "So, what can we do for you?" Silently, she wondered if he too felt the chemistry between them.

He examined her for a few seconds. "Do you enjoy your job, Ms Ashe?"

She sat back in her chair. "Please – call me Allegra."

He smiled, revealing deep dimples. "Allegra."

She took a moment to steady her voice. "Yes, I enjoy my job very much. ImageBox consists of a small but hardworking team. Each of our clients receives its own designer – I would be yours. We work with our clients in a synergetic way. We take *your* ideas on board and–" She stopped, mid-gesture, halted by Michael's raised hand.

"You don't have to give me the hard sell," he said, eyes boring into hers. "Just talk to me."

She nodded, caught off guard by his sudden informal manner.

"So tell me, Allegra, is what you do important?"

"Graphics design?" She paused. "It's important to a lot of people."

"Is it important to you? Not just because it provides an income, but the actual work you do."

"Yes, of course."

"But there are more important jobs you can think of?"

She bit the corner of her bottom lip, suddenly annoyed with her boss for sending her to this meeting with no information. How was she supposed to sell to a client she knew nothing about?

She shrugged, uncomfortable beneath his gaze. "Yes, there are doctors and teachers and policemen – they have important jobs."

He nodded, pleased with her answer. "Allegra, I want you to come and work with me."

She blinked in surprise. "We would be delighted."

He held up his hand again. "No, you misunderstand. I don't want ImageBox – I want you."

She felt her cheeks redden. "I'm not sure what you mean."

He glanced around the near-empty restaurant. "Allegra, I work for a small government unit which targets criminals – a very specific type. We do good work. You could say we're like doctors and teachers and policemen all rolled into one."

She looked at him blankly.

"Part of my role is recruiting new field agents. I'm a head-hunter of sorts. I would like to recruit you."

She waited a few seconds. When he said nothing, she started to laugh. "Is this one of Jonathan's tricks?"

Michael shook his head. "I apologise. I used ImageBox to set up a meeting with you. I know it was unethical but I needed to talk to you on mutual ground to explain my proposal."

Allegra bristled. "I delayed a rare dinner with my family to come and meet you this evening. You're telling me I'm wasting my time?"

Michael reached forward and touched her arm, sending sparks across the pit of her stomach. "Hey, listen, I'm sorry. Please just hear me out." His eyes held hers.

Fragments of an old song ran through her mind:

Your eyes are burning holes through me. I'm gasoline. I'm burning clean. "I'm sorry, but I really am very happy in my job." She stood to leave but he stepped in front of her. "I've given you my decision," she said falteringly, unnerved by the magnetism between them. As she drew back, Michael took hold of her wrist in a grip so hard, it almost hurt.

"Don't go." His face was inches from hers.

Taken aback, Allegra struggled to free herself.

He tightened his grip on her wrist and pushed a card into her hand. "Take this," he urged. "Please just think about it." With this final plea, he released her.

Allegra looked to the card, cheeks burning with indignation. The name 'VOKOBAN' was written along the top with 'Michael Stallone' printed beneath it in small letters. *No wonder he thinks he's Rambo,* she thought indignantly. By the time she looked back up, he was gone.

She blinked in his wake, still able to smell his smell and feel his fingers wrapped around her skin. Her body shook as the knot in her stomach crept down her body, inching past the navel, and settling in the tight curve between her legs. Gathering her thoughts, she slipped the card into her bag and stalked out of the restaurant.

"Baby sister, you're late," accused Sienna.

Allegra winced and crunched up her shoulders in mock shame. "I'm sorry. I texted you. Jonathan sent me to a last-minute meeting."

"It's okay, I'm used to you. Just don't complain if the meat's too tough."

Allegra smiled. "I *never* complain about meat being too tough," she replied with a dirty laugh.

"Incorrigible." Sienna ushered her in with a hug and closed the door.

"Speaking of incorrigible, where's the rugrat?"

With perfect timing, Reese poked her head into the hallway. "Who're you calling 'rugrat'? I'm already taller than you." At 5'3", she was an inch taller than her aunt.

"*Well, nobody's perfect,*" replied Allegra, challenging her niece in the Movie Quote game they often played.

Reese raised a brow. "That's *easy* – 'Some Like It Hot'."

Allegra sighed exasperatedly and bowed in defeat. "Alright kiddo, I'll get you with the next one," she threatened.

Sienna slung an arm over Reese's shoulder. "Right, you two. Food's ready so let's eat. And Allegra, no hard meat jokes – not in front of the 13-year-old, however precocious she may be."

Allegra laughed. "I promise." She followed her sister to the dining room and took a seat at the grand oak table.

"Speaking of precocious, I'm gonna need to go up a bra size," said Reese. At 13, she had her mother's dark hair and hazel eyes, and was already beginning to echo her hourglass figure.

"Wish I could say the same." Allegra glanced down at her size six frame with its non-existent curves. "This milkshake ain't bringin' no boys to the yard," she said, adopting a heavy American accent.

Sienna and Reese laughed in unison. "Why would you need to bring any boys to the 'yard' when you have Andrew?" asked Sienna, referring to Allegra's boyfriend of two years.

"Oh, Andrew. He's my rock, but it doesn't hurt to catch the eye of a handsome stranger now and again – maintains the ego." She paused and gestured towards Reese. "I'm not being a bad influence on the rugrat, am I?"

Sienna laughed. "This rugrat has her life's ideas, goals and principles already set in stone. I don't think you, me *or* her father can sway those in any way!"

Reese smiled with wide-eyed innocence, making the two adults laugh.

"Anyway, enough about milkshakes," said Allegra. "This wine is delicious and the roast – perfect."

"Why, thank you, baby sister." Sienna raised a glass. "To good times, handsome strangers and, er, potent milkshakes." They laughed and clinked glasses.

The lights flickered on as Allegra walked into her apartment. "Andrew?" she called. "Are you here?" There was no reply.

She surveyed the empty sofa in the empty living room and looked wryly at the red wine stain on an armrest. Andrew had warned her against choosing the cream corner suite but she hadn't listened. Walking in, she noticed that the haphazard pile of books on her coffee table had been straightened. She walked over and knocked a few off the top. *Better.* Her apartment, while neat, was distinctively lived in. Her bookcase was crammed with books, her kitchen table was littered with newspapers, and her walls were adorned with conflicting pieces of art, flown over the oceans by her best friend, Sahar. She *chose* to live with discord and passion. Andrew's place, on the other hand, was an exercise in minimalism; everything was clean, neat and sterile. Everything was *too safe.*

Shrugging off her coat, she switched on her answering machine.

"Hi Allegra. You have two new messages. One is from Andrew and the other is from Sahar. Would you like to listen to them?"

"Yes."

"The message from Andrew was sent today at 5.30 p.m."

"Hey sweets. Listen, I'm still caught up with the Carter case. I doubt I'll make it out at an earthly hour so I'll crash at mine tonight. You can call me at the office if you want. Talk to you soon. Love you." The machine clicked through to the next message.

"A Leg Rash, how's it going?" Sahar's smooth voice filled the room. "Listen, I'm in New York but I'm flying back tomorrow for three days. I haven't seen you in ages. We have to meet up, okay? Call me."

Allegra glanced at the clock. 11 p.m. It was too late to bother Andrew and she could call Sahar the next day. She showered, changed into a slip, and lay back in bed, stretching luxuriously. As the satin sheets caressed her skin, she began to think about Andrew. She missed his bulk and shape next to her in bed. She pictured him kissing her, his dark hair brushing against her neck, his full lips on her skin, his weight crushing hers. She missed his arms and his body and his forceful touch. As she drifted off to sleep, her thoughts faded and curled away but not before whispering, *Andrew doesn't have dark hair.*

CHAPTER TWO

Allegra walked up the corridor towards the ImageBox offices. As the double doors slid open, she nearly crashed into Christian, the youngest member of their small team.

"Oh, gosh, sorry Allegra. I, uh, I wasn't looking where I was going," he stammered.

"That's okay." Allegra smiled. "You haven't seen Jonathan, have you?"

"Jonathan?" He looked at her blankly.

"Yes, Jonathan. You know, 6'2", massive mop of curly black hair, Director of our company? Sits opposite you every day?"

Christian blushed and pushed his glasses back up the bridge of his nose. "Okay, no need to take the piss. Yes, he's in already."

"Is he in a good mood?"

"Seems to be," he said unsurely.

"Okay, great. Thanks, Christian."

Allegra walked into the office and greeted Jonathan brightly. Barking orders into the phone, he waved in response. As she tossed her bag onto her desk, the last member of the team, Luka Karev, walked in. He looked Allegra up and down.

"Ha ha, Andrew must have done something right last night," he said with a dirty smile.

Allegra scowled. "Must you be so vulgar first thing in the morning?"

"I'm just saying. You're looking good, babe. Like some kind of glow."

"And that kind of stuff usually works, does it?"

"Come now, I'm being genuine."

"Genuine? Surely there isn't a solar eclipse outside. That *is* the only time you can be genuine, right?"

"Ouch. You break my heart every morning," he said with a grin.

Jonathan stood and interrupted their exchange. "Listen kids, can I have a few minutes?"

Allegra smiled at the way his head almost touched the ceiling.

"What's up, Chief?" asked Luka.

"Christian, come over here and sit yourself down next to Allegra." Jonathan waited. "Okay, I need you all to just relax for a minute because I've got something important to tell you."

Allegra bit her lip nervously. *The Panacea decision must be in.*

"Okay. So you all know how much ImageBox

means to me and you are all like family. You have amazing qualities and between you, you have taught me more than you know. I like to act like the big boss around here but the truth is, without you all, I'm nothing and ImageBox would be nothing and that's why I'm so indebted to you.

"In the five years since its birth, ImageBox has grown from a twinkle in my eye to a real business serving hundreds of people all because you guys work like dogs to make it happen. I know you are dedicated to it one hundred percent and that's why it's heartbreaking for me to tell you this." He paused.

"Tell us what?" Allegra prompted.

"I've had an offer from BNAB," replied Jonathan, referring to the second largest advertising company in the UK.

"For ImageBox?" asked Luka. "Are you kidding me?" When Jonathan said nothing, he shot up out of his chair. "This is a joke, right? You're not serious. You want to sell ImageBox to those corporate, sterile, impotent bureaucrats?"

Jonathan grimaced. "They heard that we landed the Panacea account and were really impressed."

"We landed Panacea?" Allegra's eyes grew wide with surprise. She had worked day and night to perfect the Panacea pitch.

Jonathan nodded. "BNAB were considering a takeover for a while. Panacea was the decider. I resisted for a while but as you know, my father's really ill. This way, I get to be with him in Paris." He paused. "Listen, I know this is messed up. Believe me, if I thought I could do this any other way, I would, but I need to wrap up all loose ends. I've got to get my priorities straight."

Allegra felt light headed. *Is this really happening?*

Jonathan continued: "As I'm sure you've figured out, BNAB will streamline our processes, meaning that your jobs will be assimilated into their existing structure. I wanted to tell you about this earlier but, to be honest, I wasn't even sure I was going to go through with it – not until it came down to signing on the dotted line."

"Jonathan, have you thought of maybe appointing a new director that can take care of things while you're in Paris? Someone who wants to keep ImageBox instead of..." her voice trailed off.

"Instead of bastardising it," Luka finished bitterly.

Hurt fleeted across Jonathan's face. "Listen guys, I need you to understand. I didn't want to do this but I had to. Family is important. You're all fantastically talented. You'll easily find other jobs."

"How long do we have?" asked Allegra.

"Each of you will get three months' gardening leave and substantial severance pay. I need you to know that I really, truly appreciate all the hard work you have put in."

"Yes, but how long do we have together?"

He coughed. "They want us to halt everything.

They have representatives coming down today to secure all the data."

"Which means?"

"Which means this is it. I didn't think they would be so heavy handed about the takeover but they want to wrap it all up."

"So we're out of a job, as of today?" asked Luka.

Jonathan nodded, eyes downcast.

Allegra was torn between sympathy and disbelief. She willed herself to say something kind, to show him that she respected the decision. Instead, she said, "I'll back up my personal emails and be gone in an hour."

He looked at her in dismay. "Allegra, please."

"Jonathan, it's *fine*. People let each other down – it happens every day. I'm a big girl. I can deal." She turned to her screen. Despite her words of nonchalance, her cheeks burned with anger. *Not you too,* she wanted to say. *The one man I've relied on these past four years. Now you too?*

Steaming water boiled over the top of the pan, landing with an angry hiss on the stainless steel of the cooker. Allegra yelped and turned down the heat. As she stirred in some salt, she heard the apartment door open. Andrew walked in and greeted her with a kiss.

"What's cooking?" he asked with a warm smile. Even after a long day at his City law firm, he seemed fresh and happy, blue eyes bright and alert, blonde hair still glossy from his morning shower.

"Just making some pasta. Sit down. It's almost ready."

He sighed contentedly. "This is the life – a beautiful woman cooking a homemade meal. What more could I ask for?"

She smiled faintly. Andrew really was a man of simple desires. It was what attracted her to him when a mutual friend introduced them two years ago. She was typically drawn to men who were dark, mysterious and edgy, but found her barriers breaking down in the face of Andrew's warmth, honesty and sincerity.

"How was your day?" he asked, forking in a mouthful of pasta.

Allegra sighed and shook her head.

Andrew's face clouded over as he immediately realised that something was wrong. He reached forward and gently placed a hand on hers. "What's happened?"

She sighed. "Jonathan. He's selling ImageBox. I've lost my job."

Andrew's eyes grew wide with shock. "He's selling up? But how can that be? He loves that place."

"Evidently not." Allegra took him through the morning's events; a rambling account punctuated by Andrew's frequent murmurs of consolation and assurance. "It was such a perfect job," she finished resignedly. "I'll never find something like it again."

Andrew shook his head. "Crazy girl, of course you will. You're young, unbelievably beautiful and scarily smart. The world is at your feet."

She met his eyes. "You think I'm perfect, Andrew, but I'm not."

He smiled and squeezed her hand. "Well, you're as perfect as it gets. It's going to be okay."

She bit her lip, annoyed by his assurances. His unwavering belief in her left no room for self-doubt. As soon as she questioned herself, he swooped in, sealing the leak, ignoring the fact that sometimes, she needed the outlet.

"Hey, it's going to be okay," he repeated, mistaking her solemnity for anxiety.

"Yeah," she nodded. "It is." She drew her knees to her chest and wrapped her arms around them. Her pyjama bottoms were torn at the knee so she pulled her loose black T-shirt over her legs, masking the hole.

Andrew watched her with concern. Her cheekbones, normally structured and defined, seemed to protrude, giving her a gaunt appearance. With her long hair tied up in a messy bun and a face free of makeup, she looked like a scared young child.

"I have an idea," said Andrew, eyes suddenly bright. "Let's move in together."

Allegra stiffened. "Move in together?" she echoed.

"Yes. It's perfect. I practically live here anyway. We'll share the mortgage so there's less pressure on you to find work and we'll get to spend more time together. What do you think?"

The idea filled her with fear. She was absurdly territorial about her space and time. The thought of owing half of it to Andrew terrified her. "I'm not sure," she faltered. "We shouldn't move in together just because I lost my job."

"No, that's not it," he said eagerly. "I've been thinking of asking you anyway. We've been together for two years – it's not like we're rushing into this."

She hesitated. "Can I think about it?"

Hurt flashed in his eyes. "You don't want to?"

"I do but I just..." She shrugged. "I just need some time to think about it." She loved Andrew but this was too much too soon.

He nodded. "Okay. That's okay," he said as understandingly as he could.

"Go take your shower. I'll clean up in here," she urged.

Andrew stood and left the room in silence. As she heard his footsteps on the stairs, she thought back to the early days of their relationship. Taking showers separately had been a ridiculous notion. *People settle into each other,* she thought wistfully.

Feeling guilty and conflicted, she decided she knew how to make him feel better. She padded over to the bathroom and stripped out of her clothes. Reaching up, she loosened her waist-length hair and shook it out. She stepped into the bathroom and was hit by a cloud of steam. It created a soft film on her skin, making it glisten with moisture. As she stepped into the shower, Andrew turned in surprise.

"Hey–" he started.

"Sssh," Allegra stopped him. "Don't talk. Just fuck me."

He blinked in surprise. After a momentary silence, he reached forward and drew her close.

"Andrew," she murmured, pulling him against her as her back hit the wall. "Fuck me." She could feel the steam on her shoulders, on her hips, between her legs.

She gripped him hard, willing him to do the same, but his touch remained soft; frustratingly gentle. She burrowed into his chest. It made her forget that while there was love and warmth, she felt no excitement, no butterflies in her stomach, no spark ripping her in half. With a wilting sigh, she let him melt into her.

Allegra Ashe cleaning on a Saturday night, she thought wryly. The date was originally set aside for Jonathan's birthday drinks but after the sell-out disaster, Allegra had decided to give it a miss. It was too late to organise anything else so she had resigned herself to an evening of cleaning.

She picked up the armful of paper she had put to one side and opened her front door to dump it in the recycling bin. As she struggled with the pile, half of it slipped out from under her arm.

"Dammit." She bent down to gather the loose bits of paper. As she piled everything into the bin, she noticed a small card. 'VOKOBAN' was printed in bold letters along the top. Beneath it in smaller letters was the name 'Michael Stallone'. She flashed back onto deep green eyes and a disarming smile. She remembered the exact tone of his voice and the exact shade of his stunning eyes. She remembered every ridge of his beautiful face and the way he had made her feel – overpowered, overwhelmed.

She shook herself free of his memory and studied the small print on the card. There was a phone number but no address. Back in the apartment, she switched on her PC and opened a browser. She typed in the letters V-O-K-O-B-A-N and pressed 'Search'. Small letters across the screen read, *Your search - VOKOBAN - did not match any documents.*

She frowned. How could Google not find anything about this supposedly wonderful company which comprised doctors, teachers and policemen all rolled into one? She then searched for 'Michael Stallone'. This time there were 3,400,000 results. After skimming through the first few pages, she decided there was nothing useful there. She tried a few different search terms and even searched for his telephone number, but found nothing.

"Weird." She glanced at the time – 7 p.m. She debated with herself for a few minutes before curiosity got the better of her. Grabbing her phone, she dialled 141 followed by the number on the card. *I'll hang up. I'll just see who picks up and then I'll hang up.*

The phone rang precisely two times before a smooth, rich voice answered "hello".

Allegra froze.

"Hello?" the voice repeated.

Flustered, she hit the 'End Call' button and backed away from the phone. *I'm such an idiot.* As soon as the thought left her mind, the phone began to ring. Her heartbeat quickened. *It can't be him. It won't be him.* She grabbed the phone. "Yes?" she asked, sounding curter than she had intended.

"Allegra?"

She breathed in deeply but her voice still shook. "Yes?"

"It's Michael Stallone. You called me a minute ago."

"I did? Erm, I did." She paused. "How did you know it was me?"

"Caller ID," he said simply.

"Caller ID? But you don't have my number and I..." a pause, "I dialled it from a private number."

He laughed. "Sorry, I should have explained when I gave you my card. Our phone technology overrides the masking function on incoming calls. It's important because we need to know who's calling us."

"But..." her voice trailed off, thick with embarrassment.

"You called for a reason?"

"Yes. Well, no. I..." She paused. *Who the hell is this guy? What technology?*

"I take it you have reconsidered my offer?"

She shook her head. "No, no, I haven't."

He waited.

"I called because, well, because I was curious. I Googled Vokoban and I couldn't find anything and I was just curious. I didn't know you had some voodoo scheme going on over there where you could find out who's calling you and where they're calling from and everything down to the colour of their underwear."

"So you're not interested in working for Vokoban?"

"I..." She sighed. "I lost my job recently and I was thinking about your offer but I don't even know anything about the role so I'm not quite sure where I stand."

"Tell you what. If you come down to HQ, I'll run you through everything – the job description, the benefits, the conditions and pay."

"Why me though? You said you head-hunted me."

"I can't really explain unless I explain everything. If you come to HQ, I can give you a full briefing."

Allegra thought it over. Maybe this was a real opportunity.

"It won't take more than 30 minutes of your time. If you like what you hear, great. If not, then you don't lose anything."

She tried to focus on the words he was saying rather than the sound of his voice. "Okay," she agreed without further thought.

"Great." The smile was evident in his voice. "When is good for you?"

Allegra had all the free time in the world. "How is Monday morning? Maybe about 11?"

"Perfect. I'll arrange a pickup."

"Okay," she said breathlessly. "I'll see you then."

"Okay." He paused. "Oh, and Allegra?"

"Yes?"

"Black and cream."

"Excuse me?"

"The colour of your underwear. Black and cream."

Her eyes grew wide.

"I'll see you tomorrow," he said with a hint of amusement in his voice. With that, he ended the call.

Allegra closed her gaping mouth. She looked around her apartment nervously and shook her head. "Bloody lucky guess." She switched off her PC and mulled over what she had done. Part of her was excited about the prospect of getting a new job. Part of her was apprehensive. And part of her just wanted to see Michael Stallone one more time.

On Monday morning, Allegra woke to an empty space next to her in bed, exactly the same as the day before. Only this time, there was a small post-it-note on the nightstand. She picked it up it and read, "Hello my pretty, off to work. Just wanted to say that you look beautiful when you sleep. Love you lots. Cradle Snatcher x."

She smiled. Andrew had given himself the moniker after Allegra had been asked for identification on the way in to an 18-certified film. "Do they think I'm dating a 17-year-old?" he had asked indignantly.

She got out of bed and padded over to her closet. Reaching to the top, she pulled out a shoebox and picked out a bundle of post-it-notes. During the early days of their relationship, Andrew would leave notes for her in the strangest of places. She would take something out of the freezer and notice a note stuck in there, probably left for weeks before discovery. Or she would put the lid down on the toilet and find a note stuck on the top, telling her how much she was loved and adored.

As she added the new note to the pile, her fingers brushed the corner of an old photograph. She took it out carefully and stared at the image beneath the white cracks of age. It was one of her favourites but she couldn't bear to leave it on display. It pictured her mother in a long skirt and loose top, long dark hair flowing to her waist. In her arms was a four-year-old Allegra. A seven-year-old Rafael had his arms wrapped around her legs and an 11-year-old Sienna had one arm hung loosely around her, smiling brightly into the camera. They all looked so happy, eyes shining with youth and hope.

When their mother died of breast cancer at 39, the children suffered a crushing blow. At 15, Rafael became withdrawn and rebellious beyond the adolescent norm. Their father had walked out on them a long time ago so Sienna had been given legal status as her siblings' guardian, and though she did her best to fill the void left by their mother, it was simply impossible. The love and warmth that was once so abundant gave way to quiet grief and silent sorrow.

Rafael moved out as soon as he hit 16, burying his

pain in a field of distance. Sienna and Allegra regularly tried to draw him back into their small family unit but their mother's death had built a wall around his heart that neither of them could break.

Allegra stared at the little boy in the picture and realised that she missed her brother deeply. She resolved to call him, maybe even try a Sienna-style dinner and beg him to attend. She carefully put the photograph back into the box and placed it at the top of her closet. With a deep breath, she shut the door and readied herself for the day ahead.

As she finished dressing, the shrill ring of the doorbell interrupted her thoughts. She walked to the intercom, balancing a booted foot with a bare one.

"Ms Ashe?" a man questioned. "I believe you have an appointment."

"I'll be right down." Pulling on her other boot, she grabbed her coat and allowed herself one last look in the mirror. She was wearing a short-sleeved black top teamed with tight jeans, which accentuated what little curves she had. She didn't want to admit that she had made extra effort but her glossy hair was pinned up in an intricate style, her sparkling hazel eyes were highlighted with dark eyeliner and her full lips looked luscious in a light shade of rose she had never worn before. Satisfied, she left her apartment and greeted the gentleman at the door with a handshake.

"I believe you're expecting me?" he asked in a mild Scottish accent.

Shaken, not stirred. "Yes, I am. Thank you." Settling into the luxurious seat, she tried to calm the butterflies in her stomach. She hadn't told Andrew about the meeting, certain he would disapprove of meeting a potential employer without thoroughly researching the company first. She didn't know what to expect but either way, she had nothing to lose.

When they reached their destination, the driver brought the car to a smooth stop and opened her door. "I will walk you in, Ms Ashe."

"That's okay. I'm sure I can find my way."

"I insist," he replied.

Allegra followed his long strides to the daunting double doors of an impressively grand building; a cross between the Old Bailey and the Bank of England. As they approached, the doors swung open slowly. The entrance hall was wide and grand but deceivingly modern; all glass, chrome and black leather.

The driver led Allegra to a large bank of security desks. "Ms Ashe, this is Leo. I'm going to leave you with him. Leo, this is the 11 o'clock inductee. If you give me a call when she's back out, I'll come and pick her up."

Leo was a 6'4" Samoan, built like stone. He asked for her driver's licence, which he stared at intently for a full minute. "They're definitely onto something with you," he said, nodding approvingly.

"How so?"

Leo didn't elaborate. Instead, he ran her through a

number of security checks and then told her to "turn left and head on through the double doors. You will be escorted by the gentleman waiting there."

Past the doors, she walked through a second metal detector and was thoroughly frisked by a stern silver-haired woman. A guard came forward and led her by the arm towards a bank of lifts. She shrugged her arm out of his grip and waited with him in silence. The lift arrived and they began their ride up, stopping at the 15th floor.

"Your stop." He pointed at the opening doors.

"Thank you." Allegra swallowed nervously and stepped out. There, she froze, struck by the vision of Michael Stallone. Dressed in a sharp black suit and a crisp white shirt, he was more gorgeous than she remembered. His luscious hair was freshly cut and his smile revealed his deep dimples. Allegra suddenly felt completely underdressed. She held his gaze and shook his proffered hand.

"Thank you for coming. Was the ride in okay?"

His voice reminded her of warm honey. "Yes it was, thank you." She thought of a statistic she had read somewhere – that 93 percent of communication is non-verbal. Their words seemed so banal compared with what she was feeling. It was strange and heady – completely intoxicating.

He led her down the bright corridor in long, powerful strides. She followed him, boots too loud on the hardwood floor. The stark white walls were adorned with several paintings, offsetting the sterile feel of the place. Stopping at a large set of double doors, Michael entered a seven-digit code into a keypad. He then moved into position in front of a small black box mounted on the wall and had his retina scanned, finally gaining entry.

"Sorry about all the security," he commented. "The powers-that-be are a little over-zealous about their privacy."

Allegra raised a brow, but said nothing. She let him lead her through the building's twists and turns. "This place is like a labyrinth."

"Yes, it can be confusing for visitors. Only people who know their way around can work out where they need to go."

"Huh. And where is it that *we* need to go?"

"We're going to a training room." He stopped abruptly at an unmarked door and went through another set of security checks before leading her into a large meeting room. Carpeted in cream, it was flooded with light from its floor-to-ceiling windows.

So much for security, thought Allegra. Just then, Michael pressed a button, bringing down shutters over every window. Artificial light filled the room, turning Allegra's skin a pallid hue.

"I apologise for the lack of sun in here. Unfortunately, we will be spending a lot of time in this room. It is what we call the 'Hub'".

There were 20 black high-back chairs around a solid

oak table, each with a laptop, paper pad and pen set out in front of it. The distance between the pads and pens was identical. *Does someone go around with a ruler?* Allegra wondered.

"Please sit," said Michael, more a command than an offer.

"Thank you." Allegra chose a seat opposite him. "So when does the fun start?"

Michael hid the grimace on his face. "First, I need you to sign a few confidentiality agreements." He waited as she signed the forms, and then sat next to her, swerving his chair to face her. She did the same until they were directly facing each other. "Allegra, I have made you sign all those forms but what I really need is for you to make a promise to me. I need you to look me in the eye and promise that you will not tell anyone what you learn here today."

"I won't."

"You promise?"

"Cross my heart and hope to die," she replied, smiling.

"Allegra, I'm serious," he said, green eyes dark and sombre.

"Yes, I promise."

He stared at her for a few moments and then nodded. "You remember the Madison McCall case a few years back?"

She nodded. "Of course. It was splashed all over the tabloids for a whole year."

"You remember how they caught Jason Carr, her killer?"

Allegra thought back. "He molested another girl. Annie or Anna somebody."

Michael nodded. "Anna Taylor. 12-year-old girl from Hammersmith."

"Yes, that's right. What about it?"

"My unit, my operation, caught Jason Carr. Here's the crux: Anna Taylor was not Anna Taylor, 12-year-old girl from Hammersmith; she was 24-year-old Sara Kunis, a field agent from my unit."

Allegra's brow furrowed in confusion. "I don't understand."

"Okay, here's the complicated part. Two years ago, new clauses were added to the Sexual Offences Act 2003. You may remember some press about the major changes to the statutory rape laws?"

Allegra nodded.

"Okay, with these changes, there were a number of smaller amendments which passed through largely unnoticed. We refer to one such amendment as Clause 160. Are you okay so far?"

"Yes," she said unsurely.

"Before Clause 160, an adult male could be convicted for having intercourse with a minor even if he wasn't aware of her age. So, for example, if a 30-year-old man had sex with a 12-year-old girl even though he thought she was 18, we would have a case against him. Clause 160 allows us to do the opposite."

"The opposite?"

"Clause 160 allows us to convict a man for having sex with a woman who is over 16 but one who he *thought* was a minor."

She frowned. "I don't follow."

"Picture this. An adult male meets a 17- or 18-year-old. He likes her because she looks young. She tells him that she is 14 or maybe 15, he gets all hot and heavy over this and initiates a sexual relationship. Technically, it isn't a crime because the girl is legal, but in his mind, this girl is 14. In his mind, he knows he is committing a crime but doing it regardless. These are the men we pursue."

"But," Allegra paused, trying to process what he was saying. "The girl is over 16. Why would she tell him she's 14?"

"Well, she doesn't. This law wasn't designed for the general public. It was made specifically for us, to allow my unit to target suspected paedophiles, gather concrete evidence and convict them based on our investigations."

"Why are you telling me this?"

"Well, that's where the field agents come in. My job is to recruit women that can pass for young teens. Women like you."

Allegra's eyes grew wide. "You want to use me as *bait?*"

"I wouldn't–"

"But... that's entrapment. You're dangling something in front of someone and enticing them into crime."

Michael shook his head. "Clause 160 is exempt. It cannot be subject to the laws of entrapment since the sole reason for its existence is to allow investigations like the ones we conduct."

"How is it that I've never heard about this Clause 160?"

"If you do some research you will see that these laws exist. They're not at the forefront of public knowledge because we do our utmost to keep it that way, implementing the new DA-notices and media blackouts if and when necessary."

Allegra pushed her chair away from the table. "I'm sorry. You– this is crazy."

"Allegra, I know it sounds crazy but this is a real opportunity to make a difference. The pay is probably over twice what you make now. It's intense but we do good work. We need you."

"You need me?" she questioned. "Why me?"

"Because, Allegra, you're 25 but you look 15. With the right clothes and makeup, you could look as young as 13."

She grimaced. "But how did you find me?"

He sighed. "I was in the queue behind you in Waitrose a few weeks back. They asked you for ID when you tried to buy some wine. When I saw your face, I knew I had to have you."

His choice of words made her stomach seize up. Mad as he sounded, he was the most beautiful man she had ever spoken to.

He continued: "Since Vokoban's inception two years ago, we have convicted 84 offenders. We failed to secure convictions in 13 cases. In general, that counts for a massive success rate. Sexual abuse cases are notoriously difficult to prove. We have 527 targets but only 72 field agents. The men that don't have an agent on their trail are out there chasing young children and feeding on the vulnerable. We are in a position to create 'pseudo-victims' who won't fall apart because they are specially trained to deal with this."

"There are 72 girls who have agreed to do this?" Allegra asked with disbelief.

"63 of those are female. The remaining nine are male field agents. Male recruitment has proved to be far more difficult as there is a huge paucity of adult males who look pre-pubescent."

Allegra shook her head. "I'm sorry. This is," she paused. "This isn't right."

"You're right – it isn't. It isn't right that men groom, rape and destroy defenceless young women, but we are in a position to stop them. Our field agents are supported one hundred percent of the way. We offer round-the-clock surveillance, high-level security, intense training, and therapy sessions to help you adjust. Our field agents have a failsafe system in place that will do everything possible to accommodate you. Field agents can take advantage of a huge range of benefits and have six-figure starting salaries."

Allegra stared at him, shocked that he could discuss

salaries in the same breath as these atrocities. "Where does this money come from? And if you have so much of it, why don't you just put a tail on each of your suspects?"

"We receive funding from a number of different sources. We can't passively trail these men. The only way we could convict them is if they go out and actually molest a young girl and we're not going to wait for that to happen."

"So you let them molest an agent instead?"

Michael grimaced. "Allegra, our agents have a support system in place. They are trained to deal with it – actual victims are not."

She met his eyes. "And what exactly do agents have to do for their *six-figure salary?*" she asked mockingly.

His eyes flashed regret or sorrow or maybe anger. "The more you can do, the better."

"'More'?"

"We can't convict a man just because he has a few conversations with a girl who he thinks is underage. It doesn't matter how sexually charged those conversations are – we can't touch him. There has to be... physical evidence."

Allegra grew cold. "Physical evidence?"

"Yes. Field agents are under surveillance at all times during their contact with the target in question. If we are able to witness or record a sexual act between the two, we can secure a conviction."

"A sexual act? What is specified as a sexual act?"

Allegra felt goosebumps rise on her skin. "A kiss? A touch?"

"No. That's not enough. Clause 160 sets very specific criteria on what will qualify."

She waited in expectation.

Michael rubbed his temple. "Oral sex, either given to or administered by the field agent; vaginal or anal penetration either penile, digital or using a foreign object; and in cases where we have a good grounding, kissing and fondling."

Allegra was stunned. *What kind of organisation is this?* She ran Michael's words through her head. "So, in other words, 'field agent' is a glorified way of saying 'prostitute'?"

Michael winced at her sharp tone. "Allegra, I can understand your reservations. Many of our agents have the exact same reaction you are having right now. It *is* a bizarre and crazy project but we are effective. It *works*. We have uncovered more of these bastards than the normal justice system has in the past five years put together."

Allegra felt horrified by what she was being asked to do. She stood. "I'm sorry, I can't do this."

"Allegra, let me finish the session."

"I can't." She headed towards the door, but he blocked her path, shadowing her small frame.

"Before you run away and think we're a bunch of madmen, let me finish, okay?"

"No." She had heard enough.

His eyes bore into her. "Think about what you're doing. You are in a real position to help the victims of crimes you can't even imagine."

She shook her head. "That's not my responsibility."

"Whose responsibility is it, Allegra?" Michael's voice rose. "The government's? We *are* the government. It is *our* responsibility, but we can't do it without you."

"I'm sorry, it is not my responsibility," she repeated calmly.

He stared at her in angry silence. Then, quick as a light switch, his eyes grew cold. "I see – I'm sorry I wasted your time." He gathered the papers on the table. "I'll have Leo send a guard up to collect you."

"Michael," she started.

"Thank you for coming and letting me have your time. Have a safe journey home." With that, he walked out.

Allegra sat, drained and, strangely, rejected. She looked at the massive clock on one side of the room. It was only 11.30. It felt like she had been there for hours. What were they asking her to do? What was going through the minds of the 72 agents that were already working for Vokoban? *Mad place. This is a mad place and I need to get out.* Allegra headed towards the exit. Just as she grabbed the handle, the door flew open.

"Mr Stallone tells me he's done with you, Ms Ashe," said the security guard.

Allegra nodded. "I believe he is."

"Godamn it!" Michael slammed his door shut. It swung back open which only aggravated him further. His assistant, Lyla, stuck her head in the doorway with a questioning look. Michael shook his head.

"What happened?"

"Stone cold wall. Impenetrable."

"Well, it's a lot for a girl to take," said Lyla soothingly. "And she's not the first to go running from this place."

"But she's different. She has what it takes." Michael slumped into his chair. He swivelled in it from left to right as he contemplated the thought of losing Allegra. "You've seen the surveillance pictures of her, Lyla. She looks like a kid. With the right clothes, she would look even younger. Girls like her don't come around every day." He paused. "She could be the one for Drake."

Lyla's eyes widened. "This girl went running and you're thinking of assigning her to *Drake*? Are you kidding me? We need to put a seasoned agent on his trail – it's not going to work otherwise."

Michael shook his head. "No, that's the completely wrong thing to do. Drake likes his girls young and fresh. You can't say to me that some of our long-timers have that freshness. You can *see* the cynicism in their eyes, Lyla. You can see what lies beneath, the ice that has formed. Allegra has a quality that no amount of training can produce."

Lyla leaned against the doorframe. "Perhaps you're right. He *has* proved to be a difficult bastard to nail."

"And Allegra could be the one that reels him in. I know she can do it. You've seen the profile of Drake's victim – brunette hair with pretty hazel eyes."

Lyla tapped her pen against her thigh, thinking it over. Finally she nodded. "Then pull out the stops."

He looked up in surprise. "Really? So you see it too?"

Lyla nodded. "She could be the one."

Michael sat back in his chair, a slow smile spreading on his lips.

CHAPTER THREE

Allegra ran into the small restaurant on the South-bank. Shaking off the rain, she spotted Sahar straight away. Dressed in a figure-hugging black T-shirt and black slacks, her best friend looked like a movie star.

"Goddess." Allegra hugged her tightly and slipped into the booth. It had been months since they had seen each other.

"What's up, Leg? You seem washed out."

"Gee, thanks."

"No, I'm being serious, babe. What's going on?" Sahar took a sip of wine, drawing the attention of every man in the restaurant.

"I'm okay, just had a rough few weeks."

"Andrew?"

Allegra shook her head. She had barely seen him since he suggested moving in together, two weeks ago.

"The job? It's being out of work, isn't it? Idleness always did drive you mad."

Allegra shrugged. "Maybe. I've been job hunting desperately but there seems to be absolutely nothing."

"Why don't you go travelling? Go somewhere nice with lawyer-boy and if he's too busy, go on your own."

Allegra sighed. "I don't know, Sahar. It's a nice idea but I've grown up a bit and have responsibilities – a mortgage for starters."

"Leg, if that's what you're worried about, fuck it. I'll buy that hole of yours for you."

"Don't be crazy. You know I wouldn't let you do that." With regular modelling work on top of the lavish gifts various men insisted on forcing upon her, Sahar could very well buy Allegra's apartment a few times over.

Sahar scoffed. "You and that stupid chip."

"Chip?"

"That chip on your shoulder that proclaims, 'Stand back for I am Allegra the Brave. I shall wander the Earth and all Creation on my Own and gather my means on my Own and live my life on my Own and need no one for I am happiest on my Own'."

Allegra shook her head. "It's not like that."

"It is *so* like that," Sahar insisted. "You don't let anybody help you."

"Of course I do."

"Oh, yeah? When? I mean, jeez, you couldn't even ask Andrew to put up that cheap-ass monstrosity from Ikea – you had to do it yourself. You remember that?"

Allegra grew silent.

Sahar's expression grew soft. "Listen, I don't mean to be so hard on you. You know I love you, right?"

Allegra nodded.

"Even though you *are* an obstinate little heifer."

"And I love you even though you're a bitch."

"Who knew a dog and a cow could get along so well?" mused Sahar in seriousness.

Allegra laughed. She always felt at ease in Sahar's company. She thought back to their days at university. On first meeting, Allegra, short and awkwardly thin, had felt painfully inferior to Sahar, statuesque and stunning with her Kenyan exoticism. Through their first few months as roommates, however, they became close friends, helping each other through the trials of university and then life in the real world. Allegra knew she could always rely on her friend, but also that she never would.

"So how *is* lawyer-boy?" Sahar interrupted her thoughts.

She shrugged. "He's well. He's just been busy with work."

Sahar studied her for a second. "Tell me."

Allegra sighed in acquiescence. "He asked me to move in together."

Sahar's eyes grew wide. "He asked *you* – child of darkness, misanthrope extraordinaire – to move in together? Is he crazy?"

Allegra shook her head. "It's not that I don't want to. It's just that..."

"You don't want to," finished Sahar. "Leg, don't feel guilty about it. We all have issues – he should know what yours are."

"I don't–"

"Hey, this is *me* you're talking to," Sahar said before her friend could voice denial.

Allegra sighed and nodded. "You're right. I don't know what he was thinking."

"Listen, I'll kill you if you ever tell anyone I quoted Marilyn Monroe, but she said this thing once, which made a lot of sense: 'I make mistakes, I am out of control and at times hard to handle. But if you can't handle me at my worst, then you sure as hell don't deserve me at my best.' That's you. And, in some ways, that's me. That's all the people who are a little bit screwed up, but who are also interesting and passionate and engaged. But it's not Andrew. I've always thought he was good for you but I sometimes wonder if you don't need someone who *does* make mistakes, who *is* hard to handle, someone who's hard to figure out, who's passionate and wild and hard to tame." She paused. "You *do* want to be with him, right?"

Allegra frowned and nodded. She lifted her empty glass. "I think it's time for a top up," she said, not quite ready to acknowledge the truth in her friend's words.

Sahar nodded and sat back. She knew what Allegra was like. She knew she needed space and time to move at her own pace. She lifted and peered into her own empty glass. "I think so too," she agreed quietly.

Lyla Stannard hated workaholics. She hated people who carried the office around 24/7. After a failed marriage to an A&E doctor she knew how overworking could infest and destroy one's personal life. That is why she made her best efforts to switch off from Vokoban when she went home and that is why her shoulders drooped when she saw who was calling her mobile.

"Michael. Do *not* tell me that you're still in the office."

"Lyla, I just wanted to run my plan past you."

She groaned but Michael ignored it.

"As you know, I've been going over all the recon and the surveillance on the Ashe case. I couldn't find anything usable in her history or Crawford's history so I took it all to a few of our psychs. They think the niece angle could work."

Lyla rolled her eyes. "Michael, you have other agents to look after. Allegra is monopolising your time."

"Lyla, this will work. I just need to execute it properly."

"It won't be enough. She practically went screaming from the place."

"Yes, but this is our way in. Personalising the problem always works."

Lyla sighed exaggeratedly.

"Okay, okay, I get the picture. I'm going. I just wanted to let you know that I'm going to be in the office over the weekend so if anything comes up, let me know, okay?"

"Yes Michael," she said in monotone. She had no

idea what could possibly come up that would make her call him in the office on a Saturday but she argued no further.

"Thanks Lyla."

"Michael, take it easy, okay?"

"You too," he said, knowing full well that she said it as a warning rather than a parting. He hung up the phone and sat back in his chair, satisfied.

Allegra awoke with a hangover. Sahar had persuaded her to venture away from the usual choice of mocktail – a decision she was now paying for with a throbbing headache. She had had a restless night and felt groggy and lethargic. Yawning, she stepped out of bed and tried to shake the feeling of uselessness from her veins. She didn't want to spend another Saturday alone so she called Sienna and arranged dinner.

Fixing a cup of coffee, she switched on all the heaters in an effort to warm her apartment. She picked up her mail and sifted through it. Among the junk was a plain white envelope with no postmark. Inside was a newspaper clipping. 'Girl of 14 commits suicide after years of molestation', read the headline. Allegra felt her stomach knot. *Michael.*

She skimmed through the article. Melissa Hart, a 14-year-old girl in Norfolk, had slit her wrists in her bedroom. A simple note was found with the words "Ask Dick" written on it. The article went on to describe how Melissa had been molested from the age of five to 14 by her neighbour Richard Jones. Police had found 84 pictures of a naked or near-naked Melissa at varying ages in Jones's house. He had been arrested and was currently in custody.

Allegra felt compelled to read on. Thirty-seven of the pictures reportedly showed full and graphic penetration while five depicted 'sadistic sexual acts'. Allegra felt her stomach churn. This was obviously Michael's sick attempt at changing her mind. She screwed the envelope into a ball and flung it into the kitchen bin. She thought of practical things – emptying the garbage, buying groceries, paying her bills – and slowly pushed Melissa Hart out of her mind.

Allegra washed her hands and surveyed her reflection next to Reese. They were both wearing black jumpers and both had their hair tied up in a ponytail. To the casual observer, they looked like school friends.

"Are you okay?" asked Reese. "I mean, I know you're beautiful and all, but staring at yourself like that is pretty egotistical."

Allegra smiled. "No, I was just thinking."

"'Bout what?"

She shook her head. "Nothing important." She slung an arm over Reese's shoulder. "C'mon. Let's go. You know how your mum likes to order as soon as we sit down." They headed out of the bathroom and joined Sienna at a corner booth.

Tassili's, a small Italian restaurant in Soho, served

the best calzone in the city. All the waiters could speak Italian and would flirt amorously with customers and celebrate boisterously whenever a rookie dropped and smashed a plate or glass. It was a warm, inviting place that served up good food with excellent service.

Visits were bittersweet for Allegra and Sienna. The smells and sounds reminded them of their mother who often spoke to them in Italian, determined that her children should learn their mother tongue. Anything they had managed to learn was now diluted into fragmented words and phrases.

Sienna gave their order to a particularly handsome waiter and rolled up her sleeves, ready for a hearty meal.

Munching on some bruschetta, Allegra turned to Reese. "How's the violin going? How long 'til the concert?"

"Three months. It's okay. I'm playing the Devil's Trill Sonata, which is giving me a permanent headache. I'm practising for hours every day. It's slow but I'm getting there."

"Am I gonna get a preview?"

"*Patience Iago.*"

Allegra laughed. "That's easy. You're quoting 'Aladdin'. Jafar says it to Iago when they're talking about getting rid of Princess Jasmine."

Reese huffed. "Okay, smarty pants. Next time it'll be some pretentious French film that'll completely catch you out."

"Bring it on." Allegra grabbed Reese in a mock headlock and messed up her hair. "So how are you finding time to practise what with your French classes and karate classes and ballet classes?"

"I do *not* do ballet!" said Reese indignantly. "You make us sound like some terribly clichéd middle-class family."

Allegra laughed. "You *are* a terribly clichéd middle-class family!"

"Hey, *you're* the one who's dating a lawyer."

"Ouch," conceded Allegra.

"Speaking of Andrewnicus, how come he didn't come out tonight? I haven't seen him in ages."

Allegra shrugged. "Busy as usual. What about Stephen? Where's he?"

"In Bruges on business," answered Sienna. "Be careful," she threw at Reese who was on her way to the lobster tank, part of her Tassili's ritual.

"When's he back?"

"Tonight. You know he doesn't like to be away too long. I'm lucky that way." She glanced at Reese. "*She's* lucky. What I wouldn't do to have had dad around when we were growing up."

Allegra snorted. "We did just fine without him."

Sienna nodded. "No, I know but," she sighed, "it just would have been easier on all of us, you know? To have him here to help us figure things out."

Allegra said nothing.

Sienna folded and refolded her napkin until it was a tiny triangle in her hand. "I know we've gone over this but do you ever think about finding him?"

Allegra scowled. "He *chose* to abandon us. He had a wife and three children and he decided that it wasn't the life for him. We haven't changed our names or locations. If he *wanted* to find us, he would have."

"But, it's not so easy."

"Open your eyes, Sienna. It's the twenty-first century. We're on the electoral roll for God's sake! It doesn't take a brain surgeon to figure out where we are."

Chastened by Allegra's outburst, Sienna grew pensive. Their father may have been low on responsibility but he was still their father. She resented herself for admitting it but they *had* needed him. They had needed someone to guide them, someone to lead them and discipline them, someone to take control.

Reese bounded back, oblivious to the sudden tension at the table.

Allegra plastered on a smile. "Here's one for you," she said brightly. "*Not another word – and I am never, never to hear of you going to the surface again. Is that clear?*"

Reese laughed. "I see what you did there – clever but not subtle."

Allegra raised a brow.

"I was playing with the lobsters which led you to Sebastian in 'The Little Mermaid'."

Allegra groaned in defeat. "Okay, you little freak, who says the quote?"

Reese smiled triumphantly. "Triton. Ariel's mighty, all-powerful father."

Allegra nervously tapped her fingers on the counter as she eyed the white envelope. It had no address and no postmark, just like the one she had received yesterday. She didn't want to play this game with Michael. Opening the envelope would be like rolling the dice. She traced her fingers along the edges. A stray thought wondered if he had used his tongue to moisten the seal. Visions of his green eyes and powerful arms flashed in her mind.

Making a quick decision, she tore open the envelope and reached inside. She took out a Polaroid and winced at the image. It was of a young girl spread-eagled on a bed. Her arms were tied to the bedpost above her head and she was completely naked. Her breasts were mere buds in her chest and her crotch only had a light smattering of hair. She was looking straight at the camera with vacant, unfeeling eyes. Along the bottom of the picture, a handwritten caption read, 'Melissa Hart: Picture 68'.

"He–" Allegra caught her breath as anger flooded her veins. She stormed to her bedroom and pulled her purse out of her bag. Rifling through it, she took out Michael's business card and punched his number into her mobile.

"Michael Stallone." He sounded breathless. Panting, he audibly steadied his breathing.

Was he? Could he be? The thought that Michael Stallone could have a girlfriend hadn't even crossed Allegra's mind. He seemed so focused on his work.

"Is– is this a bad time?" she faltered. *It's a weekday morning.*

He breathed in deeply. "No, I just ran up the stairs to get to my phone."

The relief usurped her anger.

"Are you okay?" he asked.

She tried to form the words she wanted to say but was still thrown by the sound of his voice. "The things you've been sending me – I want you to stop."

He coughed. "Allegra, I want you to see the kind of thing we're up against."

"There is no *we*, Michael. It's what *you're* up against."

He sighed. "Vokoban needs you. You can help us stop men like Richard Jones."

"It's not my responsibility."

"Is that the attitude you take to everything, Allegra?" Anger grew in his voice. "Global warming? Nothing to do with me. War crimes? Nothing to do with me. Man raping a child on the street? Nothing to do with me."

"You are *out* of line."

"It exists, Allegra. I didn't send you that picture to get a rise out of you. I sent it to show you that it exists."

"I'm not stupid, Michael. I *know* it exists but I can choose not to be a part of that world."

"Exactly! You have a *choice* – girls like Melissa Hart don't," he countered.

"I am ending this conversation." Allegra fought to control her rising voice.

"Allegra—"

"Do *not* send me anything else, Michael," she said coldly. "If you continue to harass me, I will tell the world about Vokoban." With that, she hung up and flung the phone onto her bed. It wasn't so much the words he said that shook her defences, but the anger and intensity in his voice. She lay back on her bed and covered her eyes with the palms of her hand, shielding out the morning sun. A film quote wandered into her mind: *The flame that burns twice as bright burns half as long.* She closed her eyes. "Screw him," she said quietly.

A week went by and Allegra settled into a routine. Andrew, if he was staying over, would kiss her goodbye. She would then spend the day job hunting, watching television and creating errands to keep busy before eating a lonely dinner and heading to bed.

On a few occasions, she walked to Crossharbour to clear her head. She would stare into the water and question why she wasn't happy. She knew that unemployment was making her increasingly lugubrious, but she had a lot more going for her. She had a man who loved her, a best friend who would kill for her and a family that cared for her, so why did she feel so empty?

She needed something to do. She needed excitement, pace and passion. She hated these days that seemed to stretch for weeks.

At 4 p.m., Andrew's phone rang for the 27th time that day.

"Andrew Crawford," he answered, suppressing a yawn.

"Andrewnicus, it's Reese."

"Hey, what's up?" he said brightly.

"I wanted to remind you that it's Allegra's birthday on May 14th. I know how useless men can be with these things."

He laughed. "Thanks kiddo, but I have it covered."

"Oh yeah, what are we getting her?"

"I can't say."

"Come oooon."

"Sorry kiddo. I can't say."

"A clue?"

"No."

"Something big? Something small?"

"I can't say."

Reese gasped. "Oh my God. It's a ring, isn't it? You're going to propose!"

Andrew's shoulders drooped. *Damn these women and their intuition.*

Reese waited, patient in the face of Andrew's silence. Finally, he sighed. "Do you think she'll say yes?"

Reese screeched on the other end of the line.

"Reese. Reese, ssh. Someone might hear you."

"Don't worry, mum's out in the garden." A whoop of delight. "Man, it's about time someone tied her down!"

Andrew flinched at her choice of words. "Reese," he said, deadly serious. "Do you think she'll say yes?"

She paused. "Why wouldn't she? You guys are totally in love."

"Yeah," he replied wistfully. He loved Allegra deeply but sometimes he felt like a stranger, locked out of the rawest parts of her.

"Can I tell mum?" Reese interrupted his thoughts.

"No! You can't say anything to anyone – promise me."

She groaned. "Okay, but it's gonna be hard keeping this to myself."

"Reese, promise me."

"Okay, okay, I promise. Let me know what happens as soon as."

"I will."

After hanging up, Andrew thought over the conversation. He was so caught up in Allegra. Growing up, he had never had to fight for female attention. His easy charm mixed with his affable character allowed him to make friends, both female and male, easily. When he had started dating Allegra he knew she had barriers but he was also confident that he could break them down. After two years, he was still trying. It wasn't that she was cold or emotionless but rather that you never really knew what she was thinking. There was a part of her that rejected emotional intimacy and shielded her innermost thoughts. Wasn't love all about removing the masks we put on for strangers? Andrew still felt shut out. He hoped that asking her to marry him would finally break through and make her his, permanently and completely.

Allegra blew on her hot coffee and curled up on the sofa. It was when she placed her cup on the table that she spotted the DVD case neatly placed next to the morning paper. She frowned, trying to remember if she had seen it there this morning. She reached over and opened the case. Inside was an unlabelled DVD. Perhaps Andrew had put it there without telling her? She debated whether to watch it or not. Maybe it was one of Andrew's quirky little surprises he used to spring on her; some cheesy message telling her how much he loved her.

She slipped the DVD into the player and pressed play. A young man with sandy blonde hair and blue eyes appeared on screen. He was dressed in a white cotton T-shirt and khaki trousers, and stood in a kitchen holding a cup of coffee.

Allegra frowned and looked over the DVD case again. There was no indication of what it was.

Suddenly, a baby's cry emanated from the screen. The young man set down his coffee cup and ran upstairs. The point of view changed to the top of the stairs and showed him running up, concern etched onto his face. He walked into a nursery and up to a bed on which the baby was placed. He began to coo at his daughter soothingly. Like magic, she stopped crying. Allegra smiled.

The scene cut abruptly to a young woman in a darkened living room curled up on a sofa, uncannily reflecting Allegra's own position. The woman looked at the baby monitor and listened to her husband coo to their baby. After a short moment of silence there was the distinct sound of bedsprings creaking. The baby started to shriek. The creaking became louder and louder but the camera remained on the woman's face. The baby's screams were drowned out by the animalistic grunts of adult pleasure. A single tear fell from the woman's eyes.

Two simple words appeared on screen: *Stop rape.*

Allegra drew back as if hit physically. 'NSPCC' appeared in small green letters across the screen. A moan of disgust escaped her mouth as her mind traitorously repeated the scenes on the DVD. Deep moans of guttural male pleasure rang in her ears.

Furious, she took out the DVD and tried to split it in two. When it refused to break she stormed to the kitchen and threw it in the bin. She lifted the bag, walked out of her apartment, and threw it into the communal bin outside. She didn't want it in her living room. She didn't want it in her apartment or under her skin or in her life.

She turned back towards her apartment door and did a double take. There, in all his righteous glory, stood Michael Stallone. Clad in a perfectly tailored wool overcoat, his powerful frame towered over Allegra.

"You bastard," she snarled, stunned into aggression.

"How dare you?" Lost in fury, she launched into him physically, forcing him away from her apartment, away from her body, away from her life.

Michael held her arms, containing her anger effortlessly. "Allegra, calm down."

"Don't you tell me to calm down!" she spat, struggling in his grip. "You sent me that disgusting tape. What the hell did you *think* my reaction would be?"

"Allegra, please just listen to me," he said soothingly.

"No!" She freed her arms and backed away.

"Ten minutes of your time is all I want."

"Nothing you say will make me change my mind so just leave me alone."

"Hear me out Allegra, please." He advanced on her slowly.

She shook her head angrily. "Just leave."

"Listen, what if Melissa Hart was Reese?"

Her head snapped up as anger bubbled to her throat. Before she had a chance to respond, Michael continued.

"We go through life thinking, 'that can never happen to me' or 'that would never happen to the people I love', but it *does* happen, Allegra. Cancer happens. Road traffic accidents happen. Burglary and murder happen. *Rape* happens. We are trying to put these sick bastards away and we have finally found an effective way to do it. Why am I pursuing you? Because even though we have 72 field agents, it's nowhere near enough. We *need* you, Allegra. I'm just saying give us a chance. If you feel doubt at any point during an operation we will accommodate that."

She shook her head. "You expect me to agree to being *touched* by these disgusting men? Men like Richard Jones? Men who get off on tying up 14-year-old girls and acting out their sicknesses?"

"Allegra, we put away men like that. That's the whole point. For every target of yours we convict, that's one fewer victim out there in the world."

"And what about *me?* What about all your so-called 'field agents'? Are we not victims? What makes us different?"

"You're not helpless and alone. Allegra, I will be with you every step of the way. I will pull you out as soon as you start to feel uncomfortable. We can give you a repeat offender – you won't need to engage in proper physical contact." His green eyes implored her.

I'm gasoline. I'm burning clean.

He reached out and touched her chin, lifting it slightly. "Come on, what do you say?"

She stared back at him, suddenly wishing she could give him the answer he so desperately wanted. "I can't. I'm sorry."

He exhaled deeply and shook his head. "Just know that I'm not ready to let you go." With that, he turned and walked away.

Allegra watched him leave, both riled and comforted by his parting words.

"Hey, you okay? You seem a bit pale." The whites of Andrew's eyes shone in the darkness.

"I'm okay." Allegra's smile failed to reach her eyes.

Andrew propped himself up on his pillow. "Cabin fever?"

"Something like that."

He smiled comfortingly. "Tell you what, how about we go away at the middle of the month? Just you and me. Maybe a weekend in Paris or Rome or Venice? What do you think?"

Allegra brightened. She loved Italy. The smells and sounds reminded her of childhood. She smiled up at Andrew and nodded happily.

"Oh, she smiles!" he joked.

"Thank you," she whispered, curling up against his body beneath the duvet. He spoke to her gently about the sights they could see and the things they would do, and watched her slowly drift off to sleep. *I will wait forever if that's what it takes to make her ready.* He kissed her forehead and wrapped her up in his arms before closing his eyes and succumbing to slumber.

She was in a dark place and could hear the slow drip drip of a leaking tap or pipe. There was a small light in the distance. She started towards it but felt her bare feet squelch into something warm and wet. She looked down to see dark liquid seep through her toes. It made her shiver in disgust. Her flimsy slip did nothing to shield her from the icy chill that curled around her skin. She crossed her arms over her chest and continued towards the light.

As she got closer she heard the low murmur of voices. She hesitated for a moment before slowly pushing the door open. She froze as she took in the scene before her. A man, or what looked like a man, stood in the middle of the room. He was topless and had enormous bulging muscles. His head was bald, save two thick ropes of hair growing from the top. The nose ring hanging from his nostrils made him look like an angry bull, snarling at the corner of the room. Allegra's heartbeat quickened at the sound. She wanted to turn and run but a morbid fascination chained her there. Her gaze followed his and she gasped as she noticed the small white figure on top of a rock-like slab. It was a young girl chained at the wrists. She was lying back, naked, with her legs splayed open. *Melissa Hart.*

The man turned, revealing his fully engorged penis, red with angry, pulsating blood. He walked to the slab and stood behind Melissa, crotch level with the top of her head. He grabbed her face and clawed at her mouth, ripping it open with his powerful fists. Her screams only made him hungrier, made him want to hurt her more. Holding her nose and throat, he rammed himself into her mouth, making her writhe with pain and fear.

He pushed deeper and deeper, causing her to choke. Heaving himself onto the slab, he placed his knees on either side of her face and ground himself against her tongue and throat. His actions grew violently frenzied until finally, he shook and juddered and exploded in her mouth. The girl twisted on the slab and spat, choking, gagging and crying. Her head rose and she made eye contact with the woman in the doorway.

Allegra screamed. The girl didn't resemble Melissa; she had Reese's face, Reese's hair and Reese's eyes.

The man's head snapped towards Allegra. He smiled manically, revealing bloody red teeth. As he ran towards her, she saw the whip in his hand. He drew it back and then whipped it forward. Allegra screamed in terror.

She shot up in bed, her nightgown soaked in sweat. Gasping for air, she frantically fumbled for her lamp and snapped it on. Andrew, breathing softly beside her, was still asleep. She could have sworn she had woken up screaming.

She stepped out of bed on shaky legs and walked to the bathroom. There, she paused, leaning against the sink to catch her breath.

"Dream. Just a dream." Splashing cold water on her face, she wiped away the stringy strands of hair stuck to her forehead. "Just a dream." The demonic face of the man in her dream flashed in her mind, his muscles bulging with frantic movement.

"Reese," Allegra's shaky whisper evaporated in the stark light. Reaching out, she lowered herself onto the cold porcelain edge of the bath. There she sat until the shivers subsided and the images in her head blurred into incoherent greys. When her breathing finally steadied, she forced herself back into the bedroom.

Resting her head next to Andrew's, she breathed deeply and closed her eyes. *Just a dream.* Her heartbeat slowed but her mind refused to quieten. It whispered a thousand thoughts, each one fighting for space before drowning in a sea of voices. She opened her eyes and the clamour grew silent. Turning on her side, she stared at the slats of her closet, silently counting the white panels. *Sixty.* Tentatively, she closed her eyes and tried to focus on the number – *sixty, sixty, sixty* – but found it slipping away beneath wet sounds of gagging and vomiting. Familiar eyes, now shallow and vacant, looked up to meet hers.

Her eyes snapped open, pushing away images of bloody red teeth smiling at her demonically. She wasn't ready to face her thoughts. She couldn't. Turning on her back, she stared at the ceiling, tracing and retracing a huge 6-0 on its dark cream surface. The spindly arms of slumber curled around her chest and throat but she refused to succumb. Instead, she lay there until traces of dawn filtered through the blinds and Andrew stirred beside her. She hid her face as he rose from bed and went through the motions of his morning routine, only momentarily closing her eyes when he silently kissed her cheek. She heard the front door close and lay still for a while. After a long moment, she stepped out of bed and walked to the kitchen. She reached for the phone and punched a set of numbers in quick succession. One ring, two, three.

"Yes?" asked a crisp, clear voice.

"Do you really think I can pass for 14?" Silence. "*Tell me.* Do you really think I can pass for 14?"

"Yes," said Michael Stallone.

"Then I'm in."

"I'll have a car pick you up at 09.00," he said without missing a beat.

"I'll be ready."

"Good." A pause. "Allegra?"

"Yes?"

"You're doing the right thing."

"Of course," she replied sardonically. Ending the call, she walked to her closet and slowly, methodically, laid out her clothes. Undressing in silence, she stepped into the shower and set the water just below scalding.

The lift's swift ascension made Allegra giddy. Smoothing her black skirt, she raised her chin and swallowed hard. She was determined to get through the day unscathed. The silver doors opened to reveal Michael standing alone, every pore of his skin exuding ease and confidence. Dressed in a slate grey suit with a salmon coloured shirt, he looked like one of those Ralph Lauren models with their dark eyebrows perfectly arched over smouldering eyes.

Allegra shook his hand firmly and noticed a tiny beauty spot by the corner of his right eye. It somehow offset his flawless features, stopping them short of sickeningly perfect.

"Everything okay? You feeling alright?" he asked.

"I'm fine."

"It's going to be a long day today. If at any time you feel like a break, let me know and we'll take time out for as long you like. It's important that–"

"I'll be fine," she interrupted.

Michael paused and then nodded. In silence, he led her to the hub and watched her take the same seat she had last time. He followed suit and turned to look at her.

"Firstly, I want to say a real deep thank you for getting up today and coming here. It took a lot of courage. Not many people would–"

"I don't expect this bleeding heart stuff from you so let's just get on with it," Allegra interjected.

Michael stopped and watched her eyes, challenging him to challenge her. Instead, he nodded and moved on: "Today I'm going to run you through all the details of Vokoban, all the ins and outs and inner workings of what we do and how we do it. Later today you will have a chance to talk to some of the field agents who have worked some of our harder cases. We want you to get a thorough and close-up look at what life will be like at Vokoban."

Allegra said nothing.

"Ready?"

Her eyes met his. "Of course. My life is but to serve you."

68

He stared at her for a long moment and then, with a sigh, continued. "We have a presentation that covers induction but I always talk my agents through it instead. It is of the utmost importance that you and I connect."

Again, she said nothing so Michael continued. "The basics: Vokoban was put together just under two years ago. We employ 72 field agents, 30 special agents, 10 therapists, five lawyers, two media relations officers and a host of auxiliary staff. I am a special agent. It is my team's job to research the targets in our database and assign a field agent to them. We are the ones that co-ordinate the operations and we look after two to three agents each. The field agents have one primary target to begin with. As they gain experience, they can be assigned two to three other targets which increases over time, depending on circumstances."

"Where do you get information for this database from?"

Michael brightened, pleased that she was responding. "From several different sources; past crimes and convictions, police records and reports, referrals from social workers and therapists, teachers, doctors, friends, relatives – basically everywhere and anywhere."

"And how do you know which ones to follow?"

"The special agents are responsible for the research stage. We obviously can't chase up every lead by placing a field agent so we run them through other databases and liaise with surveillance units. We are extremely thorough because 'Mr Regular Joe with his blonde locks and disarming smile' could be raping his daughter every night. We suspect everything and excuse nothing."

Allegra grimaced and waited for him to continue.

"Our field agents receive three weeks of thorough training; weapons, negotiation, intelligence, psychology and acting classes."

"Acting classes?"

"Yes. Those are actually one of the more important classes. You go through three weeks of acting classes before we put you in the field. We teach you how to look, act and even *think* like a young girl. We need to adjust your language, not only verbal but your body language too. We need to make you into something other than what you are. We need to toughen you up mentally to equip you with what you need to deal with your targets. This will involve a process of desensitisation to make it easier."

"Desensitisation?"

Michael met her eyes. "Basically, we show you things to get you used to what these men are capable of."

"'Things'?"

Michael nodded. "Images, videos, leaflets, accounts from victims and police reports."

"From child abuse cases?"

"Yes."

"Why am I not surprised?"

He frowned. "Allegra, it's a really important part of your training. It, perhaps more than anything else, will equip you with the tenacity you need for this role."

She raised a brow mockingly but said nothing.

"Listen, I know you're angry and I know you're confused. I know you're questioning what you're doing here but that you're not able to walk away – I understand that, but please know that you're doing the right thing."

Allegra said nothing, partly annoyed that he had an answer for everything, but also impressed that he was so in tune with her feelings. He displayed this uncanny ability throughout the rest of the session, answering questions and easing concerns before she voiced them. He took her through the various stages of training, ran her through past successes and gave her a timetable of classes. She was quietly comforted by the structure of it all.

After the morning session, he took her to lunch on the first floor of the building. She almost laughed when she saw a canteen that looked like any other. She was expecting a glass-chrome deal with security checks just to buy food. She sat down with a sandwich and relaxed, glad to be out of the hub. Here she could pretend that this place was normal and that the things happening beyond the walls of the canteen were okay. She watched Michael take a bite of his sandwich. He had let his professional guard down. It felt strange watching him act like a normal man with none of the secrecy and suspicion usually present in his eyes.

"What's your favourite colour?" she asked.

He looked up with surprise and shook his head to indicate 'Why?'

"I just figure if we're going to be spending a lot of time together and relying on each other, we should know the basics about each other."

Michael smiled. "Blue."

Despite herself, Allegra basked in his smile. "Mine too."

He raised a brow. "Not black and cream then?"

She blushed and averted her gaze. "Not black and cream."

"Favourite movie?"

"That's easy. 'The Godfather'."

Michael held up his hands. "Hey, I'm not going to argue with that."

"You have Italian in your blood too, don't you? With a name like Stallone?"

Michael nodded. "Yes. My father was mixed Italian and Sicilian. He came over here in the late 1960s and married my mother – she's Danish. It was a weird combination but they made it work."

So that's where he gets his gorgeous looks from. "Do you speak Italian? Or Danish for that matter?"

"I don't, no. You?"

Allegra shook her head. "My mother tried to teach me when I was young but," a pause, "she passed away before we could make any real progress."

"I'm sorry to hear that." Thin lines of concern creased his forehead.

Allegra waved it away. "Favourite book?" she changed the subject.

"'The Count of Monte Cristo'."

She laughed. "Such a man's man," she said in a gruff voice.

An hour flew past as they shared stories and anecdotes over the rest of their lunch. When they got up to leave, as if it was set to clockwork, Michael's guard came back up, his eyes became professional and his posture businesslike. The transformation intrigued her.

In silence they walked back to the hub. As she stepped in, Allegra saw that there was already a group of people in there.

"Everyone, this is Allegra. Allegra meet Caitlin." Michael indicated a slim, fragile-looking girl with long blonde hair and translucent skin. "Sophie," a slight brunette with shoulder-length hair. "And Rayla," a petite South-Asian girl with luscious black hair. "They make up three of our 72 field agents," finished Michael.

"Hi," said Allegra nervously. All three girls were beautiful and had a certain quality about them. Allegra couldn't quite put her finger on it. They were all extremely slim and very petite. Then it occurred to her: they looked like children. They looked like beautiful children rather than grown women. It was uncanny and unsettling.

"How old are you all?" Allegra asked falteringly. "If you don't mind me asking," she added quickly.

Caitlin, the blonde, stood up. "I just want to introduce myself properly, Allegra. As Michael said, my name is Caitlin. I have been with the unit from its inception. I am 24 and am currently placed with three targets." The assertiveness in her voice betrayed her doll-like appearance. "Basically, the three of us are here so we can have a chat and hopefully provide you with some insight that you haven't received so far," a brief glance at Michael. "Michael will slip away and come back at the end of the afternoon."

Allegra looked to him with sudden panic. He wasn't going to leave her with these strange, otherworldly creatures, was he?

He touched her arm and smiled reassuringly. "I'll be back at three. Use this time, Allegra. These girls live in the world you're about to enter. They can tell you things I'm not equipped to."

She nodded hesitantly. "Okay."

He exchanged partings with the other girls and left with one last glance at Allegra. She turned to the girls and smiled, trying to hide her anxiety. She felt like an outsider thrown into some strange clique.

Rayla stood and surveyed Allegra coolly. "Rayla Nagra. I work in the Special Interests Group under Agent Rasel Kundra. Men with very particular tastes, be it a taste for 'exotic' girls or a certain fetish, are assigned to us. I'm 25 and have been with the unit for a year."

Allegra nodded and offered a small smile of acknowledgement.

Lastly, the skinny brunette stood up. "Sophie. I'm 20 and I just joined the unit five months ago." Her voice was so soft that Allegra could barely hear her. "I am also assigned to Michael. He wanted me for a target called–"

"Sophie," interrupted Rayla. "We're not allowed to discuss targets with each other. You know that."

Sophie looked stricken, her gaze torn between Rayla and Allegra. "I'm sorry," she said into the air between and fell silent.

It was Caitlin who spoke next. "Allegra, we're here to answer your questions about the workings of the unit. We can't divulge any specific information about the targets we are working on because as you know, everything within the unit is highly classified. Having said that, please do ask if you have any questions and we will try our best to answer them."

Questions whizzed through Allegra's head. She asked the most prominent one: "Why?"

Caitlin frowned thoughtfully but it was Rayla who spoke. "That's exactly the right question you should ask: 'Why?' Some of these special agents drum the importance of *responsibility* and *duty* into your head but that's mainly bullshit."

Allegra blinked, taken aback by her abrasive honesty. "Then why? Why did you join?"

Rayla raised her head defiantly, chin jutting out as

she spoke. "I was date-raped two years ago. The bastard got away with it because there wasn't enough evidence."

Allegra's eyes grew wide. She started to speak but was silenced by Rayla's scowl.

"Don't apologise. It wasn't your fault," she said curtly.

Chastened by her tone, Allegra said nothing.

"Anyway, Vokoban got wind of my case and got in touch. I made a deal with them: I work for you, you set an agent on the tail of the cunt who raped me. They told me it was a waste of time – that the fucker didn't fit the profile of a paedo – but I wasn't gonna give up. They put a sweet little blonde thing on his tail and guess what? He happily fucked himself over like a moth to a flame. He's rotting in jail as we speak," she finished triumphantly. "These fuckers deserve to rot in prison and if we're not going to put them there, the bastard politicians certainly aren't gonna do it."

Allegra processed the information, secretly relieved that agents were made to see a therapist. She looked to Caitlin, glad to turn from Rayla's searing gaze.

"I wish I could say my intentions were as noble." Caitlin's soft blonde lashes fluttered. "I did it because no other job would pay a 22-year-old the kind of money I was offered. I was in a lot of debt. My parents retired, bills were overflowing, the bank was calling me every day. I was depressed, manic, just totally apathetic. Then I met Michael and it all went from there. I was in a tight spot and that's why I started. I have stayed because I genuinely believe in the work we do."

"Do you regret your decision?" asked Allegra.

Caitlin shook her head vehemently. "Not one bit. I can't say what we do is pleasant or even tolerable but it *is* important and it makes a difference."

Allegra nodded and looked to Sophie who was sitting meekly in the corner. The others looked at her expectantly.

"I, er, well, I did it because..." she paused, "I knew a girl who needed help but didn't know where to turn." Her soft voice was barely audible. "When I was young, my next-door neighbour, Mary, used to climb through my window at night. She told me it was because she was scared of the dark. I didn't think too much of it. Years later, when I was about 12, I realised that I had never climbed into her room – it was always the other way round – so I decided to try it. When I got to her window, I saw... her father." Sophie took a sharp intake of breath.

"You don't understand – he was so *big*, like a rugby player. He– he was on top of her, pulling off her nightie, shushing her, telling her to be quiet, telling her that he loved her, that she owed him. 'This is the rawest, most natural thing we can do together – you know that,' he told her.

"She was as still as a doll. He turned her around on her hands and knees. She looked so tiny beneath him."

Sophie's voice wavered. "She kept moving away when he tried to get inside her so he wrapped his arm around her stomach, forcing her to stay still. When she squealed in pain, he clasped his hand around her mouth, telling her that her mother would be jealous and angry with her if she found out. I remember the tears rolling down her face but she said nothing. She didn't even struggle; she just succumbed to him."

"He took so long. I know I should have done something but I was frozen and it went on for so long until finally, he... finished. Afterwards, when he was done, he kissed her goodnight and said he loved her. I ran home. All that time, like an idiot, I hadn't realised what was going on; why Mary always begged me not to tell my mum that she was staying over. I wanted to talk to her about it. The next time I saw her I tried to talk to her but I couldn't." Tears rolled down Sophie's cheeks. "Two months later they moved away. I can still remember the fear in Mary's eyes when she told me they were leaving. I saw it and I said nothing."

Sophie stopped to catch her breath. "I tried to find her two years ago but I couldn't. I didn't help her while I had the chance but there are others I *can* help and *that's* why I do this."

Caitlin walked over and put an arm around Sophie.

Allegra stared at her with sorrow. "But... how do you handle it? How do you deal with that kind of man being near you?"

"It will freak you out, Allegra," said Rayla. "I won't

lie to you and say that it won't. The first time will leave you cold and sweaty and like a mad dog in the summer, just going crazy, but when you find your feet, you will be fine."

"How many have you had?" asked Allegra, wincing at her choice of words.

"I've taken care of five over the past year. Some of the more experienced agents are assigned up to 10 targets a year, depending on how quickly they finish each case."

Allegra nodded. "Have you dealt with a guy that has escaped conviction?"

Rayla's eyes dropped to the floor. "Yes. It happens. It makes you furious because it was all for nothing but some men get off on a technicality, others look too much like Tom Cruise or Brad Pitt for anyone to ever believe they're sick in the head."

Allegra tried to formulate a new question as she digested the answer to her old one. "What about the ones you do manage to put away? How long do they stay inside?"

Caitlin took over. "It depends. Some get life sentences. Others are freed within a year."

"A year? It hardly seems worth it."

"Don't ever question that, Allegra," said Caitlin emphatically. "Don't ever question the worth of our work. What you will see during training will shock your system. You will meet victims of child abuse cases and you will realise that during your time in the unit, if you put away *one* guy for even *one* year, you will be helping some little girl out there from becoming the battered shells we come across."

Allegra drew in a shaky breath. "I'm just a little overwhelmed."

It was Sophie's turn to speak up. "Caitlin is right," she said softly. "Allegra, we meet the worst kind of men in our work but you have to believe it's worth it. Me telling you that won't make you believe it but hopefully once you have finished your training you will have that sense of belief in what we do."

"What is–" Allegra stopped, reconsidering her question. "What is the worst encounter you have had?"

Sophie's eyes turned to ice and she turned, deflecting the question to the others. Caitlin, the leader figure, stayed silent and even Rayla's hard exterior seemed to crack.

"I don't want to bring back nightmares for any of you but I'm really really scared here. I'm scared of these monsters and what they can do and if you tell me the worst, I will be prepared."

"Your training will run you through all that," said Caitlin.

"I'm not interested in the training. I'm interested in *you.*"

Caitlin sighed. "I've been here the longest so I guess I'll field this question." She took a deep breath and crossed her legs in her chair. "I think your first is always the worst but there was one guy who just made me sick. It wasn't anything violent or even unusual when you think about it but he used to like licking my skin. I mean, all the way down, everywhere – my stomach, my arms, my neck. Not kissing but licking it and I could feel his saliva drying on my skin, goosebumps growing underneath. Every time I was with him I felt disgusted afterwards."

Allegra saw the vulnerability in Caitlin's eyes and wondered if she could really expose herself in this way. "How many times did you... how many times, on average, does a field agent have an encounter with a target?" she asked, adopting their language to make the question more clinical.

"It varies," answered Caitlin. "It can be from three to 10. It depends on how good the field agent is, how quickly the target responds and the severity of the act that happens between them."

"Have you all slept with one of these men? Michael said it helps the conviction."

The girls fell silent again.

Allegra gulped, swallowing the lump in her throat. "How many?"

Caitlin looked up slowly. "Nine."

Allegra drew back in her chair as if physically pushed.

"One," said Sophie.

"One," echoed Rayla.

Caitlin looked at her in surprise. "One?"

Rayla nodded. "I nail them with oral," she said with a hint of pride. It made Allegra feel queasy.

"Do you have any other questions or worries?" asked Caitlin.

Allegra drew her eyes away from Rayla. "Do you ever worry that these men will track you down once they are out? I mean, you *do* have to testify, right?"

"Targets with spent convictions will be kept under loose surveillance. But you have to understand that these men are not violent per se. They are sick with sick habits but more often than not, they are cowards who wouldn't dream of tracking down an agent."

Allegra asked about the process of convicting a target from beginning to end and began to relax in the other women's company. For the first time, she saw herself as others did: a strange being, not a woman but not quite a girl. The others, like her, looked 14 or 15 despite being in their twenties.

At precisely 3 p.m., Michael knocked on the door and looked in. "Do you need more time?" he directed at Allegra.

She shook her head, comforted by his presence. As he walked in, she caught a subtle exchange of glances between him and Caitlin. She didn't quite know what it meant. She thanked the three women for their time and help, and watched them file out of the room one by one.

"Okay?" asked Michael.

She nodded. "Yeah, I'm okay."

"You have anything else to ask me?"

She shook her head.

"I hope you're not too overwhelmed." He tried to gauge if one last pep talk was needed.

"I'm okay." Allegra met his eyes, reassured by his concern.

He decided against the pep talk. "Let me take you home." When he caught the look on her face – a mixture of surprise and concern – he immediately amended it: "I mean, let me call the driver who'll take you home." He led her back through the labyrinth of corridors down to the foyer where he discharged her for the day.

"I'll see you tomorrow," he said with a smile that looked sad to Allegra.

"Bye Michael." She stepped out into the cool May air and felt familiar butterflies in her stomach. A part of her was so scared, it froze the blood in her body, but another part was strangely excited about the journey she was about to begin. She knew it would be frightening and dangerous, but, to her own surprise, she felt ready. In spite of herself, she felt determined to be a part of something important, to make herself proud. And yes, to make Michael proud.

CHAPTER FOUR

"Hey sweets," Andrew kissed Allegra's cheek. "Where were you today?"

She smiled. "I got a job."

He broke into a wide grin and pulled her close. "Really? Where? When did this happen?" She let him hug her, breaking eye contact, and spoke the words Michael had given her: "It's a graphics job for the Home Office. I'll be helping design their internal documents and annual reports, and working on their website."

Andrew frowned. "It doesn't sound very creative. Are you sure it's what you want?"

She shrugged. "It doesn't sound as interesting as the stuff I was doing at ImageBox but it's a start."

"Well, in that case, I am taking you out to celebrate!"

Allegra shook her head. "I'm actually really tired. Can we just have a night in?"

He smiled. "A night in with my beautiful, stunning,

employed girlfriend? You think I'm going to complain?"

They ordered takeaway and nestled in front of the television. As she rested her head on his shoulders, Allegra realised that she felt no guilt about lying to him.

"Genius," Lyla greeted Michael as she walked into the office at 8.30 a.m.

He looked up questioningly.

"Melissa Hart. I couldn't figure out what you did to make Allegra say yes but then I saw Melissa Hart on your file access history."

Michael shook his head. "It took a lot more than Melissa Hart."

"Oh?"

"Yes." He elaborated no further.

"Do you think she's in for the long haul?"

"I can't say yet. You know you can't really tell until first contact – the classic fight or flee. If they're okay after that, they're usually in for the long haul."

"Did she talk about any history of sexual abuse in her family?"

"No." Michael shook his head. "We just got very lucky."

"Hmm." Lyla nodded thoughtfully. "Well, she's braver than me. I sure as hell couldn't do it."

"That's because you love working with me too much and couldn't bear to leave me," said Michael in uncharacteristic jest.

"Ha!" Lyla laughed. At 47, she was 12 years older than Michael. "If that were true, you'd have to lock me up along with all the other paedophiles you catch!"

"*They* catch," he said with sudden solemnity. He looked at Lyla sadly. "The field agents do all the work. They do the catching. I just sit and watch. Sometimes, I..." He shook his head.

"Sometimes you?" urged Lyla. She saw torment in his eyes every day but he never spoke about his feelings or how he was affected by Vokoban.

"I sit and watch our agents being touched, violated, *destroyed* by these men and I... hate myself for it."

Concern crept across Lyla's face. "Michael, none of these women would be here if they didn't want to be. They understand that we – *you* – do good work."

He shook his head. "I know it's the big picture that counts but it's in *real time,* Lyla – that's the thing. I'm not watching a piece of collected evidence like those used in desensitisation; I'm watching an agent get molested *right now,* as I watch, and I can't do anything about it. I can't run in there and grab the guy by the throat like I want to. I can't beat him to a pulp like he deserves. I can't pull that woman out of there because *I'm* the one that's put her there. I have to sit and watch every touch, every stroke, and I have to take it. I have to just let it happen and it makes me–" Michael shot up from his desk and paced across the room. Face red with restrained aggression, he flexed his fingers and his jaw.

Lyla watched him prowl the room, stripped of the cool he so carefully maintained in front of others. She blinked, trying to think of something calming to say.

"I'm fine," he snapped. "I'm fine. I'm just anxious about Drake. I just want this case over and done with and then I'll be fine."

Lyla nodded. "Okay. Allegra will be here in half an hour so I'll leave you alone to prepare." She closed the door in silence and walked away.

Allegra silently counted Michael's eyelashes. *What is he doing here?* she wondered. *Shouldn't he be on a film set somewhere? Not here with me, standing so close.*

"We have a packed day for you," he interrupted her thoughts. "I hope you had a good night's sleep,"

Allegra thought of herself in bed last night, hot and sleepless in the stifling darkness. "I did," she lied, feeling a tingle run through her body. He didn't seem to notice the blush spreading on her cheeks.

"You already have a copy of your timetable. For the first week you will meet with me at the beginning and end of every day. This will be reduced to evening meetings only in the second week which may be further reduced thereafter. Does that sound okay?"

"Yes. Sounds okay." She fell in stride with him as they walked to the hub.

He pulled out a copy of her timetable. "As you can see, training is divided into four sections. 'Psych' involves therapy sessions and desensitisation seminars.

'Acting classes' are self-explanatory. These sessions will also run you through media relations and communication. 'WSN' is pronounced 'Wesson' and involves Weapons, Self-defence and Negotiations training. Lastly, 'Intel' covers the basics of gathering intelligence, and trains you with the technical equipment you will be using. We will train you with wires and surveillance methods, and teach you how to optimise your time with a target by eliciting as much damaging evidence as possible. It will be an intense first week but I will be here for you to turn to. Depending on your progress, you could be making contact with your first target by the 15th."

Allegra did a double-take. "But that's in two weeks."

"Just first contact," said Michael soothingly. "You will continue to train but we will allocate one day where you make contact with the target. But at this point, it is entirely dictated by your pace and what you feel comfortable with. No one is going to rush you into anything, okay?"

Allegra felt her stomach churn. "But two weeks? That's not enough time."

"Hey," Michael touched her arm and looked into her eyes. "When you say 'go', we go. When you say 'stop', we stop. That is a promise."

His touch was warm, reassuring. She nodded. "Okay."

He checked his watch. "It's almost 10. I believe you have your first Psych session in a few minutes.

Think you can get there alone?"

Allegra hesitated. "Fifth floor, out of the lifts, right, cross the atrium and third door on the left."

He nodded, impressed. "You're going to be alright," he said with a smile.

"So this is where we part ways?"

"Until 4 p.m, yes. Be good."

She smiled. "I'll try."

"It's open," called a voice from the other side of the door.

Allegra opened it hesitantly and was surprised by what she saw. Instead of a stern woman in a stark office, she was greeted by one no older than 30 in an office that resembled a living room.

"I'm really sorry about the mess." The woman kicked an overflowing bag underneath a table. She leaned forward and offered her hand. "Marianne Faithfull."

Allegra shook it hesitantly. "Allegra Ashe. Not quite as, er, interesting as your name."

Marianne smiled. "My father had a thing about rock stars." She gestured at the sofa. "Please sit."

Allegra tried to make herself comfortable – the session was going to last an hour. Marianne sat in a chair opposite and crossed her statuesque legs. With long blonde hair and stunning blue eyes, she looked more like a model than a therapist.

Maybe everyone needs to be beautiful to work in this place.

"Allegra, Michael Stallone is your special agent, is he not?"

"Yes."

"Gorgeous, isn't he?"

Allegra looked up in surprise.

"Hey, I'm just telling it like it is," Marianne held her hands up in defence.

"Well, he isn't exactly the hunchback of Notre Dame."

"If I liked men, I would have had that man 10 times over."

Allegra fidgeted, immediately uncomfortable with the forced intimacy.

Marianne picked up on it and smiled. "Sorry, I'm getting carried away. The reason I ask you this is because you will fall in love with him."

Allegra prickled. "Are you a therapist or a clairvoyant?"

"Bit of both." Marianne laughed. "Allegra, during your time within the unit, Michael will be your first form of contact. I will always be here for you but inevitably, Michael will become the one you rely on. With a man that gorgeous, those feelings of dependence will naturally form into what you think is love."

Allegra shook her head. "I'm already in a relationship."

Marianne opened her mouth to speak but then closed it again and nodded. "Okay. Now that the pleasantries are out of the way, it's time to get down to business. As you know, this session is written in every Tuesday morning. It's there for us to have a chat. It can be about work, about the training and what you're going through or we can sit and talk about re-runs of 'Sex and the City'. It is entirely up to you. Nothing you say will go beyond these four walls. If you want to have a quiet place to sit and think, you can use this space to do so. I'm totally flexible and will work around you."

Allegra nodded. She couldn't decide whether she liked this woman or not. There was something about the whole therapy thing that got her back up.

"For this session though, in typical shrink fashion, I'm going to ask you to tell me about yourself. I'd like you to tell me about your background, about your friends and family so I can get an all-round picture of you."

Allegra was amused by the question; by the situation. *I may as well tell her what she wants to hear.* "My mother died when I was 12. I have one elder sister, Sienna, and one elder brother, Rafael. Yes, I was devastated by the death but I got over it – people do. I was a graphics designer but was made redundant and so here I am."

Marianne looked at her with an expressionless face. "And your father?"

Allegra grew still. "I don't know my father and I never did."

"How come?"

A vein in Allegra's temple contracted. "He walked out on us when I was very young."

"Has he ever tried to get back in touch?"

"Never."

Marianne nodded. "Do you ever think you might look for him?"

"Never."

"Because?"

"Because he doesn't deserve us. Sienna has a beautiful and happy family. Rafael is doing well now and I'm, well, I'm here and we're okay and we don't need him in our lives."

"So you've never really had a father figure?"

She shook her head. "I've done perfectly well without one."

"What about relationships? You say you're in one at the moment? How is that?"

"It's healthy. He's a lawyer."

Marianne nodded. "Do you love him?"

Allegra bristled. "Yes," she said emphatically. "I love him very much."

"Are you *in* love with him?"

"Of course I am." She sounded more defensive than she had intended.

"How do you feel about keeping the workings of the unit from him?"

She shrugged. "I'm just taking it as it comes."

Marianne nodded. "And why are you here?"

Allegra searched herself for an answer. "Because if I

wasn't, the next time I heard about one of these cases, I'd feel... responsible."

"Guilt is a powerful emotion."

"I guess."

Marianne surveyed her for a few seconds. "Any other reasons you took on this role?"

Allegra thought of Michael. "My first reason isn't good enough?"

Marianne shook her head. "Of course it's good enough. I'm just trying to get a complete picture."

"That is the complete picture." She held Marianne's stare.

"Okay. Tell me what you expect from this job."

"In what sense?"

"In any sense."

Allegra sighed. "I expect to walk through a lobby, ride up in a lift, talk to people, eat lunch at the canteen and get a monthly pay cheque."

Instead of the annoyance Allegra was aiming for, Marianne's laughter expressed amusement. "Very good," she commented. "Have trouble expressing your feelings much?"

"To strangers, yes," Allegra shot back.

"Let me guess, but to friends, you're a gushing ball of uninhibited emotion?"

Allegra swallowed. "People are comfortable with different degrees of intimacy. Didn't they teach you that in Psych 101?"

Marianne smiled. "Hey, I'm not trying to antagonise

you. I'm just trying to figure out a way we can help each other. Working life at Vokoban isn't pretty – even for me who experiences most of it second hand. I just want to make sure you're gonna be okay."

Allegra stood up. "I'm gonna be okay."

Marianne glanced at her watch. "We're not done."

Sighing, Allegra sat back down. "Okay. I want to talk about re-runs of 'Sex and the City'," she said insolently.

"I reckon I would have chosen Aidan over Big. I mean, he *was* the nicest guy, but women are so exasperating sometimes. They just can't help but go for the powerful but arrogant alpha male. I can understand the allure of the elusive, but when we beat ourselves up over a guy who won't commit or who likes to play about with our emotions, it's just embarrassing to continue demeaning ourselves by chasing them. But that's just me – what do you think? Who would *you* have chosen?" asked Marianne without missing a beat.

"I'm Yasmine." The whisper came from a young Asian girl with the biggest, most soulful eyes Allegra had ever seen. With luscious lips and long dark eyelashes, the girl looked like a younger, more beautiful version of Rayla.

Allegra smiled unsurely. "Allegra."

"First week, right?" Yasmine tilted her head, sending her long black hair cascading over her shoulders.

Allegra nodded.

"Who's your special agent?"

"Michael Stallone."

"Score! I hear he's scrumptious."

Allegra raised a brow and smiled. "Scrumptious?"

"Yeah. You should see Rasel, my special agent. He's about 45, horn-rimmed glasses, dresses like he's still in the eighties, craggy face and an even craggier disposition. The stories I've heard about Michael Stallone though... Is it true he has the dreamiest eyes?" The girl sighed in a doe-eyed reverie.

Allegra ignored the question. "You say your agent is Rasel. Does that mean you're in the Special Interests group with Rayla?"

"You've met Rayla? She's great, isn't she? *There's* a girl who knows what she wants and takes no shit from anyone. I'm told I look a bit like her. All I need now is that kick-ass attitude."

"So you *are* in Special Interests?"

"Oh, sorry," Yasmine laughed. "Yes, I am. I talk a mile a minute. I'll talk forever if no one shuts me up."

At that precise moment, the door to the conference room shut with a loud thud. A woman in her mid-forties walked in, dressed all in black.

"Good morning agents," she said, clearly and confidently. "My name is Jessica Taylor. I have been formally trained as a psychologist and work closely with the therapists you have been assigned. I organise and implement the desensitisation seminars. Along the way you will also meet Cory who is my 'deputy' if you will. When I am absent or unable to attend a seminar, Cory will take over.

"It may have been some years since you were in education or in a classroom-based setting so I want to establish a rule: when I am talking, everyone listens. No one talks over me. Everyone understand?"

The eight girls in the room nodded, some muttering a "yes".

"Good. Now a word of warning: some of what you see in this room will make you feel sick. It is designed for this purpose. We want to squeeze every single ounce of anger, sadness, outrage, frustration and disgust out of you during training so that these emotions do not surface out in the field. Sometimes when we watch things, you will want to leave the room or close your eyes. It is intrinsic to the success of these sessions that you are exposed to as much material as possible so I don't want any of you turning away from the screen. We don't want to dehumanise you, we simply want to arm you. Do not be frightened of what's to come. We do good work here and as long as we stick together as a unit, we will succeed. Any questions?"

Yasmine raised her hand.

"Yes. You are?"

"Yasmine."

"Hello Yasmine. What would you like to know?"

"The footage that we're going to see, is it all real or is some of it made up?"

Jessica shook her head. "None of it is fake. It is *all* real. Some of it has been found on the internet, much of it was seized from collections belonging to convicted paedophiles, some of it is CCTV footage or pictures from police reports, some of it was sent to us from other crime organisations across the globe. Our database of this material is vast and varied. It contains every sick thing you can dream up, and then some."

Yasmine nodded and offered a quiet "thank you".

"Any more questions?" Jessica glanced around the room. When no one spoke, she continued. "Okay. Well, I hope you're sitting comfortably for we are about to begin."

Jessica Taylor didn't plan to ease the agents into anything. Her technique had been criticised by a few special agents, specifically because there was a danger of scaring off newly recruited field agents but Jessica Taylor did things her way. There was no pussyfooting to be done in her sessions. She was determined to equip her agents with steel in their nerves. It was the only way they would survive Vokoban.

She pressed a button and the projector lit up with a brutal picture of a young girl's bloodied corpse. A round of disgusted gasps resonated across the room. The girl's blonde hair was soaked in blood and her nose was a mushy mess. It looked like it had been smashed in by some sort of blunt instrument. Her eyes were open, dead and vacant.

"Sarah Philips," boomed Jessica's voice. "Twelve

years old. Raped and murdered half a mile west of Clapham Common on September 5th 2009. The assailant was one Josh West, a 38-year-old banker from Camden. On surface, a 'typical' case but this had one specific sticking point." Jessica looked around the room, making sure the agents were focused on the picture. "Josh West was in our database of suspected targets since August 10th 2008. He was untagged by a field agent as all of them were occupied with more high priority cases."

A wave of whispers passed through the room.

"Sarah left behind her parents, two younger sisters and a younger brother. Vokoban could have prevented her death if we had more field agents; agents like the ones you will become. She died because *we* failed." She let this sink in.

The screen clicked. The picture was replaced by another, this one showing a profile of Sarah's body. There was a palm-sized bruise just above her hips. Disturbingly, it reminded Allegra of blueberry pie.

Jessica continued. She gave them a biography of Sarah's early years and followed it up with close-up shots of her naked corpse. The presentation ended with a clip of Sarah's parents giving an emotional statement to the press. It was the kind of case that made your blood run cold. The agents would be dealing with cases like this, time and time again.

Blanking the screen, Jessica looked at each individual agent. "This is the first of many to come. It is not the worst case you will see but it is particularly poignant for us at Vokoban because of the circumstances surrounding the perpetrator. Before we close for today, I just want to point out that sometimes I will take a hard line approach and make you watch things you don't want to see or remember. I will make a point of searing these things into your brains but I am doing it for your own good. You have a lot of support here within the unit. Mine is just a different sort."

Quietened by the images soaking into their minds, the girls sat in silence.

"Okay, agents. Thank you for your attention. I will see you tomorrow morning at 11."

The agents filed out of the room and disbanded. Yasmine, however, stayed by Allegra's side.

"You wondering how we're gonna survive this?"

"Yes," said Allegra honestly.

"Me too." Yasmine momentarily fell quiet before brightly announcing, "Hey, it's almost lunchtime."

"Yes."

"You wanna head down to the cafeteria? Maybe Mr Stallone will be there," she said in a singsong tone.

Allegra smiled. "Sure."

As they ate, Yasmine filled Allegra in on some of the details of her life. She was 22 years of age and had grown up in East London before studying history at Manchester University.

"After graduating, I couldn't find a job. There was

fuck-all," Yasmine exclaimed in disgust. "I was unemployed for a year and that's when I met Rasel."

"How did you react to him? How did he approach you?"

"I was in a bloody library of all things. I was in the adult learning lab when Rasel came up to me and boldly asked how old I was. I thought he was one of the attendants so I told him I was 22. His eyes lit up – it was actually kind of creepy. Anyway, he gave me his card, said his organisation could use women like me. He was pretty vague but I called him up anyway. My parents were getting on my nerves. Every day would bring the same arguments; the same questions: 'Yasmine, what did you go to uni for? Why did we waste our money?' After a while, it became unbearable."

Allegra thought wistfully of her mother. She would endure all the criticism in the world if she could just have her back.

"So I did the only thing I could do," Yasmine continued. "I took this job and I moved out."

"Where are you staying now?"

"I'm renting this shabby place in Forest Gate but I didn't have many options, being as skint as I was. Hopefully when our first pay packet comes in, I'll be able to wave bye-bye to the skank-hole I'm living in. It will show up my parents good and proper."

Allegra raised an eyebrow.

Yasmine sighed. "Don't get me wrong. They're my parents and I love them but they can be so overbearing.

They're classic over-achievers – run their own law firm and everything – so they expected the best from me. It always felt like 'we'll love you just the way you are if you're perfect'." She shrugged her shoulders and smiled sadly.

As Allegra began to respond, Yasmine's head shot up. "That's him, right?"

Allegra followed her gaze. Her stomach seized as she spotted Michael. Every pair of eyes in the room followed him as he strode over to the conveyer belt and put his tray down.

Guess I'm not the only one who can't take my eyes off him.

The audible lull in the cafeteria was broken as soon as Michael left.

"Jeeesus Christ. Mama, give me some of that!" Yasmine all but panted in Michael's wake. "You lucky mare," she shot at Allegra. "How come other girls get all the breaks?"

"It's actually quite difficult working with him," Allegra commented.

"What? Difficult like walking on searing hot coals with shards of glass stuck in your eye? 'Coz I tell you, I'd walk over miles of it just to wank in his shadow."

Allegra's jaw fell open.

Yasmine caught herself. "Jeez, I'm sorry. I'm oversharing. I do that."

Allegra shook her head. "I don't know quite what to say."

"I shouldn't be so vulgar." Yasmine lifted her chin and put on a posh English accent. "My darling, that fellow is so divine, one does acquire the sudden proclivity to foray over miles of potentially harmful materials so that one may pleasure oneself in his divine penumbra."

Allegra burst out laughing. "You're mad."

Yasmine laughed too and shrugged her shoulders. "Only on Tuesdays."

The two of them spent the rest of the day together like two schoolgirls, only with classes in weapons and intelligence instead of science and maths. As the day ended and she said goodbye to her new friend, Allegra sighed wistfully, wondering if they really would survive all that was to come.

"I love you."

Andrew looked up sharply. "I love you too," he said, trying to shake the surprise out of his voice. Unaccustomed to hearing Allegra say it voluntarily, he couldn't help but ask, "What's brought this on?"

She shrugged. "I just..." She stopped and adjusted her body against the kitchen counter. "There's just so much ugliness in the world and so many horrifying things happening every day – I'm just happy that I have a slice of something good."

Andrew walked to her and gently took her hand. "Is everything okay?"

"Everything's fine." She nodded and wrapped her

arms around him, leaning against his chest. "I love you," she repeated, holding him tight.

He kissed her hair, hiding the lines of concern snaking across his face.

The next day, Allegra sat beside Yasmine in their first acting class. Their teacher, a wild redhead dressed in a lime green kaftan with multi-coloured paisley-patterned leggings, greeted the class with a toothy grin.

"Okay kids, settle down," she called. "I am Moesha Evans. You may call me Moshe. I will be taking care of your acting sessions for the next three weeks. Thereafter, you may have some refresher sessions but the bulk of your lessons will take place now. Have any of you ever done any acting before?"

"Well, I deserve an Oscar for some of the lies I've told my parents," said Yasmine, making the class laugh.

"Thank you, Miss?"

"Miss Ali. Yasmine."

"Thank you, Yasmine," said Moshe with a smile. "Anyone else?" After a pause, she continued. "The purpose of these lessons is to teach you about getting into character, about changing your body language and how to switch it on and off. Changing into a character is one thing; changing back to yourself – switching *off* – is infinitely harder. We don't want you to lose your identity so these lessons are very important." She looked around the room. "Everyone ready to start?" A pause. "I can't hear you. Are you ready to start?"

"Yes," called a chorus of voices.

"Good. Okay, I want you to come on down from those seats to the centre of the room. Take off your shoes and sit in the middle. Don't worry, I'm not going to make you hold hands and sing 'Kumbaya'. I just want you all to be comfortable."

There was a bit of chatter as the agents did what they were told. Once they were settled into a ragged circle, Moshe leaned forward. "Acting lessons will fall into one of four categories: popular culture, verbal language, body language and sexuality. Popular culture because the shows you watch are not necessarily the shows a 13-year-old watches; the music you listen to will not be the music schoolgirls are listening to. We're going to get you up to date with the latest trends in music, film, fashion, the internet and even text speak. We are going to change the way you speak and use language, and slowly graduate onto physical movement. The most important thing you will learn is how to change your body language. The way a 12-year-old girl moves is different to the way a 24-year-old woman moves. The way she talks, smiles, laughs, walks, everything is different.

"Then comes sexuality. We will cover it in depth but one important thing to note right from the start is that we want you to act like *normal* teenage girls. We are not trying to teach you to be young seductresses, enticing these men with your forbidden fruit. There'll be no 'light of my life, fire of my loins'. Entrapment laws are waived for Clause 160 but if our evidence shows an agent dressed up like a young hooker, giving it all of this," Moshe flicked her hair and stuck her chest out, "It won't go down well. It destroys or, at the very least, reduces our credibility. I'm not going to bombard you with too much right now, but just bear it in mind."

Allegra was both impressed and unsettled by the scale and depth of their training. She looked over to Yasmine. *Will we recognise ourselves on the other side?* she wondered.

Moshe pulled out an A2-sized piece of paper with some words written on it. "Come closer." The girls crawled forward and scanned the piece of paper.

Similar words
Effect/Affect
Bought/Brought
Dependent/Dependant
Further/Farther
Lose/Loose
Peddle/Pedal
Principle/Principal
Stationary/Stationery
They're/Their/There
Your/You're

Plural v Singular
Fish
Data
Media

"What you see in front of you is a collection of words that children often confuse," said Moshe. "You will start to incorporate some of these into your speech while in character. The second section shows a list of words that people, even adults, get confused about. Words like data and media are plural so saying 'the media is' is wrong. Again, we will teach you to drop a few of these into conversations with your targets. This change in language is a small and subtle thing but it is effective. It adds to the whole package of making you seem younger than you are."

I bought my sister along, said Allegra in her mind.

Moshe continued: "What I want to do today is examine your speech patterns. All of you obviously speak differently and I need to know how to work with you on an individual basis to 'correct' your patterns. I'm going to call each of you to the front of the room and give you a subject to speak about for a minute or so. It won't be anything difficult, just your thoughts and opinions on very simple subjects. You think you can handle that?"

The girls nodded.

"Okay, good." Moshe pointed at Yasmine. "Miss Ali. You're up. Can we have you talking about a pet hate please?"

Yasmine nodded and walked to the front of the classroom. "Hi. I'm Yasmine and I'm an alcoholic." The class laughed. "Okay, my pet hate is reality TV. You'd think it would have died down by now but they've been going on for what? A frickin' decade and half? They've got everything from dustbin men to amputees being followed around. It's so unbelievably stupid. The other day I was watching TV and there was a show about the life of priests. I mean, *come on,* how interesting can a priest's life really be? Unless, of course, you're one of those perverted priests but it wasn't even like that – it was just a show following them around church and quarters. I couldn't believe it."

Moshe nodded, pleased, and made some notes. She put her pen down and pointed to Allegra.

"Miss?"

"Ashe. Allegra Ashe."

"Allegra, you're up. Can we have you talking about," Moshe scanned the paper pad on her lap, "relationships?"

Allegra stood nervously and walked to the front. "I, uh, okay. I think relationships are overrated."

Moshe looked amused. "Go on."

"In a way, they're like size zero. The media tell us that size zero is the pinnacle of beauty so, even though we *know* a size eight or ten looks so much better, we begin to worship size zero. It's the same thing with relationships. I mean, don't get me wrong, some relationships are great, but it's this idea that we should *all* be looking for someone and that we are incomplete without a matching pair that really gets to me. Singles are forever searching for 'the one', envying paired-up individuals when, in reality, so many couples are only in a relationship because they feel they should be."

Moshe smiled. "Well, I know where my work lies with you."

Allegra looked at her questioningly.

"A 25-year-old can just about be excused for that amount of cynicism. A 13-year-old most certainly cannot."

Allegra started to respond but then just nodded and returned to her spot.

Yasmine shot her a sideways glance. "Dude," she said under her breath. "You need to get laid."

Allegra couldn't help but smile. She glanced back at Yasmine. "Maybe I do." She shrugged. "Maybe I will."

Allegra's last meeting of the week was on Friday evening with Michael. To her surprise, he had asked her to go to his office instead of the hub. As she walked in, a satisfied smile spread across her lips. His room was just as she thought it would be: a big black leather sofa paired with stained oak furniture; a leather chair in front of a meticulously tidy desk; a number of abstract paintings hung perfectly straight on the wall; and, of course, a large bookcase filled to the brim with psychology and crime analysis books.

"Please sit," Michael gestured towards the black sofa.

Allegra chose a chair instead, lowering herself into it with a grimace. Her first WSN class had put her through a gruelling fitness test, leaving her with sore muscles everywhere.

"I hear you're doing really well."

"From who?"

"From your tutors. Moshe thinks you're a character."

"Thanks – I think." Despite her casual tone, she still wasn't comfortable around him.

He ran a hand through his perfect hair. "I want to talk to you about the target I'm thinking of assigning to you."

Her heartbeat quickened. "Okay."

He pulled his chair closer to her. "I want first contact to be made on the 18th."

Allegra's face tightened with apprehension. Up to now, she had been drifting along, making friends with the other girls, and even enjoying the learning experience. The thought of first contact made panic rise in her throat.

"Allegra, it's just first contact. We will just trickle you into the target's consciousness. You may not even have to talk to him. He just needs to be aware of you."

She shook her head. "But the acting sessions, we're still just talking about language and speech. We haven't even spoken about boundaries or the way I should carry myself or all the things Moshe said we were going to cover."

"I know her schedule. By next week, you will have covered first contact. The last week covers the rest of the operation and how to react when the target engages in physical activity with you. That you don't need to know until much later."

She stiffened. She wanted to succeed in Vokoban, but the prospect of meeting her first target so soon made her burn with anxiety. "Surely it's better to have an all-round idea of what goes on and how to act – a complete training period – before throwing me in the deep end?"

"I know you can handle it, Allegra."

She shook her head. "You said we'll stop when I say 'stop'," she accused.

"You will be ready by next week." He leaned forward and touched her arm. "If you say 'stop' then, we'll stop."

She took a deep breath. "Who is this target? Surely he can wait just one more week?"

Michael sighed. "We–" he paused. "We have placed a few agents with him before but none of them worked. I want to test you out as soon as possible to see if you match. If not, I'll prime you for another target altogether."

Allegra was confused. "I don't understand. You say the other agents didn't 'work'. What do you mean they didn't work?"

"He didn't initiate any sexual activity with them."

"Well then... doesn't that just mean he's *not* a paedophile?"

"Usually, yes, but this one has very particular tastes. The other three agents didn't work because they weren't his type."

Allegra was taken aback. "*Three* agents? What are

you going to do? Keep throwing women at him until he finds someone he fancies? You do that to any man, you'd probably end up reeling him in."

Michael shook his head vehemently. "I *know* he's guilty."

"How?"

"Casework. His file. His history. His habits. Allegra, I have seen hundreds, maybe thousands of paedophiles in my time. It's just that *thing,* the one thing that I can just pick up on. We need to nail him."

"But what led you to him? You just saw him on the street and thought, 'Hey, *he* looks like a pervert'?"

Michael swallowed his frustration and then, calmly, began to speak. "Last year, a young girl called Jemima was killed and dumped near Hampstead. Initial investigations found short periods of time where Jemima's whereabouts were unknown. She would tell her parents she was at her best friend's house when she wasn't. She would say she had detention when she didn't. At first, we suspected she had a secret boyfriend but all evidence indicated the presence of an older man."

"What evidence?"

"She suddenly had expensive gifts that her parents had no idea about. Her diary mentioned 'HIM' a few times. We think 'HIM' was the man that groomed her and eventually killed her."

Allegra processed this information. The knot in her stomach tightened. "But why kill her?"

"Because it couldn't last forever. Even when a young girl is willing to sleep with an older man, eventually the truth comes out. She may want more from him or she may want to stop it. She may threaten to tell someone – any number of reasons."

"But how do you know we're targeting the right guy?"

"When we went through the objects in her room, her parents pointed out things they didn't recognise. We came across a blank postcard originating from a gallery in Hampstead. Recon work on the owner – his actions and habits – led me to believe that he's our man."

Allegra heard the words he was saying but still didn't *know* anything. "Michael, I really would rather just finish training first. It's just a week."

His eyes softened. "Hey, look at me." He reached forward and touched her chin, lifting it gently. "I would never give you something you couldn't handle. I know you're capable of this. All you have to do is make him see you – you don't even have to talk to him. I will be looking after you every step of the way. I won't let anything happen to you."

Allegra, comforted by his words and his touch, nodded in acquiescence.

The relief was clear on Michael's face. "You have made the right decision. I've wasted so much time on this guy but I *know* he isn't as clean-cut as he comes across. I *know* it."

Allegra was unsettled by the growing excitement in

his voice. He sounded strangely like a man with a vendetta. "You don't *know* this guy, do you?"

Michael shook his head. "No, but I know his type; the kind of guy who looks so clean, no one would ever imagine he has dirty secrets to hide."

Allegra bit the corner of her bottom lip and nodded.

"So everything is settled. Don't worry about anything. Carry on with training as usual. Do pay a lot of attention to the acting and Intel classes. Intel will show you exactly what you need to do to secure a conviction. I will work behind the scenes and set up the circumstances for first contact. I will talk to Moshe about prepping you and ask her to talk to the wardrobe and make-up people."

Allegra felt apprehension spread through her veins but she didn't want to disappoint Michael. She nodded simply and said, "Okay."

"Oh, my Lord, I don't believe it."

Allegra smiled. "Ta-da!"

"Allegra Ashe? Early?" Sienna poked her head out and looked around. "Where is she?" she called out. "Where is my sister? Take away this imposter, punctual as she may be."

"Okay, okay, that's enough." Allegra ushered her sister into the house and followed her in.

"No but seriously, you're early? I have never known you to be early for anything. This new job must be teaching you the laws of discipline."

Allegra bristled and offered a weak smile.

"Grab a seat on the sofa. You can keep Reese company while I finish dinner. She's trying to get a section of her solo right but she's struggling."

"Sure." Allegra walked into the living room to find Reese slumped on their massive sofa with her violin lying in the middle of the room. "What's up, kiddo?"

Reese brightened at the sound of Allegra's voice. "Hey! You're here."

"I'm here." Allegra kissed Reese's cheek and took a seat next to her. "So what's up?"

She sighed. "I just can't seem to get the middle section of my solo right. The pitch has to be perfect and I keep messing it up."

"Let me hear."

Reese stood resignedly. She took a moment to position the violin on her shoulder and then began to play. Her piece was renowned for technical difficulty but she swept over the introduction beautifully and then seamlessly segued into the crescendo. It was pitch-perfect and only wobbled slightly in the last few seconds. Reese stopped playing and looked up with red cheeks, delighted. "I did it! I did it. It was right, right?" she asked.

Allegra wasn't really musical but it had sounded perfect to her. "It was right."

Reese whooped. "You're my lucky charm. I've been trying to nail this since morning and not once have I got it right. I nearly had an asthma attack 'coz I was getting so stressed out." She bounded over to Allegra and grabbed her hand. "This means you *have* to come to the concert."

Allegra smiled. "I'll be there. July 21st, right?"

"June 21st," corrected Sienna, joining them in the living room. "Well done sweetheart." She ruffled Reese's hair. "Anyway, la cena e' servita!"

"Great. I'm starving." Allegra stood and followed the others to the dining room. Stephen was at a friend's stag-do so it was just the girls.

"How's the new job?" asked Reese.

"It's good." Allegra took a quick sip of wine. It burned in her throat.

"Any cute guys?"

"No, not really." She coughed. "How about you? Any cute guys at school you haven't told me about?"

Reese shrugged. "Not like it'd make any difference. There's no way Führer Major and Führer Minor would let me date anyway."

"Hey," Sienna interjected. "Your dad and I haven't said no yet." She looked to Allegra. "There's this apparently 'scrumptious' young guitarist at her music school that has shown an interest in her. We've vetoed one-on-one dating but she's been begging us to let her go on a group outing."

Reese looked at her mother dubiously. "And even then, you're going to run me through rules and regulations akin to UN negotiations, right?"

Allegra laughed as Reese indignantly shovelled a

spoonful of chicken salad into her mouth. As she watched her niece, she wondered how effective her acting classes would really be. Look how different Reese was from the typical 13-year-old. Could Michael or Moshe or *anyone* really say what a typical 13-year-old was like? Could she really pull it off and make someone believe she was that young? She shook away thoughts of Michael and tried to focus on dinner instead. With all that was to come, she needed as much family time as she could get.

As Allegra steeled herself ahead of the desensitisation seminar, she felt a hand on her arm, pulling her aside. Moshe, dressed in a purple kaftan and silver leggings, led her to the wardrobe department for her first fitting.

Despite feeling anxious about first contact, Allegra was curious to see if they really could make her look like a young teenager. She followed Moshe to the basement of the building and into a big square room with approximately 50 rails of clothes. A woman and two men descended on Allegra, pulling her forward into the middle of their circle. The woman reminded her of Velma from Scooby Doo. She had short red hair, thick-framed glasses and was even wearing an orange jumper. The two men were tall and lanky. One had short brown hair with a box beard while the other had long blonde hair tied up in a ponytail. They looked at Allegra critically, not even bothering to introduce themselves.

"Hair needs cutting, maybe an elfin sort of look," commented one man.

"No, too short. Just a trim will do. And if we must cut it, no shorter than her chin," said Velma.

The second man agreed. "Yes, she looks young anyway. The hair doesn't matter too much."

The first man shook his head. "Agent Stallone said the matched target likes the elfin look."

Allegra scowled. It seemed that these cronies knew more about her target than she did. "I don't want short hair," she told the three stylists.

All three stopped and looked at her. "It's settled then," said the woman, turning her back to Allegra. "A trim it is."

"Do we know the setting?" asked the ponytailed man.

"No. Agent Stallone hasn't briefed us on that yet."

"Tsk. Well then how are we meant to complete her today?"

The three spoke amongst themselves. Allegra looked at Moshe helplessly.

Moshe simply shrugged in response. "They're very good," she assured.

After a few minutes, one of the three finally turned to Allegra. "I'm afraid we're going to have to ask you to come back either tomorrow or later in the week. We need some more information from Agent Stallone before we complete you."

I don't need 'completing', she wanted to say. Instead,

she nodded. She followed Moshe out of the basement and walked back to desensitisation. As she took her place in the seminar room, Yasmine raised a questioning brow.

"Tell you later," Allegra mouthed in response.

Jessica Taylor's voice interrupted her thoughts. "You're all doing well, agents. Today's session will be a short one. I will show you an advert and leave you to discuss it amongst yourselves. Then you are free to go to lunch."

Jessica hit a button and the screen at the front of the room sprang to life. It showed a handsome young blonde man standing in a kitchen, drinking coffee. Suddenly, a baby's cry filled the room. The man set down his coffee cup and headed towards the baby's cries.

Allegra closed her eyes, realising what she was watching.

"Allegra, eyes open please," said Jessica's voice.

Damn that woman. She opened her eyes but watched the edge of the screen, wishing she could block her ears as the deep moans filled the room, slicing through the cries of pain.

As the text appeared on screen, Allegra looked around the room. Yasmine shook her head in disgust. One girl further down the row had tears in her eyes.

"You can talk amongst yourselves." Jessica stopped the tape and exited the room.

"Fucking sick wankers," Yasmine said to no one in

particular. "Fucking wankers. How the fuck can they *do* stuff like that?" She turned to Allegra who sat expressionless. "What's wrong with you? Are you okay?" Yasmine stared at her dispassionate face.

"I'm fine." Allegra realised that the second time around, it hadn't affected her as badly. There was none of the churning nausea she had felt when she first viewed the clip.

"You saw that, right? How fucked-up can people get?"

Allegra nodded in silent agreement.

"I'm gonna nail as many of these fuckers as I possibly can and hope to God they spend their lives behind bars being raped and brutalised."

Allegra sat back in her chair. "That's a bit extreme, isn't it?"

"Not at all," Yasmine said with total conviction. "They should get their balls cut off. Forget chemical castration, they should be *properly* castrated. That would stop these fuckers in their tracks. It's all well and good having their fancy laws to catch these bastards but you introduce corporal punishment and I *guarantee* these fuckers will think twice before they touch a child."

Allegra tried to dredge up the same level of enthusiasm, but all she felt was a vast emptiness.

So this is it. I finally get to find out who he is.

"Sit," Michael gestured to a chair.

Allegra settled in it and looked at him expectantly.

"I believe you met the wardrobe team earlier today."

"What? The three stooges?"

Michael smiled. "Yeah. Them."

"Yes, I did."

"I need to get back to them with a specific brief about how we want you to look so they can figure out all the intricacies."

"So I'm finally going to find out about Mr *'Is he a pervert or isn't he?'*"

Michael grimaced. "His name is Joseph Drake."

"Joseph Drake," Allegra rolled the name off her tongue. "Sounds like a movie star or a movie star villain."

"Well, you're right about the 'villain' part," he commented.

"So who is he? What is he? Why? How? Etcetera."

Michael pushed a manila folder towards her. "He's an art dealer. Thirty-five years old. Very rich. Has properties in London, Oxford, Cambridge, the Cotswolds and a number of international locations. Highly intelligent. He studied Philosophy, Politics and Economics at Oxford and has an IQ of 160."

Allegra raised her eyebrows and whistled slowly. "Wow."

"There's a full bio of his in that folder. I was in two minds about giving it to you. On one hand, I need you to be studied up on Drake. I need you to know his ins and outs, his strengths and weaknesses so you know what buttons to push. On the other hand, I don't want you to let slip by accident that you know something about him."

"So I know 'what buttons to push'? I thought this wasn't about being provocative. Moshe keeps drumming that into our heads. We can't come onto the targets. *They* must take an active role in initiating a sexual relationship. So why are we talking about which buttons to push?"

"You're not gonna make this easy, are you?" Michael rubbed his temple.

"I'm not being difficult for difficulty's sake. I just want to understand and align the different things I'm being told."

"It was just a figure of speech. I'm not saying you should be provocative. It's just that he's proved very hard to nail and we need to get this right."

"Isn't there some sort of guideline about how many attempts we can have? This guy has already had three agents tailing him and he hasn't taken the bait."

Michael nodded. "We've only been wrong about four guys in the past. We used two agents each on those guys before we accepted that they were clean."

"So what's different about Drake?"

"I told you – instinct."

Allegra remained unconvinced. She opened the file and sifted through the first few documents. There was a short bio about him followed by a longer, more detailed one. His education records, health records and tax records were all in the folder. She turned another page in the file and froze when she saw the A4 colour photo of Joseph Drake. Her head snapped up to Michael and then back to the picture before finally, her eyes settled on Michael.

"Who– who is he?" she stammered.

"I told you who he is. His name is Joseph Drake."

"But..." Allegra looked at the man's green eyes, full lips and dark hair. "But he looks so much like you. Do you know him? Is he a relative?"

Michael shook his head.

"You seem totally unfazed. Can you not see the resemblance?"

"I see it," Michael said without emotion.

"And he's totally unrelated?"

"Of course."

Allegra stared at the picture. Drake had thinner eyebrows and more prominent cheekbones but they could easily pass for brothers. She shook her head in bewilderment.

"Nothing's going on," Michael assured her. "It's just a coincidence. It did register with us both when I interviewed him in his home. A normal person's instinct would have said, 'He's like me, of course he can't be what I think he is,' but Allegra, there was something about this guy – something I can't put my finger on – that makes me positive he killed that girl."

"What are you trying to prove? That evil can come in a gorgeous package?"

Michael looked at her in surprise.

122

She winced as her words sank in. Before the blush could spread on her cheeks, she turned her head down to the file, flipped the photo over and continued leafing through the documents. She turned a page and found another photo. This one was of a young teenage girl. The caption read 'Jemima Bradbury, age 14'.

"This is the girl he killed?"

"That's her."

"Well, now I understand why you were so keen to recruit me." Allegra looked at the girl's dark hair and hazel eyes.

Michael put a hand over the file. "Allegra, I really want this to work. Jemima's family have had no peace since her death. They've moved out of the area but the memory haunts them. They need a resolution."

She looked down at Jemima's picture. One eye was covered by Michael's hand. The other seemed to be giving her a knowing wink. She looked up at him. "I won't let you down."

He smiled, green eyes sparkling. His approval made her glow with pride.

They spent the rest of the afternoon preparing for first contact. Michael played a few home videos of Jemima. He had booked a slot with Moshe so that she could help Allegra pick up some of Jemima's body language and traits. They then drew up an outfit for the stylists to create, one loosely based on what Jemima was wearing the day she was killed.

By the end of the week, Allegra felt she knew

everything there was to know about Joseph Drake. She had been trained and tested by Moshe, Michael, Jessica, and her WSN and Intel tutors. She went home on Friday in a mixture of apprehension and excitement. With her head filled with coy expressions and innocent gestures, she was determined to snare Drake.

Come closer, my pretty.

Allegra smiled and peeled the post-it-note off her front door. Walking into her apartment, she called out for Andrew but there was no reply. On the desk, she found another note. *Ring ring,* it said. Just as she read it, her doorbell rang. She answered the intercom.

"A cab for Ms Allegra Ashe, commissioned by Mr Andrew Crawford."

"I'll be down in five minutes." *What is he up to?* She dashed to the mirror and looked at her dismal attire. She did usually try to make an effort at work but she had run late this morning and was dressed in old jeans and a grey sweater. She ran to her closet, praying that something decent was ironed. *He should have warned me.* She grabbed a black dress that was casual but smart. It had a twisted knot at the front, which pulled the dress over the breasts, bringing them into existence. She quickly brushed her hair, put on some mascara and rushed out the door.

"Good evening, Miss." The driver held the door open.

"Good evening. Do you know where we're going?"

The driver smiled. "Mr Crawford told me you would ask me that. He also told me not to tell you anything."

A post-it note in the backseat said, *Ssh. It's meant to be a surprise.*

A 15-minute drive took her to the Royal Docks. When she got out of the car, a young man dressed as a waiter approached her.

"This way, Ms Ashe. Mr Crawford is awaiting your arrival."

Allegra gasped when she saw the boat gliding on the water, aglow with fairy lights. She walked up the steps onto the deck and spotted Andrew. He was standing by a candlelit table with a bunch of white orchids in his hands.

"Happy birthday."

Allegra blinked back unexpected tears. She took the flowers and gave him a long, slow kiss. He handed her a small package.

"Can I open it now?" He nodded so she unwrapped it carefully. Inside was a GraphPad, a state-of-the-art graphics tablet. She remembered moaning to Andrew that she needed a GraphPad, but that Jonathan refused to buy the ImageBox team a set. She smiled and hugged him. "Thank you. It's perfect."

"I know it's not the most romantic thing in the world but you don't like jewellery and I thought it would come into good use with your new job and everything."

"Ssh, it's perfect." She brought a finger to his lips. "Let's not talk about work."

Andrew frowned as he spotted a purplish plum-sized bruise on her forearm. "What happened?" he asked, gently wrapping his fingers around her arm.

"Oh, this. It's nothing." Allegra pulled away, hiding the bruise she had been given by her over-zealous sparring partner in a kickboxing WSN session. "I banged it against a cabinet when I was turning from my desk."

Andrew smiled comfortingly and gestured for her to sit down.

"This is beautiful." She was truly overwhelmed by his effort. He was always an attentive and loving partner but no one had ever put this much effort into pleasing her before. "Where did you get the idea?"

"I wanted to take you out to dinner and thought about alfresco because the weather's finally turning. Then I figured where better for alfresco dining than here?"

They enjoyed a meal of oysters with champagne, topped off with a perfect crème brulee. Looking out at the water, Andrew curled his arms around her. She leaned back into his chest and watched the water ripple hypnotically.

"I love you, Allegra."

She shifted around in his arms to face him. "And I love you."

"We've been together for two years now and no one has ever made me happier than you."

She smiled. "I'm glad."

He hesitated. "I know we've had our ups and downs. I know that sometimes I crowd you and that's why you didn't want to move in with me."

Allegra reddened. "I–"

"No, it's okay. It's okay because I know you. And you know me. I'm a simple man, Allegra – you know that. All I want is to be with you, to be near you and close to you and keep you safe. You mean the world to me."

Allegra nodded. Rather than comforting her, his words only unsettled her.

He released her from his embrace and reached into his jacket pocket.

Allegra's smile froze on her face. "Andrew!" she barked.

He looked at her, startled.

She grabbed his hand and squeezed it. "Thank you so much for this. I really really appreciate it."

He began to speak but she shook her head. "No, I know you're going to wave this all away as if it was no effort but it's amazing. And you're great. And you're doubly great for understanding and accepting my host of neuroses and for letting me take things at my pace."

"I know but–"

Allegra rubbed her shoulders. "Oooh, it's getting chilly. Shall we make a move?"

He started to take off his jacket to give to her.

"No, it won't be warm enough. Is the car waiting?"

"Allegra," started Andrew but she was already halfway across the deck.

She reached out her hand to him. "Let's go. I want to show you how much I appreciate this."

"But if you just wait a minute, I..."

She walked over to him, kissed him hard and began to pull him across the deck. "I don't want to wait." They stumbled down the stairs and into the waiting car.

Allegra's heart was beating fast. "The food was delicious," she murmured. Andrew nodded in a subdued manner. She felt a tremor in her heart as he looked up with sadness in his eyes.

"Allegra, what are you doing?" he asked.

She leaned forward and kissed him. She wasn't ready for words. She wasn't ready for this conversation. She loved Andrew. She wasn't ready to marry him but she didn't want to let him go. Her kisses grew hungry on his lips.

"I love you," she whispered, kissing his neck to hide the tears in her eyes. "I need you."

Andrew closed his eyes and began to return her kiss.

Allegra forced another bite of quiche into her mouth. First contact would be taking place in a matter of hours and she was too excited for lunch. She could feel the adrenaline pumping in her veins. She felt powerful and strong, completely the opposite of what she had expected when she got out of bed this morning. She was excited about finally meeting Drake, the movie star villain she had spent a week analysing.

After lunch, she headed to the basement for her meeting with the three stooges. They led her to a separate room where they trimmed an inch off her hair.

"You're lucky," said Tristan, the one with the blonde ponytail. "We wanted to give you a fringe but Agent Stallone said it would look too obvious."

Allegra shuddered. "A fringe? Not for love nor money."

They dressed her in a pair of faded jeans, Kickers trainers and a light blue T-shirt underneath a grey zip-up top.

"Agent Stallone said your target likes 13-year-old girls that dress like they're 13 rather than 23 so we've kept it very simple. We're not putting any makeup on you because your skin is young as it is. Any coverage will just make you look older."

They primped and prodded her for another 20 minutes. When they were finally satisfied, they sent her to Intel to get wired up. Allegra said her thanks and headed upstairs. As she did, she caught a glimpse of herself in the mirror and did a double-take. They hadn't done anything in particular – they had simply cut her hair and changed her outfit – but suddenly, even to her own eyes, she looked like a child. She touched her face and opened her mouth.

"Hi," she said to her reflection. "Hi Amy." They had built a whole life around her undercover personality,

Amy Petronas, so that Allegra would be ready with answers to questions that Drake may ask.

She visited Intel and then readied herself for Michael, whom she hadn't seen all day. She knocked gently and entered his office.

"Wow. They're good." As he stood to greet her, she leaned into him, breathing in his sexy smell, feeling him seep into her. It was intoxicating.

"I knew you would be perfect for this the first time I saw you," he said softly.

She felt the burning adrenaline course through her.

"Are you okay?"

Allegra smiled. "Yes."

"You know your back story?"

"Yes."

He took a step closer. She watched his Adam's apple dip out and in as he swallowed hard. "The hair twirling? You've practised that?"

She nodded. "Yes."

"Are you sure?"

She looked up at him, her face mirroring his. "Yes."

He took a ragged breath, straightened, and then stepped away from her. "Okay, your transportation will be here in exactly five minutes." He ran her through last-minute details and then led her down to the car.

She settled into the backseat and fastened her belt.

"Good luck." He squeezed her hand and shut the door.

With her churning stomach, she felt like a boxer before a big fight; nervous but strangely powerful. She met the driver's eyes in the rear-view mirror and said, "Let's go".

Joseph Drake spent Monday evenings in his gallery on Hampstead High Street. Allegra was to pose as a rich kid from the local area out to buy some art for her mother's birthday. The gallery was usually manned by a hired assistant but Drake always visited on Mondays to review the week's business.

Amy Petronas. 13. I'm 13. I can pull this off. She stepped out of the car and looked up at the building. The Drake Gallery was a tall white building with a large glass entrance. The space inside was long and rectangular, approximately 60 by 40 feet, with impressive wooden floors.

The Vokoban team had debated whether to give Allegra a bike so that she could ride up to the gallery but decided it was unnecessary. The same veto had been put on a school uniform. It was too obvious, Michael had said.

Allegra took a shaky breath and steeled herself. *It's just first contact.* She walked in and blinked in the bright white light. There were three other people milling around. At the far right corner, there was a curved oak desk with a dark green banker's lamp and a stark white Apple Mac on it. Behind the desk was a young man, no older than 20. He glanced up at

Allegra, held her gaze for a second, and went back to his magazine. Allegra scratched her head in a childlike manner. She stepped over to the first painting on the wall. It depicted an elderly woman at a creaky old table, eating a piece of fruit. She was looking off to the distance with a poignant look in her eyes. Allegra mulled over it for a minute before moving onto the next one.

She looked at the back door through the corner of her eye. There was no sign of Drake. She wondered how long she could stay in the gallery and what would happen if Drake didn't materialise. She turned back to the painting. This one showed a vast blue sky with a woman in a green bikini lazing underneath the shade of a tree. It was a completely different style from the first painting and seemed out of place.

As she walked to the next painting, she heard the back door open and close, making her heart slam in her chest. She took a shaky breath and glanced back as casually as she could. In a mixture of relief and disappointment she realised it was only the young man at the desk walking out. As she stared at the rectangle of the closed door, it opened again. Time froze as Joseph Drake stalked into the gallery.

Allegra's stomach seized as she stood, staring at his face. Dressed in black trousers with a black jumper, Joseph Drake was lean, tall and imposing. He looked like Michael but with a tougher face somehow. His green eyes had a hard edge to them and his sharp cheekbones created an overly harsh effect. With his hands in his pockets, he walked into the main body of the gallery and met Allegra's eyes.

She willed herself to turn back to the painting but found that she couldn't move. Shaking off her fear, she offered him a smile. He nodded at her before walking over to a middle-aged woman who was looking at a painting. He spoke with her in murmured tones for a few minutes before approaching a man who shook his head and then left the gallery.

Allegra stared through the painting in front of her and tried to calm herself. *Why here?* she thought. *Why on his ground? Why not somewhere neutral?* She swallowed hard as she heard footsteps approach behind her.

"Hi there," said his deep voice. His tone was warmer than she had expected.

She turned. "Hi," she replied, feigning casualness.

"How are you?"

"I'm good. This place yours?" *Stay calm.*

Drake nodded with a smile. "Guilty."

"No. It's beautiful." She paused. "It's really cool."

"You're an art connoisseur?"

"A what?" *Too obvious? Reese knows what a connoisseur is.*

Drake laughed. "A connoisseur. It means someone that appreciates the finer aspects of a certain field."

"In that case, I can't claim to be a connoisseur. I guess I'm just a regular person who thinks art's kinda cool."

"So are you interested in buying for yourself?" he asked with an amused smile.

"No. It's for my mother. She's a bit of an art nut. Would die for a Kandinsky – that type of person."

Drake nodded, impressed. "Well, I can't say we have any Kandinskys here but we have very similar works by a local artist called Neena Sarson. Would you like a peek?"

"Sure. That'd be great." *I'm doing okay.*

"Great. The Sarsons are in the back," Drake gestured towards the back door. "I can't heave them out here but I'll let you come out back if you want to take a peek?"

Allegra panicked. She didn't expect things to go like this. At most, she expected a quick conversation with him, maybe one where she could hint at a return visit. *What would Michael say? What would he tell me to do?* "I guess I could... if we're quick."

"Great. You'll love it." He walked to the door and beckoned for her to follow.

She hesitated for a split second before taking a step towards him. She followed him through the exit and down a short corridor. Her eyes searched for the young man that was at the desk but there was no sign of him. She hoped to God that her recording device was working. It was a tiny gadget the size of a pinhead that was attached to her earring. *Very 007,* she had thought when she was first trained to use it.

"So you live around here?" he asked casually.

"Yeah, I decided to pop in after school. My mother's birthday is in a week so I figured I'd get organised. Dad promised to pay for the present I chose."

"Good thinking, Batman."

Allegra smiled. "She's turning 39. One year before the big 4-0."

Drake smiled. "And how old are you?"

Crunch time. "13."

"13?" Drake's cold eyes surveyed her intently.

She froze. *He knows.*

"Exactly a third," he said quietly.

"Sorry?" Allegra tried to swallow the prickly lump that had formed in her throat.

"A third of your mother's age."

"Oh. I didn't think of that." She laughed nervously.

"Well, here we go." Drake put on a pair of gloves and then pulled the covers off three paintings. All three were of bright, colourful objects thrown together in a random, abstract way. "Beautiful, aren't they?" he asked, lost in a reverie. "Like three visual Prete Rosso arias, laid out for all to see."

Allegra nodded unsurely. "I like them. I like that one." She chose the one in the middle at random. It had a big red circle to one side with random lines of varying thickness intersecting it. Other shapes were dotted around to form a colourful array of nothing in particular.

Drake shook his head in admiration. "It's beautiful. Would you like it now or do you want to think about it for a while?"

"I think I'll think about it. How much is it? I do want it. I'm just gonna have to ask dad first."

"Six hundred pounds."

Allegra whistled, slipping more comfortably into character. "That's a lot of cash but, hey, what's the point of having a rich dad if he doesn't fork out once in a while?"

"I like the way you think." Drake laughed.

She smiled. "So, I guess I'll see you again?"

"Yes. Nice doing business with you Miss...?"

"Petronas. Amy Petronas." She offered her hand.

He shook it gently. "Amy, Joseph Drake at your service."

"So I'll be seeing you," she said brightly. He broke their gaze and led her back into the main gallery. She wondered if she could have pushed him a little, maybe been a bit more enticing, but as all agents were specifically told not to be provocative, she had conducted herself properly. *As long as Michael is happy.*

"Okay, kiddo. Be good," said Drake, holding up his hand in a wave.

Kiddo – the nickname she used for Reese. "You too." She shot him one last smile and walked out of the gallery. The burst of cold air invigorated her. She ran down the street, round the corner and practically floated into the waiting car.

With a big smile on her lips, she looked at the driver and once again, told him to "Go".

"Nailed it. She nailed it!"

Lyla raised an eyebrow. "Anyone would think you've won the lottery."

"Maybe we just have, dear Lyla. Maybe we just have."

Lyla was unnerved by Michael's exuberance. He was usually so professional, so composed. Why did Allegra affect him so much? The door buzzed. "Oh, here comes your ingénue now."

"Michael!" Allegra burst through the door with red cheeks and glowing skin.

"Allegra!" he rushed towards her and enveloped her in a hug.

Oh my God, they look like lovers. Lyla surveyed them with concern.

"Allegra, you were great. Absolutely perfect." They broke apart.

"Really?" she asked breathlessly. Like a schoolchild, she lapped up the praise.

"Really. The recce device was crisp and clear. The way you played your age into the conversation and left it open for a return visit was expert."

"Oh, I'm so glad."

He reached out and placed his hands on her shoulders. "Ready to start prepping for second contact?"

Allegra leaned towards him, steadied by his firm hands.

"Yes," she said eagerly. "Yes, I am."

Lyla stood quietly for a moment, then walked out the door.

CHAPTER FIVE

Allegra knocked, waited for Marianne's reply and then walked into her office. She was leaning against the desk, long blonde hair cascading over her shoulders as she rubbed her bare foot.

"Damn Carvalho shoes – they're gorgeous but they hurt like hell. Give it a week, I'll have bunions bigger than the wicked witch of the East."

Allegra grimaced. "Hi Marianne."

"Dammit, I'm sorry, Allegra. Look at me – I'm meant to be a professional." She slipped her shoe back on.

Allegra smiled. Since their first session together, they had met twice – enough for Allegra to decide that she actually liked the straight-talking young therapist.

"So you had first contact yesterday." Curled up in her chair, Marianne reached into a desk drawer and pulled out a file.

"I did."

"And how was it?"

Allegra beamed. "It was great. It went exactly to plan."

Marianne raised a brow. After a second's silence she said, "It *was* only first contact."

"I know. It's really stupid but I pictured some middle-aged fat man with a bald patch and comb-over. It's such a stupid way to think after all the training we've had. I guess I was relieved that it was just a normal guy."

"A *normal-looking* guy," emphasised Marianne.

Allegra nodded. "That's what I meant."

"And was it okay? Are you nervous about seeing him again?"

"You know what? I'm actually not. I'm sure it'll become stressful once things start happening – *if* they start happening – but for now, I'm okay. I actually genuinely want to see if this guy is warped or not."

Marianne frowned. "You get the feeling he's not?"

"It's not that. It's just that I haven't got the feeling that he *is*. He didn't even look at me wrong so I really don't know."

"Have you spoken to Michael about these doubts?"

She sighed. "Michael won't listen. He's adamant that this guy is guilty and he's hell-bent on proving it."

"Do you think his judgement is clouded?"

Allegra hesitated. "I wouldn't say that. Michael knows what he's doing. I trust him."

Marianne frowned at the word 'trust'. She paused

and wrote something into the file. "When do you have second contact?"

"Friday."

"So soon? There's usually a longer period in-between."

Allegra nodded. "It had to be soon based on the pretext I visited under. I said I'd be back within a week to buy a painting."

"And you're okay about that? You're not feeling overwhelmed?"

Allegra waved away the concern. "I'm fine. Honestly I am. I thought I'd feel all weird and confused about it all but like I said, I'm actually excited to see how this pans out."

Marianne nodded and broke eye contact. Faint wrinkles creased the perfect skin on her forehead as she added a note to Allegra's file.

Friday afternoon signalled the real start of spring. Warm sunshine flooded Michael's office and turned Allegra's hair a golden brown. She twirled, showing him her outfit; a short-sleeved green top teamed with a pair of jeans and her hair tied up in a high ponytail.

"Well, the three stooges definitely know what they're doing," said Michael, taking in her youthful appearance.

"Yeah, even if they can't muster up a personality between them."

Michael smiled, causing his dimples to dip deep in

his cheeks. It made Allegra want to touch his skin.

"You have the cheque?" he asked.

"Yes." She patted her right pocket.

"And the lip gloss?"

"Yes." Allegra had been instructed to apply strawberry flavoured lip gloss in Drake's presence, the same brand Jemima Bradbury was wearing the day she was killed.

"It's not designed to be provocative," Michael had told her. "It's creating a subconscious link to his previous victim. We hope that it will incite the feeling of power he felt with Jemima and ease things along."

"You get that from pop psychology 101?" Allegra had replied, immediately regretting the joke when she saw anger flash in his eyes. He really was serious about catching Drake.

"So you're set?" Michael neatened a stray strand of her hair. His fingers on her skin sent sparks shooting through her stomach.

"Yes," she replied hoarsely.

His face grew solemn. "Before we go ahead with this, I want you to listen to me. Drake has been slow in the past. He may not seem like too much of a threat but please don't forget the danger. At any given time he could decide that he wants you and he may take you to a private place and try to molest you. That could happen *today*. As an agent, it is your job to succumb to his advances with little resistance. I don't think you're prepared for that. First contact was easy. The second contact could be serious enough to complete this operation. I want you to be prepared for that. Do you think you are?"

Allegra felt goosebumps rise on her arms. She hadn't contemplated that it could become serious so soon.

Michael waited in silence.

"I..." She paused. "I won't blow it."

"I don't want to pressure you, Allegra. If you feel like you're going to crack in that situation then do what you have to do. At the end of the day, your real reaction would be pretty close to the reaction of many young girls in that position, so don't see it as blowing the op. It will, however, make it harder because after an experience like that, you would obviously stay away from him and we can't get ourselves into that kind of situation."

"I won't blow it," she reassured him. The image of Jemima Bradbury's dead body ran through her mind. If Drake really was responsible, Allegra would make sure he paid his dues.

"The second thing is slightly more serious."

More serious? The goosebumps spread across her skin.

"Drake didn't rape Jemima; he groomed her into a consensual 'relationship'. We expect him to follow the same MO with you–"

"With *Amy*," she interrupted.

Michael nodded. "Sorry. With Amy... but we can't guarantee that he won't change the way he operates. We can't guarantee that he won't try to... rape you."

Allegra grew cold.

"Of course, rape is completely different from a normal situation where an agent has consensual intercourse with a target. It is not something we will condone happening to our agents. We will have security within 30 seconds of you at all times. We had this on Monday as well but I didn't tell you because I didn't want to make you nervous but now, I want you to be prepared mentally and physically. I know you have been training hard in WSN but do run over all the defence techniques you have learnt over the past few weeks *just in case*."

Allegra felt anger rise in her throat. "You couldn't tell me this before? You had to wait until 10 minutes before I leave to go and see him?"

"Allegra, it's just precaution. I just want you to be prepared."

"Then you should have prepared me! Instead of throwing last-minute warnings at me, you should have told me *before*."

"Hey," Michael held her shoulders but she shrugged out of his grasp. He gripped her arm and waited until she stilled. "Our agents will be seconds away from you. We won't let anything happen to you. Anything. You understand that?"

She shook her head. "I might be playing a child, Michael, but don't treat me like one. I've come this far, I'm not going to flee at the first sign of danger. I'm made of stronger stuff. If you want me to perform well, you need to give me all the information I need *when* I need it."

Michael swallowed. "I'm sorry. You're right. It won't happen again." He stepped back, leaving a red handprint on her bare arm.

"I'm ready," she said quietly, feeling it burn.

The door swung shut with a heavy bang. Allegra's trainers made soft squeaking sounds on the floor of the empty gallery. The hum of the computer was the only other sign of life. Glancing at the motionless back door, she casually hooked her thumbs into her pockets and walked to a painting she hadn't noticed on her last visit. It was of a young girl, dressed in white, sitting by a lake. Her face was sad, wistful somehow. She seemed lonely.

The back door opened with a long, low whine. The sound, like a cat with a caught tail, made Allegra shiver. She turned slowly, curving her mouth and widening her eyes just a touch, the way she had been taught.

Joseph Drake walked into the gallery. Dressed in a pair of smart black trousers and a fitted grey shirt with sleeves rolled up above the elbows, he exuded an easy, effortless sense of style. He spotted Allegra and broke into a friendly smile.

"Amy. You came back."

She returned his smile. "Yeah. I really liked the painting."

"I told you you were a connoisseur. Come on round the back and we'll take care of business."

Allegra steeled herself as she followed in his footsteps. He held the door open with an outstretched arm, forcing her to pass beneath him. Her hair brushed against his bare skin but his features remained expressionless. Elongated by the shadows in the dark corridor, his face looked like a mask.

"Straight ahead. In the same room we were last time," he directed.

Allegra blinked. Her vision was speckled by the small dots that appear when you walk from bright sunshine into the dark. She followed Drake down the corridor into the musty room with the paintings. He took off the dust cover and waved her closer.

"Stunning, isn't it?

"It's beautiful," she agreed.

"Look at these lines – don't they remind you of the ocean?" He narrowed his eyes as if recalling a memory. *"The shattered water made a misty din. Great waves looked over others coming in, and thought of doing something to the shore that water never did to land before."* He looked at her with heavy eyes. "I love the water. It has such power to calm and transform – there's nothing like it." He paused and added, "Almost nothing." Reaching forward, he started to rub her shoulder, making her flinch with surprise.

His hand immediately fell away. "Cobwebs," he commented casually.

Allegra composed herself and hoped that he hadn't seen the expectation in her eyes. *Keep cool, Allegra.* "I hate spiders," she said, cursing the shrillness in her voice.

Drake laughed. "You're cute when you frown."

Allegra felt her stomach clench. She tried to think of something to say.

"So hey, how are you going to transport this home?" Drake gestured towards the painting.

"I have a driver." Allegra watched his look of surprise. Cringing with faux embarrassment, she said, "Don't. It's mortifying. My parents are your typical too-much-money-too-little-time people. They have a driver who takes me where I need to go."

"Nice work if you can get it."

"Yeah." She laughed.

"Well, tell that driver of yours to drive carefully. The painting's too precious to be knocked about in the back of a car." He paused and added, "As are you."

Allegra felt her cheeks flush. "I'll make sure he takes care of it... and me." *Are we flirting?*

He smiled. "Okay. Let's get it wrapped up." He lifted the painting, muscles rippling beneath his shirt. Allegra watched him for a second before following him out.

"How would you like to pay for this delight?" he asked.

"My dad wrote me a cheque. I know it's old-school but he wasn't gonna give me his card." She pulled out the cheque, signed by a non-existent Stephen Petronas, and felt her fingers brush the cool plastic of her lip gloss. She handed the cheque to Drake and waited until he turned his attention back to her. Taking a subtle step closer to him, she pulled the lip gloss out of her pocket, pouted and slicked it over her lips twice. She rubbed them together and met his eyes, catching his look of intensity.

"Well, Amy Petronas, it was a pleasure doing business with you."

She shook his extended hand. "Thank you. Maybe I'll come back to see if I can become a connoisseur sometime."

Drake looked at her with a thoughtful expression. "Well, if you are genuinely interested in art, why don't you come along to this exhibition I'll be at tomorrow? It's not here. It's at the Marriott hotel in Mayfair starting out at eight. It's an exhibition of the work of Simoné LaPaglia – he's the 'next big thing' and it's kind of my duty to be there. Maybe we could find each other if you turn up?"

Allegra considered his offer. How realistic would it be for her to accept the invitation? "I'd have to run it by my mum. She's at some charity function tomorrow. I reckon she'll be cool with it as long Miguel, our driver, takes me there."

"Excellent. Just wear something black and you'll fit right in. We'll scout around and find each other."

"Great." Allegra beamed. "I'll see you at eight."

He opened the door for her and touched her shoulder fleetingly, watching as she carefully placed the painting in the waiting car. Turning briefly, she waved goodbye and saw that Drake's smile was one she had seen on a hundred men: genial with no trace of anything sinister.

She sat in the car on the way back to Vokoban and ran through the afternoon's events. In many ways, she was glad she had been assigned to Drake – he seemed like a normal man, one she would probably even be attracted to if she met him outside of work. Back at HQ, she found her way to Michael's office.

He stood up to greet her. "You were a pro."

"It was okay," more a question than a statement.

"You were more than okay. You were natural, composed and convincing."

She smiled happily. "So I guess I'm going to this party thing tomorrow?"

He nodded. "Hey, I'm really proud of you. You're doing really well. And the fact that you're working so hard bodes very well for your future."

Allegra didn't know what to make of this. Her future? What would be the next step from this? What kind of promotion could she get in this place?

"I'm going to call the three stooges." Michael stopped and laughed. "I'm going to call Daria, Tristan and Sabian to come up and help us put this together."

One phone call later, the three stylists were in Michael's office along with David Ellsworth, the head of intelligence. They sat down and, together, constructed young Amy Petronas's outfit, attitude and actions.

The discussion took place as if it was an absolute certainty that tomorrow would be the day Drake would act. Allegra had trouble convincing herself of it. Drake had been completely normal up to this point with no real indication of any deviant habits. She couldn't believe that he would do such a drastic about-turn in one day. When she voiced her opinions to Michael, he silenced them with a frown.

"We need to be prepared for every eventuality," he said simply before turning back to David.

The three stooges were happy with the challenge of making Allegra sophisticated enough to go unnoticed at an art exhibition, but young and innocent enough to entice Drake. They finally settled on a black knee-length shift dress over a long-sleeved white shirt. She looked smart and sophisticated, but to a person who thought she was 13, it would look like a young girl's dress.

After a long evening of preparation, Allegra finally left the Vokoban offices at 9 p.m. She checked her phone and saw that she had six missed calls from Andrew. She swore under her breath and headed out into the dark.

"I was worried about you. You could have called," said Andrew angrily.

Allegra looked at him in surprise. He had never raised his voice to her. "I was at work." The annoyance was evident in her tone.

"How could I have known that? I was trying to call you. You could have answered. For all I know, you could have been lying in a ditch somewhere!"

Allegra reconsidered her actions. Andrew often worked late without calling her but she understood that he wasn't used to her doing the same. "I'm sorry. Things just got so hectic at work. I didn't have a second to myself."

His expression softened. He walked closer and caressed her cheek. "It's okay. We still have time."

"Time? For what?"

"To catch the plane. If you're quick to pack, that is."

"Plane?" Allegra asked in confusion.

Andrew smiled. "I booked two nights in Rome for us."

Her face fell. "You did what?"

"I..." Andrew faltered. "I booked two nights in Rome for us. We talked about it, remember? I know I should have checked dates with you but I wanted it to be a surprise and I know you're not doing anything this weekend – you said you were free – so I went ahead and booked it."

"Is it refundable?" She thought of her promise to Drake that she would be at the exhibition.

Andrew's face crumpled. "Refundable? You don't want to go?"

"I can't. I want to but I have this really important thing going on at work tomorrow and I have to attend."

"Work? But..." He looked at her pitifully. "Even *I* don't work on weekends. What's so important?"

"It's a really important training day I have to attend." Allegra's voice sounded strained, even to her own ears.

"What kind of training? You're at the top of your game. What on earth do they have to teach you?" He pushed a lock of blonde hair away from his reddening face.

"It's really important. I have to attend and there's no way I can get out of it." Allegra shook off the guilt as she took in Andrew's crestfallen face. "I'm so sorry."

He shook his head disbelievingly. He had gone to so much trouble organising the very best for her. He had planned to propose to her during the trip but here she was, cancelling it because of *work*. "Allegra, I don't ask you for much but I'm asking you, please, to make the effort to postpone this work thing. We haven't spent a lot of time together and this is really important to me."

Guilt bubbled up inside her. He was right – he didn't ask her for much. *How can I say no to him?* She wished she could call Michael and rearrange but she knew it was impossible. She would love to run away and not face what was to come tomorrow but she knew she couldn't. *Who knows when we'll get another shot at Drake?*

"Andrew, maybe next week? Can't we postpone?"

He held up his hands. "Forget it, Allegra. You do what you need to, as always. I need to leave."

"Andrew, please, don't be mad at me. It's not my fault."

"You're right," he said resignedly. "It's never your fault."

"I'll make it up to you, I promise."

He shook his head. "It's fine. I'll see you when I see you." He headed towards the door.

Guilt stung at her as she watched him leave, angry but silent. He never shouted at her, calm even at his most frustrated. He gave her the stability she had craved throughout her youth and now that she had it, she shunned it every chance she got.

As she showered, she thought about the good times they had together. He was a good man, better than anyone she had been with. She knew they could have a good life together but she worried about the way she treated him. She tried to be kind to him and take care of him but every display of affection seemed contrived; carefully constructed to prove that she cared – it just didn't come naturally. The thought of marriage scared her deeply but she vowed to say yes to Andrew. She owed him that much.

"We've been arguing about makeup. Sabian seems to think we need to put some on you because you're going to a fancy do but Tristan and I agree that apart from a little skin smoothing, you don't need squat."

Allegra shrugged. "You guys know best."

Daria squinted at her. "You seem awfully calm for

what you're about to go through. Most fresh ones are shaking by the time they get to this stage."

Allegra smiled faintly. "Maybe I'm made of stronger stuff."

Daria's blank expression gave away nothing. "Maybe a lick of mascara to lengthen your lashes and some nude lipstick but nothing more that that," she decided.

By the time they finished styling her, it was coming up to eight. Michael walked into the room just as Allegra stepped in front of the mirror. Yet again she was surprised at how young she looked. A light foundation had been used to cover her blemishes and make her skin look young and supple. Her hair had the glossy sheen that fades with age, and the dress was perfect.

Allegra thought about Daria's words: *most fresh ones are shaking by the time they get to this stage*. If that was so, why did she feel so excited, like she was almost looking forward to it?

Michael squeezed her hand as she got into the car. She nodded, hearing his unspoken question and replying: *Yes, I'll be okay*.

The journey to Mayfair was short and surprisingly traffic-free for a Saturday evening. Pulling up to the Marriott, Allegra thanked her driver and stepped out, trying to mimic the awkward disposition of a young girl. Spotting the other guests, she realised she wouldn't have to try very hard. The women wore evening gowns and intricate hairstyles while the men were all in black tie. She looked down at her loafers and cringed. *It's okay. I'm meant to be a kid.* She headed into the grand entrance.

Inside, she milled about by herself. She hated going to parties where she didn't know anyone. This was twice as bad because she actually felt like a child. After 30 minutes, she still hadn't spotted Drake. She pretended to admire the art and did her best to blend in. Every now and then, she turned from a painting to visually sweep the room but still there was no Drake.

By the time it hit 9 p.m., she started to lose her patience. She walked out of the exhibition hall to call Michael. As she passed the exit, she heard a soft voice to her left.

"Amy." It was barely audible. She turned and saw Drake standing by a window. Dressed in a sharp black suit, he looked like a movie star leaning against the wall. He beckoned for her to go over. Allegra exhaled slowly and walked to him.

"There you are," he said. "I was looking out for you. I thought you had decided to give it a miss."

She shook her head. "No, I've been here a while. I didn't see you so I was just looking around. There's some really cool stuff here."

Drake nodded in agreement. "You look cute in that dress."

She smiled a coy smile. "You look cute in that suit," she replied. On the surface she was relaxed and calm but inside, thoughts were whizzing through her head. *Can't be flirtatious. Can't be provocative.*

"Cute?" Drake laughed. "It's been a long time since anyone called me cute."

She shrugged. "Well, they should tell you more often."

He laughed. "So what time did you get here? Have you eaten?"

"Dead on eight and no, I haven't."

"You must be starving."

Allegra realised that she actually was. "I *am* a bit peckish."

His eyes brightened. "Hey, I've got an idea. I'm here for the night. I figured this thing would go on 'til late so I booked a room so I wouldn't have to drive home. We could go up and order some takeaway? Watch some TV? Get away from these geriatrics?"

Allegra felt a trickle of sweat run down the small of her back. "Sure," she replied perkily. "It'd be nice just to chill out." *Wouldn't even a 13-year-old think this is strange?* Allegra questioned.

"Great," Drake smiled. "Tell you what, I left the keys at the hotel desk for safekeeping. Why don't you go on ahead while I collect them? I'm on the third floor, room 315."

She shrugged nonchalantly. "Okay, cool."

"Excellent."

Allegra nodded and turned. As she did, she heard a voice say, "Allegra!" She stopped in her tracks and turned to look at Drake. He watched her intently. Spinning back round, she heard the voice again.

"Allegra! Hey!" The source of the voice was unavoidable in its 6'2" frame: Jonathan Malone from ImageBox. Sharp panic gripped her. He was about to blow her cover. She turned and began to walk away but Jonathan grabbed her arm.

"Allegra, hey! This is a coincidence! I haven't heard from you in ages. I spoke to Luka and Christian and they both said you had disappeared into the ether. What are you up to?"

She pulled her arm out of his grip. "I'm sorry. I–"

Jonathan continued to speak, suddenly solemn. "No, I know. I shouldn't blame you. I guess you needed some time to recover. I'm so sorry about what happened. Have you managed to find a new job? Listen slugger, maybe you'd consider joining BNAB? I know they've got some vacancies."

Allegra stepped back. "I'm sorry, I think you have the wrong person." She glanced at Drake. He seemed more curious than suspicious but she had to stop this now.

Jonathan hesitated. "Allegra," he laughed unsurely. "What do you mean?"

What would Amy do? What would Amy say? "Listen, sir, I'm really sorry but I don't know who you are. I'm not who you think I am." She didn't know what else to say. She was losing control of the situation.

Confusion swept across his face. "Are you being serious? It's me – Jonathan from ImageBox."

"I'm serious. I don't know who Allegra is. I'm not Allegra."

Jonathan drew back from her. "Uh, okay." He seemed lost for words. "I'm sorry I bothered you. It's just that you look so much like this girl who used to work for me."

She said nothing so Jonathan turned. He shot one last glance at her and then walked away in bewilderment.

In an instant, Drake was by her side. "What was that?" he asked with a hint of anger. "Do you know that man?"

She shook her head. "No, I've never seen him in my life."

"So who's this Allegra he's talking about?"

"No idea. I don't know what he was talking about." She was red in the face, positive that Drake could see through her lies. Her heart beat hard as he stared at her, cold eyes examining every shadow of her face.

"Listen. It's been a long night for you. I think you should go home," he said finally.

Her heart fell. She had to rescue the situation. Michael would never forgive her otherwise. "I'm not tired or anything. I'm fine. And it's not like it's a school night or anything."

He shook his head. "Even so. Have you called your parents? Are they okay with you being out this late on your own?"

She nodded. "They know I'm at a respectable event. I told you what they're like – far too busy to really pay attention. They're happy as long as I call our driver when I'm ready to be picked up. My dad pays him well to look after his little princess." Allegra smiled, more to reassure herself than Drake.

"What does your father do?" he asked.

She shrugged casually. "He's a consultant for Zurich Bank, whatever that means. He works all the hours under God's sun. I don't think he even realises that he never sees the family he works so hard for."

Drake's hard face slowly softened. "Well, since you have no one to go home to, I guess we could entertain each other for an hour or so."

Allegra nodded vigorously, relief awash in her veins. "So I should go up and wait for you?"

He smiled. "Yes, you should."

She turned and headed towards the exit. Taking the lift to the third floor, she waited outside room 315. *This is it. It's going to happen.*

"You found it," Drake's voice echoed from Allegra's right. He slid up beside her and gently touched her shoulder. Slipping the card into the reader, he unlocked the door and guided her inside. As darkness washed over her, she felt tension rise in her stomach.

Drake flicked a switch, making her blink in the sudden brightness. The room was large and rectangular with a king-size bed in its centre, complete with luxurious bedding and eight silk pillows. Allegra ran her fingers over the fabric absentmindedly. She looked at the massive television, stationed in one corner, and the minibar well equipped with a variety of beverages.

Drake followed Allegra's gaze. "Would you like something to drink?" he asked, walking over to the bar.

"Just a Coke, thanks," she replied. She then remembered how Reese always pleaded to have a sip of wine. She grinned at Drake. "Unless of course you wouldn't mind me having a sip of wine. My dad lets me have some but my mum hates it."

Drake raised his eyebrows. "I think the young lady should stick to Coke. For now anyway," he said with a lopsided smile.

Allegra switched on the television and placed her bag next to it, positioning her phone so that it could record video footage of the bed or anything that went on in its vicinity. She walked to the bed and sat down tentatively. Drake handed her a Coke and sat beside her. She looked into his piercing green eyes. *I'm gasoline. I'm burning clean.*

"Comfortable?"

She nodded. "Yes, this room is lovely." *Lovely?*

"Why don't you get on the bed properly and rest against the pillows? They're really comfortable."

Swallowing hard, she got on the bed and shimmied over to the headboard side. She leaned back and stretched her legs out before her.

"Better?"

"Yes." She ripped her eyes from his and forced them to the screen.

He sat still for a few seconds and then turned to her. "Can't let you have all the fun now, can we?" He crawled onto the bed and settled down on the pillows beside her. "As for that," he reached over her to take the remote, his arm brushing her chest. He changed the channel to Sky One and placed the remote between his thighs and hers. The air felt thick and difficult to swallow. Allegra's legs threatened to start shaking so she curled them to her chest.

"Cold?" asked Drake. "Here." He stretched her legs back out and began to rub her left leg with his right hand. He spent a while rubbing her thigh in long, heavy strokes before moving onto her right thigh. He had to shift closer to reach it. He spent a while rubbing it, his hand creeping higher with each stroke. "Warmer now?"

She nodded. She couldn't comprehend the magnitude of what was happening. Her mind was that of a 25-year-old and it couldn't process that Drake was in this room and doing this to what he thought was a 13-year-old. Allegra expected to feel disgust but because she wasn't 13 and didn't *feel* 13, she couldn't feel how wrong it was.

"Amy, do people tell you how beautiful you are?"

She let out a strained giggle. "Beautiful? I wish!"

"You are," he looked deep into her eyes. "You have these beautiful eyes and soft soft skin and these gorgeous lips. Your boyfriend must be the luckiest boy in the world."

She laughed. "Boyfriend? I don't have a boyfriend."

He continued to rub her thigh. "You don't have a

boyfriend?" he asked with incredulity. "I can't believe that. A stunning young woman like you has dozens of young men after her, no doubt." He wasn't looking into her eyes anymore. His gaze was set on her thigh and kept flickering a little higher.

She swallowed hard as his hand travelled further. "I– I don't meet many boys."

"It's probably best. You'd break all their hearts." He leaned in closer. When he blinked, it took him a second to reopen his eyes. He inhaled deeply, his face hovering just above her hair.

She leaned back a little and closed her eyes. Drake brought his lips to her ear. "I have something for you," he whispered with a long, shuddery breath.

Allegra's heart slammed in her chest. She opened her eyes and watched him walk to the bathroom. She sat rod-straight on the bed, looking from the bathroom door to the camera in a panic. *Fight or flight?* An old snippet of a documentary ran through her head. Drake walked back in, hands hidden behind his back. She tried to stop her body from shaking.

It was then that he revealed what he was holding in his hands. It was a beautiful single pink rose. It was a day away from full bloom and its petals grew from a striking magenta to a pale pink.

"I want to give you this: a beautiful flower for a beautiful woman."

Allegra blinked in surprise. The pounding of her heart slowed. She took it from his hands and let out a shaky breath, quite visibly relieved. *I didn't imagine all that,* she told herself. She hadn't imagined the lust in Drake's eyes, the darkness or the desire – it *had* been there. What had stopped him? Why hadn't he crossed the line?

"I think I've kept you here for long enough. Shall we call your driver?"

Allegra looked up at him, surprised by his abruptness. "Er, thank you for the flower. I, uh, I still have some time if you–"

Drake smiled. "Much as I'd love to keep you here, I think your parents will begin to miss you, as neglectful as they may be."

She wasn't sure what to say.

"You can use the phone here." Drake pointed at the bed-stand.

She looked at him questioningly but he turned his attention to the news report on the television. Hesitantly, she called her driver and spoke a few words before turning back to Drake. "He's five minutes away."

"Have a safe journey home," he said, barely glancing at her.

She stared at him in confusion. One minute he was ready to jump on her, the next he was completely nonchalant. "So... I guess I'll see you?" she asked.

"Count on it," he replied, still focused on the screen.

She turned and, with one backward glance, walked out of the room. The relief she had felt a few moments ago now gave way to the bitter taste of disappointment.

"Fuck!" screamed Michael. He pushed away the surveillance gear on the desk and shot up in disgust. Pacing the room, he felt the anger pump in his blood. He had set three agents on Drake and every single one had returned with nothing. Allegra already had him touching her. They just needed a little bit more. What had happened? As he clenched and unclenched his fist, Allegra walked in through the door.

Michael flew towards her. "What *happened?*" he demanded.

She froze, taken aback by his sudden aggression. "I–" she started.

"You what? What did you do?"

"I didn't do anything," she said defensively.

"You must have done something. What the hell turned him cold like that? It was like a goddamned switch going off. Are you wearing perfume? Expensive shampoo? He got close to you and *something* set his trigger back to 'off'. I want to know what it was. What did you do?"

"I didn't do anything," stressed Allegra. "I wasn't wearing any of that. I didn't do anything."

"Firstly, the way you dealt with Jonathan Malone was horrific. You should have shut him down *straight away.*"

"I did. I tried to." Allegra held her hands up defensively.

"You *conversed* with this character!" Michael spat the word as if it described something despicable. "You should have shut him down. You should have walked away. Instead, you started explaining yourself. You even used your name *twice* unprompted. 'I don't know who *Allegra* is. I am not *Allegra*.'"

"I panicked," she started.

"And I thought you were ready," he said contemptuously.

Allegra felt sudden anger course through her body. "Don't you blame me," she said bitterly. She stabbed his chest with an open palm. "*You're* the one who forced me to move so quickly." Stab. "*You're* the one that said we're going to go at my pace." Stab. "*You're* the one who ignored my pleas." She raised her hand again but this time Michael grabbed it and forced it against her thigh. She pushed him with her other hand but he grabbed it too, easily restraining both arms with one hand. She struggled against him.

"Stop it," he warned, placing her back against a wall.

Face red with fury, she fought his grip but he held her in place. She lunged forward but he grabbed her shoulders and slammed her against the wall.

Before she could process what was happening, he grabbed her hair and pulled it back, lifting her face to his. Fuelled by anger and emotion, he pressed his lips against hers, crushing her with physical force. Shock and anger mixed with confusion as Allegra felt herself respond to him.

His kiss grew rougher as his hands pulled at her jeans. Her fingers flew to her buttons and undid them desperately. Breathless and overwhelmed, she let Michael lift and move her to his desk. He took off her jeans and T-shirt, and pushed her back onto the oak surface.

A groan escaped his mouth as he hooked his finger beneath the crotch of her panties and pulled them aside. He pressed his fingers against her, soaking up her slick moisture. As he undid his fly, she hooked her legs around him, willing him to touch her, to push her, to crush her.

He grabbed her arms and held her down. She felt completely powerless beneath him, overwhelmed, out of control. He spread her legs and pushed himself against her. He could feel how wet she was – it taunted him, begged him. He hooked his arms beneath hers, palms on her shoulders, and pushed himself inside her with such force, it made her cry out in pain. He responded by wrapping one hand around her throat and pushing deeper, harder. She squirmed against his body desperately, giddy and lost, wild and urgent. She felt completely possessed. He drove out his anger and frustration on her, pushing them to an animalistic climax, one that shook every part of her body. Moments later, he collapsed on top of her, sweaty, exhausted, sated.

CHAPTER SIX

"Give me *something*," pleaded Michael. He looked imploringly at the panel of psychiatrists. The ensemble comprised Jason Altman and Freida Warner, two of the Vokoban's 10 psychologists, along with Marianne who was the first to respond.

"Michael, we can't give you any real analysis beyond what you have concluded so far. Either he had a bout where he simply lost control or the Jonathan Malone episode scared him off. I believe it's the former. If he was warned off by Allegra's behaviour, he would have shut it down straight away. He wouldn't have invited her to the hotel room."

"I agree," said Jason. "I think that he struggles with his desires. Perhaps he feels guilty about his feelings and therefore tries to restrain himself. He started touching Amy Petronas but when he came back from the bathroom, he was perfectly composed. Perhaps he needed that time to regain control of himself."

Michael paced back and forth behind his desk. He seemed stressed – unusual for a man who was normally so self-possessed. "So what's the solution? If he's in a struggle with himself and he's going to crack, I'd rather he do so on my watch with one of my agents than with some young girl that he grooms and molests."

"You just have to keep trying," said Marianne.

Michael looked at her. "This is our last shot."

She nodded. "Then make it count."

The next day, in her weekly psych session, Allegra noticed that Marianne wasn't her chipper self. She didn't greet her with the usual chain of rambling. Instead, she nodded and gestured to the chair Allegra usually chose.

"Everything okay?"

Marianne weaved her fingers together and placed them on her desk. "Yes. I had a meeting with Michael."

Allegra frowned. "And?" she asked curtly. *Has he told her?*

"Don't worry. I don't tell him anything that happens in these sessions," Marianne soothed. "We spoke about what happened on Saturday."

Allegra cleared her throat. "What did he say?"

Marianne sighed. "Nothing. I just... I'm just not convinced that he has your best interests at heart."

Allegra bristled. "What did he say?" she repeated.

"He didn't say anything, per se. I shouldn't even

mention this to you because it's not like he isn't doing his job properly – he is. It's just that it seems he's so hell-bent on catching your current target, he's willing to do anything. That's usually admirable but not when there are field agents involved."

"Are you saying he's compromising my safety?" Allegra had vested a lot of trust and confidence in Michael. She believed that he would put her first, before his quest for Drake.

Marianne shook her head. "No. You can trust Michael. This kind of operation is nothing if there is no trust between the field agent and her special agent."

"I can trust him, but?"

"But nothing. I shouldn't have even mentioned it."

Allegra didn't know what to make of this. She was confused enough already and the one thing she was clinging onto was her faith in Michael. She couldn't let Marianne or anyone else rock that faith. She depended on it.

Ensconced in the corner, spread across a leather booth, they looked like a group of beautiful children. Gathered there by Yasmine to "celebrate and commiserate on the last week of training", the field agents were on a rare social outing. Of course, a few special agents had taken exception – girls that looked as young as they did would not go unnoticed in a bar. However, with promises of sobriety and inconspicuousness, they had been awarded this one concession.

Yasmine welcomed Allegra to the fold with a hug. "Hey beauts, I'll get you a drink. What are you having?"

"Just a Coke, thanks."

"A Coke?" Yasmine shook her head disapprovingly. "With a twist?"

Allegra smiled and shook her head. "Just a Coke."

"Okay. Go sit down. You know most of the new agents. Some of the older ones are also here so go say hi."

Allegra nodded. She spotted Rayla talking to two of the new agents. She rounded the corner to squeeze into the booth when she spotted Caitlin and Michael sitting alone at a nearby table. A stab of jealousy pierced her skin. *What are they doing together?* She knew Michael was Caitlin's special agent but why were they separate from the group, sitting cosily at their own table?

Caitlin was all floaty white dress and long blonde hair. Michael had rolled up his sleeves and undone his tie. He looked rugged but relaxed; a look that was even sexier than his usual buttoned-up perfection. Caitlin caught Allegra's eye but turned quickly back to Michael. It made her cheeks burn with indignation.

"Hey," Yasmine put an arm around her shoulder and handed her a drink. "C'mon."

They squeezed into the booth and Allegra exchanged greetings with the other agents. She tried to focus on the conversation but her eyes kept flickering towards Michael. *He knows I'll be here too. Why isn't he looking for me?*

Deep in conversation with Caitlin, he was oblivious to his surroundings. If it was work-related, did they have to do it here? Couldn't they do it in the office?

Allegra turned to Rayla. "Is Rasel coming?"

She snorted. "Ha! No chance. He's a 9-to-5er. For a guy who continually extols the virtues of responsibility and duty, he sure does love to skip off home on time."

Michael had his hand on Caitlin's shoulder. He was looking at her the way he looked at Allegra; smouldering, burning with restraint. It made her blood boil.

Rayla followed her gaze. "Of course, *his* problem is the opposite. He comes to a party and ends up grabbing an agent to talk shop."

"They're talking about work?" Allegra's eyes flickered to Rayla and then back to the table.

"What else would it be?" Rayla shrugged and turned her attention back to the girls in the booth.

Caitlin shook her head and stood up. Michael reached forward to stop her but she had already stepped away. Rubbing her forehead, she walked to the booth.

"Hi girls." She avoided Allegra's eyes. "I've got a monster headache so I'm going to head home."

"Lightweight," teased Rayla.

Caitlin smiled faintly. "Have fun." She turned and stalked out.

Without a moment's pause, Allegra stood and walked to the table.

Michael looked up, surprised. "Oh, hi."

"Hi." Allegra gestured towards the door. "What was that about?"

He frowned. "What?"

"Caitlin. You and Caitlin."

Michael set down his drink and ran a hand through his hair. It reminded her of the first time they met. "We were just talking about a prickly case. We're having a difference of opinion." He smiled. "Kind of like you and I do all the time."

The comparison annoyed her further. She took Caitlin's place at the table and pushed aside the drink she had left behind. "It's Tuesday."

Michael nodded. "Yes."

"We haven't spoken since Saturday."

"No."

She shook her head. "Don't you think we need to?"

Michael looked towards the booth. "It's hardly the place."

"It was good enough for you and Caitlin to have an intimate tête-à-tête."

He frowned. "You're in a relationship, right?"

She nodded.

"I'm very sorry about what happened between us. I'm sorry I put you in that situation."

She waited but he said nothing. "That's it?"

He hesitated. With a sigh, he reached out and gently

touched her arm. "It was," he paused. "It was amazing. It was something that has haunted me from the first moment I saw you. It was something that was taking me off-balance and off-focus. It was something I wanted desperately and it lived up to every second of every fantasy I've had about you."

His words lit fire in her. She felt it spread to her throat, to her stomach, to her crotch. How could he do this? With mere words, how could he reduce her to this?

"But we both know it can't happen again."

She froze under the weight of his words.

He continued: "Not only because you're in a relationship but because it goes against every rule that Vokoban has in place. It compromises my professional integrity. If anyone, including Marianne, finds out, it would get us both in a lot of trouble." He looked at her pointedly. "I should have been able to control myself but..." He shook his head.

Allegra was silenced by a range of emotions; desire, guilt, anger and disappointment. She didn't know what to say to him.

"Are you okay?" he asked.

She willed herself to tell the truth, to tell him that she wasn't okay, that he filled her with an intensity and abandon that was irresistible and addictive, that she couldn't stop thinking about him even when it ate her up with guilt. She wanted to talk about what happened properly. She wanted to examine it and process it and, if need be, discard it. She was not okay. She willed herself to tell him so, but instead she shrugged, nodded and said, "Yes, of course. You're right."

"I'm sorry, Allegra." He looked truly regretful. It gave him a momentary vulnerable edge that only made him more attractive.

Allegra wondered how she was going to cope working with him so closely. "I'm sorry too." She took a sip of her drink, stood up and left the table.

Allegra's uppercut bounced off her opponent's raised fists. Frustrated, she lunged forward with a backfist, this time making contact with the side of the head. The girl reeled backwards but stayed on her feet, raising her hands high. Allegra drew back and then rushed forward with a spinning back-kick. This time the girl's petite frame, almost identical to Allegra's, flew backwards and landed with a hard thud on the mat. Shaking her head in a daze, the girl stood on unsteady feet, wiping away strands of her brunette hair.

"Time," called Jordan, their self-defence instructor.

Allegra advanced towards the girl and hit her hard with three short straight-punches.

"Time!" yelled Jordan.

She hit the girl with a straight knee-thrust followed swiftly by a sweeping kick, flooring her instantly. The girl lay splayed on the mat, clutching her stomach in pain.

Jordan stormed to Allegra's side and pushed her away from the girl. "Ashe, I said 'time'!" he yelled.

"What part of that did you not understand!?"

Allegra, eyes still focused on the writhing figure on the mat, simply said, "I didn't hear you."

"This is self-defence! That's what I teach you: how to *defend* yourself, not how to beat someone senseless!"

Allegra scoffed. "You know, this clichéd hard-ass routine is getting really tired."

Jordan recoiled with surprise. "Go," he said angrily. "Get out of my sight." When she didn't move, he stepped forward, face inches from hers. "I said, get out of my sight!"

Face flushed red, Allegra stormed out of the hall. Slamming the locker room door shut, she heard it open again behind her.

"Dude, what the hell?" Yasmine held her hands out, demanding an explanation.

"What?"

"Time of the month or what?"

Allegra flexed her fingers. Her knuckle pounded, sending sharp pains shooting through her fingers. "I'm fine."

"Yeah, but you should see the other guy."

Anguish flashed in Allegra's eyes but she refused to speak.

Yasmine sat next to her and softened her voice. "Listen, I know we're coming up to the end of training and it's über-stressful and it's freaking everyone out, but we'll get through it. I'm right here with you. I know what it's like. There are days I wonder what the hell I'm doing here, days I wish I could run away and, I don't know, become a monk in Tibet or something."

Allegra smile faintly. "Women can't be monks."

She shrugged. "Semantics."

"Anti-semantic," countered Allegra.

Yasmine laughed. "See? You're gonna be okay." She pulled her up off the bench and pushed her towards the showers. "Just tone down on the Xena Warrior Princess shit, you hear me?"

Allegra nodded and headed into the shower. She couldn't tell Yasmine that it wasn't the stress. She couldn't talk about how she had betrayed Andrew and how disgusted she was with herself, how the guilt coursing through her veins had darkened her blood with self-hatred. She couldn't face what she had done with Michael. Worse than that, she couldn't face that she would give anything to do it just one more time.

It was a week later that Allegra met Drake again. The first day of June was uncomfortably humid with its merciless sun failing to dispel the moisture in the air. It created beads of sweat that slid uncomfortably down the small of her back before dissolving into her white cotton top. Her skinny legs were exposed beneath a knee-length denim skirt and her dark hair, slightly frizzed, fell loose over her shoulders.

She bounded into Drake's gallery, hands on hips, and shook her head disapprovingly. "And just what do you think you're doing inside on a day like this, Mr Drake?"

He looked at her in surprise. "Where did you spring from?" he asked, a smile playing on his lips.

She shrugged the way all those plucky teens did in American soaps. "About," she said gaily.

"Well, I'm glad you came by. I've missed your presence."

She smiled and walked over to his desk. She leaned round to see what was on his screen: a game of Solitaire.

"Productive," she commented.

Smiling, he reached out, grabbed her arm and pulled her towards him. "Come sit with me. I'm desperate for some company."

For a second, she thought he was going to sit her on his lap but he pulled out a chair and gestured towards it. She sat down and began to swing her legs. "So what's new?"

"Nothing much. Same old, same old."

"How's business? Getting a lot of sales?"

"Comme ci comme ça," he commented.

Allegra nodded before realising that perhaps a 13-year-old wouldn't understand. She raised an eyebrow.

"Some," said Drake. "Why? Are you interested in buying another painting?"

"Maybe," she replied.

"Really? If you want, I'll take you out back. We always have the newest stuff there. It's dead out here anyway." He stood up and led her to the back of the gallery. They spent a quarter of an hour looking at the

176

paintings before Drake suddenly brightened. "Hey, you've never been upstairs, have you? I have some beautiful paintings in my study. You want to see?"

"Sure," she replied brightly. *Bingo.* As she followed him upstairs, she wondered why he was wasting his time with a 13-year-old. Surely a man like him could get a woman of his own age? She silently chided herself for the thought. It was borne of that preconceived notion that paedophiles were old, ugly and sick. Drake was successful, attractive and charming. It was hard to reconcile that with what he really was. *If that's what he is.*

He led her to a large room on the first floor. A grand oak desk stood at the back of the room with several chairs strewn around a long leather sofa. A bookcase, teeming with books, covered the entire back wall. The layout and decor reminded her of Michael's office. Sudden thoughts of him crowded her mind. She remembered the way he had forced her against his desk, the way he had climbed on top of her and pushed his way inside her, making her sick with pleasure.

Drake walked to a painting, ripping her out of her reverie. "What do you think?"

She coughed but her voice was still throaty. "They're all so beautiful. You have a good eye." Casually, she reached out and placed her bag on the desk.

Drake touched her chin, raising it lightly. "Yes, I do," he replied, staring at her with clouded eyes. "*You* are beautiful."

She parted her lips to speak but then let them hang still, half-open in a pout.

"Come." He led her to the sofa and began to stroke her cheek. "So soft," he whispered, leaning closer. He kissed her ear lightly, a butterfly of a touch – momentary, barely perceptible. His lips moved to her neck and then to her shoulder.

I want to laugh out loud. I want to scream. I want to leap on her and tear her into a thousand little pieces.

When his kisses grew hungry, Allegra leaned away, heart slamming in her chest. "Joseph, I–" She scrambled for words. "I don't think I can."

"Of course you can, sweetheart. Of *course* you can."

"I'm 13," she whispered.

"But you're a woman," murmured Drake, lost in her skin. "You're beautiful. I want you. I've wanted you from the first moment I saw you."

It's haunted me from the first moment I saw you, a fragment of speech ran through her mind.

Drake began to unbutton her top slowly, carefully. Pulling it open, he moaned when he saw that she was wearing no bra. He teased her nipples with his fingertips. Slowly, he brought his lips to them and licked gently.

Soft, so soft. *Too soft.*

He took a nipple into his warm, wet mouth. In an instant, his demeanour changed. His hands, suddenly rough, pushed her back on the sofa and grabbed at her skin. One hand, on the back of her neck, grabbed her hair, hungry and urgent.

Intensity and familiarity clawed at her; feelings of powerlessness, of submission and desire. Overwhelmed by the pace and force of Drake on top of her, riddled by guilty memories of Michael, she felt her body buck against his. He pushed her back forcefully and began to undo his jeans.

It was the sight of him, pale and rigid, that brought her to her senses. His hand snaked forward, reaching for her head to push it down. She slapped it away in panic. "No!" A scream so loud and shrill, it froze them both. In an instant, Allegra pulled herself from beneath him. Head pounding, she grabbed her bag and flew out the door.

"Amy!" Drake's frame clambered down the stairs behind her. "Amy, wait!"

She felt him gaining on her, reaching forward, ready to grab her. With a squeal, she burst out onto the street, holding her shirt closed over her slamming heart, and launched into a dead run. Finally, five streets away, she stopped and leaned against a wall, heaving in sharp, shallow breaths.

What have you done? she questioned immediately. She thought of Drake on top of her, angry and desperate. It was behaviour she had prepared for, actions she had foreseen, so why had she panicked? As she stood there, shivering and panting, it dawned on her: it wasn't Drake's actions that had caught her off-guard but her own. She hadn't expected to feel so overwhelmed. Suddenly feeling sick, she staggered away from the wall. *Water. I need water.*

She thought of Michael and knew she couldn't face him. She couldn't face anyone at Vokoban – what excuse could she give for blowing the case? She had none. Scrambling to Hampstead station, she staggered home in a haze.

Do you have any idea what it's like to crave the flesh of a lovely child? To crave her blood but not want death for her? I build these walls to cave me in. I fight with my guilt and there is guilt. I am not a monster with no conscience or moral compass. I know what is right and I know what is wrong but am I culpable simply because you refuse to blame nature? Do we vilify homosexuals for their preferences? Do we persecute them for their natural desires? No. Because it is nature that is culpable. A rogue gene or twisted DNA, it is something nature drew forth, something preordained by God Himself. It is the same for me. I am not a monster so why must I build walls to cave me in? Why must I pretend to be something I'm not? And why, when I free myself, do they run? Why do they always run?

"Hey, are you okay?" Andrew knelt next to Allegra. She looked at him through bleary eyes. "Huh?"
"Are you okay? You look..." He brushed a rope of

greasy hair off her face. His concern drew fresh tears from her eyes, already raw from hours of crying. She was on the floor, leaning against her closet, pyjama-clad legs drawn up to her chest. He held her face and tried to catch her downcast eyes. Red lines criss-crossed them, giving her a manic look. "What's happened?"

Allegra sobbed in reply, her small frame shaking against the wood of the closet.

Fear struck at Andrew's heart. He had never seen her like this before. She never cried – at least, not in front of anyone. "Is it... Reese? Sienna?"

She met his eyes briefly and mournfully shook her head before her face crumpled with yet more tears.

"Allegra, please. You're worrying me. What's the matter?"

"I want to sleep," she said, barely intelligibly.

"You want to sleep?" he asked helplessly. "Okay. That's okay but what's wrong? You have to tell me what's wrong."

"Nothing. I just want to sleep," she said pitifully.

"But what's wrong? I tried calling you but it just rang and rang. Are you okay? Is it work?"

"Andrew, don't."

"But sweets..."

"Please, just leave me alone."

"But what's wrong? I can't–"

"Just *leave me alone!*" she shouted, suddenly angry. She launched into him, physically pushing him away with such force that he fell back. "Just leave me alone!

How many times do I have to tell you? I need space! You're smothering me. I can't breathe. I don't need you here. I don't need you. Just go!"

Andrew looked at her with wide eyes. He opened his mouth but no words came out. Filled with shock, he realised he had nothing to say. He stood, waiting for an apology or, at least, an explanation. When she said nothing, he turned and silently walked away.

As she heard the door close, she screamed in frustration. The hurt in his eyes cut at her conscience but she needed time away from him. She was lost and wanted, *needed*, to find her own way. She lay down on the floor and wept.

Allegra woke with a start. "Dammit," she swore when she realised it was still dark. With bleary eyes she read the red numbers on her bedside clock: 04:00. Burrowing beneath the covers, she closed her eyes and willed herself to sleep.

When she found that she couldn't, she sat up in bed, drowsily watching shadows play on the ivory surface of her walls. Frustrated with sleeplessness, she stalked out of her bedroom. On her way to the kitchen, she tripped on a tangled wire that lay ripped from its socket. Kneeling down, she picked it up and hesitated before crawling to the socket and plugging the phone back in. After a minute, she picked herself up and headed to the kitchen for a strong cup of coffee. Today would be a day of battles.

As the coffee hissed and bubbled, Allegra noticed a small yellow square neatly stuck to the fridge. She snatched it up and read Andrew's scrawl: 'I have had enough of this. I have had enough of you. I'm tired. Goodbye.'

The words felt like a kick in the stomach. Initial shock and guilt quickly turned into anger.

How dare he leave me like this? How dare he leave me when I need him the most? As indignant anger burned in her blood, she remembered the exact words she had used last night. She remembered how she had physically pushed him away, causing that look of hurt and heartbreak in his eyes. Most of all, she remembered how, instead of fighting back or spitting ugly words back at her, he had left in dignified silence. Her heart broke as she thought of him quietly scrawling this note, leaving her apartment and softly walking out of her life.

Shouldn't you be happy? asked a bitter voice in her head. *Isn't this what you wanted?*

She felt a lump in her throat, felt it rise up into her mouth. She swallowed hard, suppressing her sobs, filing them next to every other piece of pain she refused to cry over. Determined not to dissolve, she lowered herself into a chair and drew her knees to her chest. In silence, she let loneliness wash over her, comforting in its familiarity.

It was an hour later that the motionless silence was broken by the shrill telephone. Strands of dawn filtered through the kitchen blinds, making her eyes and head ache. Lowering her feet to the cold kitchen tiles, she walked to the phone, slowly, wearily.

"Allegra?"

"Yes?" Her voice was thick with sleep and swallowed tears.

"I've been trying to ring you for the last 12 hours."

"I've been sleeping."

"What time are you coming in?" There was no hint of anger in Michael's voice.

"The usual time," she replied softly.

"Okay, I'll see you then."

"Michael."

"Yes?"

She hesitated. "I'm sorry."

"Don't worry. Just come in. We'll talk then."

She nodded. "I'll see you soon."

Michael leaned against his desk, both palms flat on the heavy wooden surface. With his head faced down, he looked like he was intently studying his shoes.

"Michael?"

He didn't move. After a long minute, he exhaled audibly and looked up to meet Allegra's eyes. She bit her lip, nervous in defence mode.

"Sit down." He walked round his desk and sat in his large leather chair opposite her. "What is your assessment of what happened yesterday?"

Somehow, she felt it would be better if he yelled at

her. This strange calm was altogether more chilling. "I– I think I blew it. Well, I *thought* I blew it but then I thought about what you said about not worrying too much if I freak out because that's likely to be more of a real reaction anyway."

"So your assessment of yesterday's events is that they went well?"

"Not 'well' but not," she hesitated. "I don't know, Michael. What do *you* think?"

He breathed deeply. "I think we need to move on this. Drake is on the edge. If we don't catch him now, we'll never get him."

Allegra's eyes widened. "You– you want to send me back there?"

A muscle in his jaw flexed. "Which of the conditions of Clause 160 were met yesterday, Allegra?" he asked coldly.

She withered under his gaze and grappled for words to say.

Michael watched the colour drain from her face. As he stood and walked closer, his demeanour changed. Kneeling next to her, he looked deep into her eyes. "Hey." He reached forward and lightly brushed her chin. "You can do this. I see your strength. I know who you are. I know your layers."

She watched his lips speak words of encouragement.

"There's tough Allegra: the one you show the world, the one that's feisty and independent and accepts nothing from anyone, the one that keeps everyone at arm's length so no one can get close enough to hurt her."

Allegra said nothing.

"Beneath her is you: scared, lonely, tired of fighting, tired of being angry, insecure and in need of the very reassurance that is spurned on the surface. And that's who you think you are. Beneath the tough exterior, that's what you think is real."

She closed her eyes.

"But hey," he touched her cheek gently. "You're wrong. The *real* Allegra is different. She's tough but she's caring. She's strong but also soft. Beneath the jaded cynicism, beneath the insecurity, she *cares* about the world and she knows she has something to give. She knows she's worthy of love – of giving it and receiving it. She's amazing and courageous and special. And much as I respect the tough one and as much as I want to take care of the vulnerable one, what I need right now is the real one."

Allegra felt hot tears well in her eyes.

"I need the real one." He reached forward and wrapped her up in his arms.

She sat in the canteen, nibbling on an apple, when Yasmine rushed to her table and sat with flourish.

"Allegra, I had my first contact this morning!"

"Really?" She was taken aback by Yasmine's enthusiasm.

"It was awesome. I totally pulled it off. This guy

totally thinks I'm a kid. He runs this grocery store in Ilford and basically, he–"

"Wait, should you be telling me this?"

Yasmine screwed up her face in annoyance. "Jeez, I don't think they're gonna shoot us if we exchange a little info. So anyway, this guy, he owns a grocery store. We got the tip-off from a mother who caught him acting sleazy with her teenage daughter. So anyway, he's Asian like me and we reckon that he reckons that Asian girls are all timid and sweet, and unlikely to blurt out that they've been molested by a sicko 'cause of the shame factor. So anyway, I go in there, all sweet and innocent, asking for some *mitai*, which is obviously perfect in an ironic way, and I'm telling you – putty in my hands."

Allegra was unnerved by the excitement in Yasmine's voice. She seemed empowered by the sexual game. "Yas, listen, it's only going to get harder."

She grinned. "No pun intended, right?" She paused to take in Allegra's sigh of exasperation before continuing. "I'm kidding. I know it's gonna get harder. I mean, fucking hell, I've seen the shit that goes on in those desensitisation seminars, but I've worked bloody hard and I'm ready to kick ass." Yasmine started to sing 'Eye of the Tiger' by Survivor.

Allegra started to protest but Yasmine was too busy boxing the air and singing.

"And the last known survivor dunks his bread in the night."

Allegra looked at her with confusion. "What on Earth are you singing?"

"Rocky, of course." Yasmine pumped a fist in the air.

Allegra shook her head. "The line is, 'And the last known survivor *stalks his prey in the night.*'"

Yasmine stopped and scratched her head. "You know, that makes so much more sense."

Despite herself, Allegra burst out laughing. It felt like the first time in months.

The desensitisation seminar was tougher than usual. The nastiest stuff had been shown during training to toughen up the new recruits but these two clips had been scheduled for post-training sessions. The first was a 50-second clip of black and white CCTV footage obtained from the Metropolitan Police. It showed a tall Caucasian man stop a girl on the street and point to his wrist. Just as the girl looked at her watch, in a flash, the man wrapped one arm around her back and clamped a hand over her mouth. Immediately she began to kick and fight back but it was clear that the man was far stronger. The footage was grainy but the fear in the young girl's eyes was all the more raw and real for it. The man punched her hard in the face. Black liquid sprayed from her mouth as she tried to scream. He kneed her in the stomach, making her double up in pain. Grabbing her hair, he dragged her off-camera.

Allegra felt silence prick her arms and slide up her back, permeating her skin and throat. Her encounters with Drake were child's play compared with what some of these young victims went through. Michael was right: it was far better for a field agent to be subjected to these men's perversions than a young girl walking home from school one day.

"You okay?" whispered Yasmine.

Allegra was surprised to see tears in her friend's eyes. "Are *you?*"

Yasmine nodded and turned back to the screen.

The second clip was two minutes long. It showed a woman, perhaps in her mid-forties, sitting in what looked like a holding cell. She wore thick-framed glasses and had tight, curly brown hair. Instead of speaking to her interviewer, she looked directly at the camera.

"Have you ever had your pussy licked?" she asked, perfectly calmly. "The feeling of a warm, wet, pulsating tongue, licking your juices, sucking it and licking it, up and down and deep inside." The woman shuddered with pleasure. "It's incomparable. Can you imagine being able to get your pussy licked whenever and wherever you like? For as long as you like? You won't find a man who will do that." She paused. "I found the perfect solution. By teaching Amber to lick my pussy, I had it anywhere, all the time. I would make her do it for hours. Every morning, before every shower, straight after school before her snack, before dinner and at night – oh, the nights were the best."

The interviewer said something inaudible.

The woman laughed. "Yes, I know she was seven – don't be a prude! If we teach our children to pleasure us, and we in return, pleasure them, then as they grow, it becomes a mutually beneficial thing – who is not to gain from that? Just because we are conditioned to think that incest is wrong and sex with children is wrong, it doesn't mean it is. Amber learned to enjoy it. In time, I would have started to do it to her too. You sit there and judge me because you have never experienced that freedom – the freedom to have what you want without game-playing, without pleading, without constraints. If you had, you would be like me." She turned her gaze back to the screen. "The whole world would be like me."

Marianne looked up in surprise. Despite running an open-door policy, she rarely had unscheduled visitors.

"Michael? Come in. Sit down." She loved looking at Michael, simply because she appreciated beautiful things.

He sat in the chair Allegra always chose and gestured towards the book in Marianne's hands. "Helene Deutsch? A bit of light afternoon reading?"

She smiled. "Beats Freud."

Michael nodded. He spread his fingers across the edge of her desk.

"Is everything okay?"

He drummed his fingers on the wood. "I wanted to ask if you've had any hint that Allegra may not be up to the job of nailing Drake."

Marianne looked at him with surprise. He knew perfectly well that she couldn't disclose any of her discussions with Allegra.

"I'm not asking you to tell me anything she's said. I simply want your professional opinion on whether or not you think she is emotionally able to go through with this."

Marianne leaned forward. "Can I ask you a question, Michael?"

"Yes," he said immediately.

"What is it about Drake? Why are you after him so doggedly? It seems that your fixation with him is some sort of personal vendetta rather than a professional interest." She saw a flash of anger in his eyes and immediately softened her approach. "I'm not saying that you're being unprofessional, quite the opposite. You're being very thorough but... it just seems like you're going an extra mile with this one."

He met her stare straight on. "What are you expecting me to say? That Drake's daddy fired my daddy so I'm hunting him down for it?"

She sighed. "I just want to know the truth."

"You want a sad story so you can file me away neatly in your psychiatrist's box," he said bitterly.

Marianne was taken aback. Michael was never this rude or aggressive – at least not to her.

He stared at her for a moment. "Marianne, say you met Drake in a supermarket or in a bar or through friends and he got to talking to you and you saw that he's handsome and charming and smart and successful. Say he asked you out on a date. What would you say?"

She smiled. "I'd say, 'Thanks but I like women'."

He sighed. "Okay, ignore that for a second. If you liked men and you were single, what would you say?"

Marianne thought of Drake's moody exterior, his jet black hair and those extraordinary eyes. "I'd probably say, 'Hell yeah'."

Michael nodded. "Exactly. Now transfer his personality into someone less attractive, less picture-perfect, and the chances you will say yes dramatically decrease. Attraction is like acceptance. You see a guy like Drake and you think, 'He can't be a paedophile – how can a guy like that be sick?' You look at the other guy and you think, 'Yeah, I see where you're coming from'. The reason I try extra hard with guys like Drake is because they're the ones that fall through the cracks. They're the ones that no one suspects. They find it easiest to catch prey. If I won't go the extra mile, who will?"

Marianne let him finish before responding. "That's noble, Michael, it is, but I'm still concerned about your tunnel vision and what it could do to Allegra."

"Well, the mere fact that I'm here, consulting you, seeking your advice, should tell you that I have her best interests at heart, shouldn't it?"

Marianne smiled. "I bet you could sell snow to an Eskimo if the need called for it."

"Meaning what?" He drew his hands away from her desk.

She waved away her comment. "Allegra is... complicated. She needs protection, Michael. She's drawn to you because you represent something she's never really had in her life; safety, warmth, protection, even discipline. She will probably do whatever you say, so you have to be careful about what you ask her to do."

"That's why I'm here. Where's the line? Can she handle another meeting with Drake?"

Marianne tapped her fingers on the file on her desk. After a moment's thought, she said, "Yes, but it should be the last one."

Michael nodded and stood up. "Thank you," he said, his voice full of relief.

Black liquid spraying from a girl's young mouth, strands of hair ripping as she's dragged to a violent death. Sordid images from desensitisation haunted Allegra as she walked to her apartment building. She imagined being grabbed by a stranger, gagged and beaten. Surely that type of terror was far worse than anything experienced by Vokoban field agents?

She walked into her apartment and ran to her ringing phone, hoping that it would be Andrew. Her pride would never let her call him first but she was ready to apologise.

"Allegra?" It was Sienna, not Andrew, on the other end of the line.

"Hi." She cursed herself for not checking caller ID.

She wasn't in the mood to talk.

"Where have you been? I've been trying to get a hold of you. Is everything okay?"

"Everything's fine. Work's just been so busy." She tried to sound as bright as possible. Sienna had a knack for seeing through her lies.

"Well, surely you're free on the weekends? We've missed you," she chided.

"I'm sorry. I'll come round as soon as I get some time."

"You're still coming to Reese's concert, aren't you?"

She winced. "Yes, of course. The 21st, right?"

"Yes. Listen, Reese wants to say hi. I'll call you tomorrow, okay?"

"Okay."

"Love you."

"Me too."

Reese's voice came on the line. "*Welly, welly, well. To what do I owe the extreme pleasure of this surprising visit?*"

Allegra laughed. "Are you kidding me? Have you even seen 'A Clockwork Orange'? And if so, how the hell did you manage to sneak that one past Führer Major?"

Reese laughed. "Believe it or not, she's lightened up of late."

"To the extent of letting you watch ultra-violent Stanley Kubrick films? Methinks not."

"Okay, no, I secretly recorded that on Sky Plus, but

she *did* let me go out on a group outing with that cute guy I mentioned."

Allegra scoffed. "With the immaculately conceived child of Mother Teresa and Gandhi? 'Cause I can't see how they'd let anyone else near you."

Reese laughed. "His name is Johnny Savant. We went to the movies – he wanted to take me to the theatre but mum didn't want us going out alone – and then we went to this really nice Italian place with fantastic ice cream and he paid for everything like a real gentleman."

Allegra smiled. "He sounds like a keeper. Is he the guy from your music school Sienna mentioned a few weeks ago?"

"Yes, but he's not like the boys in my year. He's smart and funny and sensitive. He knows everything there is to know about music – did you know that Vivaldi had asthma? An asthmatic violinist, just like me! Mum's insisting on meeting him – Johnny, not Vivaldi – asap to 'examine' him, like he needs delousing or something."

Allegra laughed. She listened to Reese ramble about the date and then, with promises of an imminent get-together, said goodbye. As soon as she hung up, her phone began to ring again. This time it was Sahar, not Andrew, on the line.

"Hello? Leg? How's it going?" Her voice seemed far away.

"I'm okay. Where are you?"

"Bermuda. Anyway, listen. I got a call from lawyer-boy. He said you were freaking out yesterday and thought I should see if everything's okay. You okay? What's going on?"

Allegra's face turned red. How could he have told someone else about what had happened? Yes, Sahar was her best friend but he had no right to talk to her about it.

"Allegra?"

"Yeah, I'm here, Sahar. It was nothing. It was stress. Work is pretty stressful and I had a bad day and Andrew was just pushing and pushing and I told him I just wanted to sleep but he just kept on so I lost it. It happens." She heard Sahar sigh.

"But what's going on? Has he split? That's the impression I was getting."

"Yeah, I guess so," said Allegra resignedly.

"You guess so?"

She sighed. "Well, yes. I guess he has. He left me a note that left little doubt."

Sahar nearly choked. "A *note*? He broke up with you with a *note*? I'm gonna wring his scrawny little neck."

"No, Sahar, I didn't pay it too much attention. Things have been rough for a while now."

"But I thought you two were okay?"

"We were. I don't know. It's me, not him. I'm just crazy." She couldn't believe she had let things get so bad.

"Leg, listen. If you want to be with him, call him, okay? Don't just leave it 'coz your ass is too goddamned stubborn to do anything about it. That man loves you – a damn sight more than any man has ever loved me. He may not be perfect but he is good for you so if there's a part of you that wants him, don't let him go." She paused. "If, however, you really don't feel anything for him, then forget his skinny ass. I mean, he's a *lawyer* for God's sake."

Allegra couldn't even muster a smile. "I don't know what I want, Sahar. I just need some time to think."

"Okay, well let me know what you decide and call me if you need to talk. I'll see you as soon as I'm back in London."

"Ok, bye." Allegra considered her options. If she wanted Andrew back, there could be no half measures on her part. It would have to be marriage or nothing. Were warmth, security and companionship enough? She could do without the passion and butterflies, couldn't she?

"Hey." Michael stood. "You okay?"

Allegra nodded. She didn't know if she was ready to face Drake again. The last two weeks had passed in a blur with different people pulling her in different directions, and yet here she was, by Michael's side, walking in the direction he pointed.

"You ready?"

"Yes." She smoothed her canary yellow T-shirt over the denim cut-offs.

"Where's your watch?"

"Watch?"

"Goddamnit, I told David to prep you with the watch."

"Oh, you mean the Bond-style watch-cum-knife-cum-drill? I've been trained with it but I haven't been given one."

Michael hesitated. "You won't need it but David should have sorted it out regardless." He waved his hand. "It doesn't matter, let's not get distracted. You remember the hair twirling?"

Allegra took a lock of her hair and pretended to absentmindedly twist it around her fingers.

Michael smiled. "Perfect. And the three stooges redid your full wax?"

"Yes." Allegra turned red, suddenly embarrassed. An avalanche of images crowded her mind: Michael on top of her, his fingers on her nipples, between her legs, rubbing, teasing; his tongue licking her, sucking, pulling her into an uncontrollable spiral. She closed her eyes momentarily. When she opened them, Michael was standing closer.

"I think about it too," he said. "Every single day. Seeing you, being near you, smelling your perfume – it's unbearable."

She felt a familiar tightness between her legs.

He took another step closer and breathed in the scent of her hair. Reaching out, he brushed a strand off her face. "You don't regret meeting me, do you?" he asked.

Allegra took a jagged breath. "Not for a second."

As she stood outside the gallery, Allegra remembered the words a field agent had told her in the early days: *Michael is a chameleon, a changeling that always gets what it wants. It's like he has this magical fairy dust. You have an issue you want him to resolve but he intoxicates you with the dust, making you forget everything. It's only when he disappears that you realise you have no resolution.*

The door slammed shut behind her and like all the times before it, Allegra felt butterflies swarm her stomach. This was her last shot.

Drake was straightening a painting on the wall. He looked around and did a double-take.

"Amy?" he asked, eyes alight with surprise and delight. Dressed in black trousers and a pale pink shirt, he looked just as immaculate as Michael always did.

"Hi Joseph," Allegra shyly lifted her downcast eyes to meet his.

He rushed forward. "I'm so glad you came. Are you okay?"

She nodded. "I'm okay. I just, I guess I wanted to say sorry for scaring you that time."

The Vokoban team had spent much time debating the way to approach this meeting. Michael had insisted that Allegra should be friendly and apologetic but David Ellsworth wanted her to be more reticent in order to build a stronger case for prosecution. As always, Michael won out.

Allegra reached up and twisted a curl of hair around a finger. "I wasn't expecting it so I panicked."

Drake looked shocked. "Amy! Darling, sweet Amy. You did nothing wrong. I'm the one who should be apologising. I got carried away. I'm sorry."

"It's okay." Allegra stood still, silent in wide-eyed innocence.

Angel. My Angel of Forgiveness. So young, so fresh. But why do you look so frightened? So stunned? I will fold you into me; I will ravage every inch of your flesh; I will suck you up until you recognise yourself no more. No, angel, do not look so frightened. I do not want you stunned. I want you to see what I am, without my mask for I see you beneath yours. No, I do not want you stunned. I want you to understand what is about to happen to you. And I want you to live through every moment of it.

Drake blinked. "Thank you for coming back and giving me a chance to apologise. I am *so* sorry about what I did. I promise it won't happen again."

Allegra frowned. If Drake restrained himself, they couldn't complete the case – had she blown the only chance she would have? How could she coax him into doing what she knew he wanted without overtly encouraging him? She smiled. "Well, I promise I won't freak out again."

Drake nodded thoughtfully. His eyes darted from her to the door and then back again. "What have you been up to?"

She shrugged. "Nothing much. School." She

pretended to rub an itch just below the cut-off of her shorts.

Drake's eyes followed the motion of her fingers. "Summer holidays are coming up. That's something to look forward to."

She nodded. She couldn't afford to let this conversation descend into banalities. "Joseph, did I leave my lip gloss in your office upstairs?" She had practised the lilting tone of the question with Michael, trying out emphasis on different words: did I leave my *lip* gloss in your office upstairs?

He stopped for a second and thought. "Not that I know of."

"Do you mind if I have a look?" She had thought about saying 'we' but had settled with 'I'.

"Go ahead, Amy. Take your time." He made no indication of following her.

"Thanks." Allegra headed upstairs. Glancing back, she saw how quickly Drake averted his eyes from her behind. In a twisted sort of way, it made her feel empowered. This man wanted her so much, he was willing to go against everything he knew was right to have her.

She walked around Drake's office, pretending to search for the lip gloss. After a minute she called out to him. "Joseph! Can you please help me move the sofa? I wanna check under it but I can't move it." Almost immediately she heard his footsteps clambering up the stairs. His appearance at the doorway, the way he stood

– tall, powerful, confident – made her heart skip a beat. His dark eyes, mysterious and silent, failed to conceal his lust. He wanted her. He wanted her so desperately, he was struggling to control himself.

He cleared his throat. "I'll lift the sofa and you look underneath it."

Allegra positioned her bag on the desk and fell to her knees in front of Drake. "I'm ready." Looking up at his strong frame, she knew she was completely powerless. She swept her arm around the space but, of course, there was no lip gloss. Sighing, she stood and brushed dust off her bare legs. When Drake replaced the sofa, she sat in it, still rubbing dust off her skin.

He sat beside her. "I'll buy you a new one."

She shook her head. "No. It's okay. It wasn't important." She could feel the warmth of his body and the weight of his desire. *Do or die.* She turned to him, every cell in her body willing him closer.

Drake leaned in and brushed a strand of hair off her face. The subtle gesture reminded her of Michael and what he had said in his office just an hour ago: *I think about it too. Every single day. Seeing you, being near you, smelling your perfume – it's unbearable.* The memory made Allegra squirm with longing. How could he resist the attraction between them? It was so heady; intoxicating; so utterly irresistible. How could she resist?

He touched her shoulder lightly and then traced a finger over her chest, across her stomach, and then down to the buttons of her jeans. His other hand moved to her face where he traced her lips. He parted them with two fingers and slipped one inside her mouth. Allegra instinctively ran a tongue over it, licking it softly, teasingly. He pushed it deeper into her mouth. Her training instructed her to move away, to voice her resistance.

She sucked his finger momentarily before pulling herself away. "Joseph, what are we doing?"

His finger crept further down the front of her jeans. "We're not doing anything wrong," he whispered.

"But you... you're much older than me and this – this isn't right."

"Doesn't it feel right to you?"

She shook her head. Thus far, she had been insulated from the true horror of what was happening because it wasn't *real* paedophilia, but as his hands undid her child-sized jeans, the magnitude of his actions hit her. He could be sitting there with a girl who was *actually* 13. It could be Reese sitting here, being stripped by a 35-year-old. It could be Reese with her hands pinned beneath her back and a writhing, hungry body growing increasingly desperate on top of her.

Images of Jemima Bradbury and Sarah Philips and Melissa Hart and the nameless faces of a dozen young girls ran through her mind. It was at that moment she realised that desensitisation was a crock of shit. It didn't desensitise anyone; it did the exact opposite. It seared the faces of past victims onto your brain so that you could never forget them, so that you would always remember them and so that you felt you owed them.

Drake's voice pulled her back to the present. "It feels right, doesn't it, sweetheart?" He undressed as he spoke.

"No." She shook her head. Inside, she was screaming but she lay still and let him continue touching her.

"Sssh, just give it some time. Just enjoy it. Enjoy me." He slipped off one strap of her A-cup bra and let it fall off her shoulder. He kissed her lightly and then slipped off the other strap. Leaning forward, he gently guided one of her bud-like breasts into his mouth. He flicked his tongue over her nipple, slow at first, but then faster, hungrier. A low, guttural moan escaped his mouth as he pushed her back onto the sofa, crushing her with his weight.

"Joseph, I don't want to," she made the final refusal, even as she surrendered to him.

"Ssh, baby. It will feel good, I promise." He ran his strong hands all over her, pulling off her panties and revealing her bare, naked body, tiny and exposed in the fading twilight. He pushed two rigid fingers between her legs, making her yelp in surprise. She was so dry it was almost painful. "Come on, sweetie. Relax. It's fun. I'll make you feel so good," he whispered. He caressed her ear with wet kisses, making her recoil away from his lips and his teeth. She felt her stomach crawl and her throat ache as hot tears burned in her eyes.

"I don't want to," she pleaded. "Please." She thought of the Vokoban team, of David Ellsworth and Jessica Taylor and Michael. She thought of them watching, listening, analysing. *How can they do this? How can they let this happen?*

She bucked beneath his weight but he restrained her effortlessly. "Baby, ssh." His strokes grew longer. He rubbed his fingers all the way down her opening and then in, expertly creating heat and tension. With one last struggle, she surrendered to his touch. *What can I do? There's nothing I can do.*

Drake pulled his fingers out of her and held them to her lips. "That's what I want from you." He showed her his glistening fingers before licking them and spreading a wet trail from one of her nipples to the other.

He violently spread her legs, making her jerk with surprise. He rubbed the tip of his penis against her, faster and faster, until he could push in easily. She dug fingernails into his arm to keep herself from screaming in pain and anger.

"See?" He grunted as he salivated on top of her. "I told you it would feel good. Look at you – you can't contain yourself."

She writhed beneath him, pushing him away, but the harder she pushed, the harder he thrust inside her. She felt overpowered by the sheer force of him on top of her. He was the roughest lover she had ever had, full of raw, unbridled desire and a pulsating passion that exceeded even that of Michael's.

They clawed at each other like hungry animals, each blow pushing them to the crest of a bigger wave. Drake gripped her throat in his hand, the pleasure of being inside her almost ripping him in two. Allegra screamed as he squeezed harder. His voice joined hers as he thrust deeper and faster until finally, he climaxed with a loud, guttural roar. He collapsed in a heap on top of her, the sweat of their bodies mixing to create one slippery mass of limbs.

"Amy, sweet, darling Amy. Thank you," he gasped through short breaths.

Allegra's chest rose and fell rapidly as she gasped in some air.

"Oh, Amy. Oh, sweet Amy. This is you. This *is* you. Oh, my God." Drake shivered on top of her.

A bead of sweat rolled a path between her breasts as her breathing began to slow. She tried to prop herself up but found that she could not. She had lost all strength, all will and all resistance.

Drake met her eyes. "Honey, thank you. Thank you so much for doing this for me. Thank you for coming to me and offering yourself to me like you did. It was a beautiful thing." Allegra said nothing so he continued. "It really touched me but, of course, other people wouldn't understand. They would call you all sorts of horrible names for coming here and bringing me upstairs and giving yourself to me. I want to protect you and the only way I can do that is by making sure that I don't tell anyone about this. You will also have to do the same. If people hear about this, imagine what they will say – you'll be labelled as promiscuous and corrupt. I don't want anyone to think badly of you. So you have to do this for yourself, okay? Promise me you will help me protect you. You won't tell anyone, will you?" Drake lifted her head so that he could see her eyes.

She shook her head, no.

"You promise?"

Allegra nodded.

"Good girl." He leaned forward and kissed her forehead.

Allegra dressed and, without looking at him, walked out of the room and down the stairs. She walked through the gallery onto the street. She turned the corner, calmly set down her bag and then leaned against the wall. She retched and then vomited violently, hit by wave after wave of nausea and hate. When she was finally done, she straightened, wiped her mouth and calmly walked away.

CHAPTER SEVEN

He paced back and forth, long strides crushing patches of the immaculate grass. Glancing at his watch, he tried to calm the elation in his veins. They had finally nailed Drake. Michael could finally look his colleagues in the eye and say, 'Yes, I was right'.

Turning to begin another lap, he spotted the dark car sliding towards HQ. Allegra's bare leg appeared from a back door. The sight of her skin made him think of her tiny naked body beneath Drake. A sharp pang of jealousy stabbed at his chest.

He took a deep breath and composed himself. He had already lost control once – he couldn't do it again. His professional veneer protected him; protected her. As much as he wanted her, as much as he craved her flesh, he couldn't surrender. He couldn't let the depravities of his work seep into his life. He wouldn't allow it.

As he watched her step out of the car, the sweetness

of victory quietly seeped away. Gone was the innocence that had seared her into his consciousness. In its place was a dead-eyed desperation, just the same as all the listless agents that floated through the halls of Vokoban.

He rushed to her side but once there, could find no words or actions to comfort her. Finally, he offered his hand. Hesitantly, she reached out and shook it.

"You did a good job, Agent."

Her face showed not a flicker of emotion. Together they turned towards Vokoban HQ. It loomed high above them, dark and eerily silent. A light in a top corner flickered, a knowing wink as the building swallowed them whole.

Allegra was taken to Vokoban's medical lab. Tissue and bodily fluids were taken from her after which she was photographed thoroughly. She was then allowed to shower and change into her own clothes. It was only after all this that Michael could sit her down and talk to her alone.

In his office, she sat in the chair she always chose. With a straight back and her legs folded neatly together, she placed her hands on her knees, palms down, and stared straight ahead.

"Allegra. Are you okay?"

She let out a short, staccato laugh, chilling in its shrillness.

"They have a warrant for his arrest."

Her eyes met Michael's. "It's over?"

He nodded. "It's over."

She stood up suddenly and walked to the window. Opening the blinds, she stared out into late dusk. It was still a beautiful day. She whispered something low.

"Sorry?" asked Michael.

"It's over." She turned back around to face him, eyes wet with tears.

He walked to her and took her in his arms. She crumpled against him, hot tears seeping through his shirt. It was a silent weeping and were it not for the occasional audible sob, he wouldn't have even known she was crying. He held her tight, gently rocking her back and forth. It slowed her breathing and quietened her sobs.

Seeing her vulnerable like this, without the barriers and pretences she maintained for protection, made him feel special and powerful. He wiped a trail of tears running from her right eye to a corner of her lips. As his fingertip brushed her bottom lip, he closed his eyes and felt a shudder course through his body. He thought of Allegra beneath him on the desk, raw and defenceless just as she was now.

She felt him harden against her, hot breath on her neck. She pulled away. "I want to go home." Her words barely audible.

Michael, torn between guilt and instinct, turned his back to her. "That's a good idea."

The shrieking seemed to perforate her skin, crash

through her skull and judder through to her very core. She sat, bolt upright – was she the one screaming or was it someone else? She turned and watched the clock vibrate on top of her desk, shouting at her to wake up, to get dressed, to go out and kick some ass.

Wearily, she leaned forward and swiped at it, halting it mid-scream. She had overslept by half an hour. Leaning back against the headboard, she pushed thoughts and accusations out of her head. She wished she could stay there, hidden behind a layer of cotton and wool, but she had to be present for Vokoban's legal preparations.

She showered and dressed on autopilot. As she readied to leave, the flashing red light of the answering machine caught her eye. Sighing, she pressed the button.

"Hi Allegra. You have four new messages. Two are from Sienna. One is from Sahar and one is from Andrew. Would you like to listen to your messages?"

Allegra's eyes flickered to the machine at the mention of Andrew's name. Isn't this what she had been waiting for?

"Yes," she replied softly.

"The first message from Sienna was sent yesterday at 6 p.m."

Sienna's voice came on the line: "Allegra, seriously, this isn't a joke anymore. Call me back, okay? You're becoming worse than Rafael–" Allegra skipped to the next message. This one was from Reese. "Hey

Auntilicious, mother dear is having a fit so could you please give her a call? I obviously don't give her enough to worry about. Anyway, also wanted to remind you that my concerto is on the 21st. Keep it free. Goodbyyye," Reese ended in a singsong voice.

The next message was from Sahar. "Leg Rash, I've been trying to get a hold of you just to check in. Call me."

She stared blankly as the machine clicked through to the last message. "Allegra, hi, it's me, Andrew," a pause, "I was hoping to collect a few of my things, namely the two black folders that I keep on your shelf in the living room and a disk I also left at your place. And, erm, I still have the keys to your apartment so I'm guessing you would like those back. Call me and I'll come round or, if you prefer, I can do it when you're at work. Okay. Bye," another pause, "Hope you're okay." With that, he hung up.

She stared at the machine for a few moments, searching for emotion but finding none. She wasn't going to cry over this. She wasn't going to cry over *anything*. She had done enough crying this year to last the rest of her life.

"Come on in," Marianne shouted at the door. She unintentionally straightened her back and squared her shoulders when she spotted Allegra at the door. "Hey, come in. Sit." She observed Allegra's slow walk and expressionless face. "Michael debriefed me yesterday.

They have Drake in custody."

Allegra nodded.

"Are you happy? How do you feel?"

She looked up wearily and met Marianne's eyes. She didn't look 13 anymore. "Happy?" she said, her voice cracking slightly. A faint smile spread across her lips. "Yes, I feel happy." *I can't let myself feel anything because then I would feel... everything.*

Marianne paused. "Can you take me through what happened yesterday?"

Allegra shrugged. "You already know."

"I want to hear it from you. Surveillance and second-hand accounts don't paint a picture of the real thing."

Her head snapped up. "You've seen the surveillance?"

Marianne back-tracked. "No. Michael has. He told me what happened, but I'd like to hear it from you."

She smiled and nodded. "He fucked me," she said emotionlessly.

Marianne's face reddened, suddenly angry. She was angry with Drake for what he was and what he had done to Allegra; she was angry with Michael for letting Drake destroy this beautiful young woman; and she was angry with herself for being here and having to tell her that everything was going to be okay.

Fuck professionalism. Marianne walked to her young patient, knelt in front of her chair and gave her a long, warm hug. Allegra didn't break down and cry as one might expect. She didn't start shaking or sobbing. She didn't even hug Marianne back. She simply sat there, still and silent.

It broke Marianne's heart. She asked herself why Allegra affected her so much. She had seen other girls go through this and if anything, Allegra was stronger than any of them. What was it about her that made people want to protect her? It wasn't her vulnerability – all the girls that came through this office had that quality. Allegra had a quiet dignity that carried her through life – the quietest and loudest thing about her. That dignity had now vanished, replaced by an air of vapid acceptance.

"How do you feel?" asked Marianne, cursing herself for using such clichéd questions. She couldn't afford to let Allegra close herself off from everyone.

She shook her head.

"You don't know?"

"I don't know."

"Allegra, are you ready to talk about it yet?"

"No," she said simply. *There's nothing to talk about.*

"Okay." Marianne nodded and walked back to her desk. "I'm going to push your Tuesday session up to Monday morning. I'll sort it out with Michael. In the mean time, if you want to talk at any time, call me. Whether it's tomorrow or Sunday, any time, give me a call, okay?"

"Okay." She stood up and began to walk out.

"Allegra," Marianne stopped her. "What you did was

a brave and wonderful thing. I just want to tell you that."

Allegra nodded, her back to Marianne, and walked out. There was no respite as she had to meet with Michael to discuss the case. She walked into his office without knocking and took the seat she always chose.

He looked at her, concern etched deep in his face. "Hey, how are you? We haven't had a real chance to talk yet – just you and me."

Allegra's gaze flickered to him before falling back to the floor.

"I want you to speak to me. I want to know that you're okay."

She opened her mouth to speak but then closed it again. After a moment's silence, she said, "I'm okay."

"What are you thinking? What are you feeling?"

"I'm not thinking anything." *I'm not feeling anything.*

Michael sighed in frustration. "Allegra, please don't shut me out like this. Something huge happened to you. I can't say I understand what you're going through but I have helped girls like you through this before. Shutting yourself in never helps. You need to speak to me. You need to tell me how you're feeling."

Allegra's face remained expressionless. "There's nothing to tell," she said blankly.

Michael began to speak but was stopped by David Ellsworth's appearance at the door. "Please come in. Take a seat."

David walked in and sat next to Allegra. "How are you, Agent?"

"I'm fine, thank you. And how are you?" she replied politely.

David frowned. "I'm well." He cleared his throat. "Agent Ashe, I just want to commend you on your performance in this operation. You have helped us build a clear-cut case. You are an asset to the Vokoban team."

"Thank you." Allegra's eyes never left the floor.

Michael turned the forum over to late arrival Thomas Aldridge who had been drafted in to take Allegra over the legalities. She had briefly met Thomas once before at a legal seminar he had given to the field agents during their intelligence training. She remembered how she had been comforted by the fatherly appeal of his salt and pepper hair.

Thomas cleared his throat. "Firstly, I want to run over the basic structure of the case. Michael and David, you will already know about this in detail. Allegra, I believe you are familiar with this as a result of the seminar given in May?"

"Yes."

"Okay. I will keep it brief. In general, child abuse cases are drawn out and difficult to try due to an all-round reluctance to put children on the stand. Clause 160 cases are streamlined and more efficient as all parties involved are adult. These cases take, on average, four to six months in comparison with a normal case that can take anything from a year up to five years.

"Joseph Drake has been taken in. Naturally, he has hired a lawyer. He is using Ethan Frost, one of the most amicable men you will ever meet but one of the most dangerous lawyers you can come up against. He is fiercely intelligent, uncovers loopholes you never knew existed and takes no prisoners.

"We have informed Frost that this is a Clause 160 case. He will, in turn, inform his client of this. The case will be tried in court like a normal case but Allegra will appear as Agent Allegra Ashe instead of Amy Petronas. Our media relations team will make sure it stays out of the papers, issuing DA notices if and when necessary."

Michael looked at Allegra in concern. He wanted to reach out and touch her pallid skin, to let her know that he was there.

Eyes trained on the floor, she thought about facing Drake in the courtroom. Would she feel scared? Sick? Angry? *Will I feel anything?*

"You think you can handle it, Agent Ashe?" Thomas interrupted her thoughts.

"I'm sorry, what?"

"Ethan Frost is renowned for his salvo style of questioning. Do you think you can handle it?"

She looked at him blankly. "And what can you do if I say I can't handle it?"

Thomas looked surprised. "We–" he paused.

"In that case, why bother asking me if it's okay?"

"Allegra," started Michael, concerned by her attitude.

"It's fine," she said quickly. "It's fine. I can handle it."

Thomas nodded wearily and continued. "I plan to submit our documents to Frost on Monday. After that, the ball's in his court. Do you have any questions?"

Michael looked at Allegra, expecting her to have a dozen but she just sat still, staring at her lap. "I think that covers everything, thank you," he replied in her place.

Thomas and David left after finalising a few details. Allegra stood to follow them. Michael wanted to stop her and talk to her but he knew it would be of no use.

"Have a good weekend, Allegra," he said instead.

"You too," she murmured quietly.

"Surprise!" Reese jumped into her sight. Allegra broke into a smile, which cracked her dry, chapped lips.

"Hey you!" She hugged Reese tightly. "What are you doing here?"

"Mum's downstairs parking the car. I ran up. We were worried about you y'know. You weren't returning any of our calls. I called Andrewnicus but he just told me to call you." Reese noticed the bags under Allegra's eyes. "Are you okay? You haven't been sleeping?"

Allegra smiled. *This girl is scarily intuitive.* "Come on in. I'll leave the door open for your mum. Is she angry?"

"Is she ever? She's been worried. She's been going on about you being the only other family we have etcetera etcetera. I told her not to worry but you know how she is."

It was at that moment that Sienna rounded the stairs and spotted Allegra and Reese chatting casually in the living room. She stormed in with her hands on her hips.

"Allegra, just where have you been? I've been trying to call you for days!"

Usually, Sienna's Mother Hen routine made Allegra laugh but today, she didn't have the energy. She shrugged apologetically. "I'm sorry. I've been so busy with work. I actually picked up the phone right now to call you but you turned up."

Sienna shook her head and huffed and puffed before settling down for a cup of tea. Reese launched into an in-depth account of her date with Johnny Savant. Apparently he had been the perfect gentlemen. According to Reese, at 15, Mr Savant was "sensitive and attentive – not like the apish 'puerilites' at school." Her cheeks grew pink with delight as she described how they held hands and shared ice cream.

These are the experiences 13-year-olds are meant to have, thought Allegra. As Reese painted a glorious picture with the minutiae of her date, Sienna suggested going for a walk along the lake in Mudchute. They bought ice cream and lazed in warm sunshine.

It was only when Reese was out of earshot,

practising her water skimming, that Sienna turned to Allegra solemnly. "What's going on?"

"What do you mean?"

Sienna sighed. "Sis, I've been here for you for 13 years since mum died. I know when something is up with you. There were dark clouds hanging over you for months when you broke up with Gabriel all those years ago but even then, it was nothing compared to this," Sienna gestured at her sister's face.

Allegra shook her head in feigned confusion. "Everything's fine. I don't know what you're talking about."

"Al, come on. What's going on?"

She knew Sienna wouldn't let this lie. If Reese was intuitive, Sienna was downright telepathic. She had to give her something to throw her off the scent. Swallowing, she met her eyes. "Andrew broke up with me."

Sienna's jaw dropped open. "What *happened?*" she exclaimed. This drew Reese's attention who meandered over joined them.

"What's going on?" she asked.

With a sigh, Allegra launched into her account of the breakup, employing euphemism and brevity to mask the severity of what had actually happened.

When she finished, Sienna and Reese looked equally heartbroken. They loved Andrew and had really hoped it would work out between him and Allegra.

"Sweetie, you're obviously cut up about it so why don't you call him?" urged Sienna.

That's just the problem. It's not him I'm cut up over. "It's fine. *I'm* fine."

"Al, I think you should come and stay with us for a while. It can't be good for you, staying here by yourself after such a big break up."

Allegra shook her head. With work so crazy, she needed a place to hide just by herself. "I'm fine," she insisted.

Amy. Sweet, forgiving Amy. Eyes deep enough to drown in. Hair so soft, caressing my skin. Betrayal just makes the sacrifice sweeter. I shall not forget the sweetness of her nor the absolution she brought forth. I shall not forget the power surrounding her, inside her. Such warm, slippery sweetness. Darkness falls and I will wait here. Days and days. Until she comes.

Allegra was jarred by the sound of the doorbell. She muted the Discovery channel and looked down at her outfit – one of Andrew's old oversized jumpers teamed with a tatty pair of pyjama bottoms. She shrugged dismissively and tied her hair up in a greasy bun as she headed to the door.

"Hey." Andrew rubbed the back of his neck the way he did when he was nervous. "I'm sorry to drop in on you like this but you didn't reply to my message and I really need some of my stuff so..."

Allegra was taken aback by how handsome he looked. His blonde hair was glossy in the sunshine and he looked casual and comfortable in a pair of jeans and a white shirt. Being away from her was obviously good for him.

"Come in," her bright tone masked her sadness. "I'm sorry the place is a mess. I've been busy."

"Thanks." He stepped in and waited, uncomfortable seeking out his belongings without her express permission.

"You said they were on the shelf?"

"Yeah." He walked over and picked up some folders and files. "Can I quickly check the bedroom?"

She nodded. This man had been her friend, lover and confidante for two years, so why did he feel like a stranger?

He collected his things and then held out his keys. "I guess you want these back?" He dropped them into Allegra's outstretched hand. "So I guess this is goodbye," he said softly. He willed her to say something, anything, to make him stay, to make him forgive her. *If you love something, set it free. If it comes back, it's yours forever. If it doesn't, it never was.* Allegra had to be the one to ask for another chance.

"I guess it is," she replied. Her eyes met his for a brief moment before drifting away. They told Andrew what he needed to know. He didn't see the sorrow or regret he expected or hoped to see. Instead, they were blank and expressionless. *Perhaps she never loved me at all.*

He contemplated one last kiss. He had given two years of his life to this woman – leaving like this felt so incomplete. After a moment's silence, he nodded, turned and walked out of her life.

As she watched him leave, she felt a small pang in her chest but it didn't register in her brain. She closed the door and returned to the Discovery channel, silently watching as a tiger tore into an antelope and dragged it to the ground, teeth in neck.

Marianne's blonde hair was tied up in an immaculate bun. With her dark red lips and designer suit, she looked like a sexy secretary. Taking a gulp of hot coffee, she told Allegra to take a seat.

"Good weekend?"

Allegra nodded. "Yes, thanks."

"What did you get up to?"

She shrugged. "I saw family."

"How was it?"

"Good."

Marianne examined her for a few moments. "But?"

"But nothing." Tiny creases in Allegra's forehead indicated annoyance or, perhaps, anxiety.

"But?" Marianne repeated.

She sighed. "I told you – but nothing. It was fine."

Marianne waited patiently.

Allegra neatened a stray strand of her chestnut hair. She picked up a paper clip from Marianne's desk and started to unwind it. After a moment she said, "I saw Andrew."

"How is your relationship with him?"

She looked up, realising that she hadn't told Marianne about the break-up. *A testament to how much he meant?* She bit her lip and said, "We broke up a while ago. I forgot to tell you."

Marianne remained expressionless. "When?"

"I don't know. A while ago. A couple of weeks maybe."

Marianne raised a brow. "How did it affect you?"

She almost laughed. "With everything going on, *that's* what you're asking me about? My *boyfriend* is what you're worried about?"

"Your ex," corrected Marianne.

She raised her chin; her subconscious way of saying *I don't care.*

"Allegra," Marianne's voice was heavy with severity. "How did it affect you?"

She took a deep breath. "I guess I just feel kind of empty. Andrew gave me everything he could. He was patient – endlessly patient – and he really cared for me. I just– I couldn't be what he needed."

"Which was?"

"Someone who is warm like him. Someone who is affectionate and caring and tactile and sweet. Someone who– who isn't like me."

Marianne squinted, as if focusing on something in the distance. "Conversely, he couldn't give you what *you* needed, right?"

She shrugged. "I guess so."

"Which is what?"

Allegra shook her head. "What do you mean?"

"What do you need in a man? What would have made you love him the way he wanted you to?"

Allegra twisted the metal wire of the paper clip around her fingers. "I need someone who is," she paused, "more than me."

Marianne waited. When Allegra failed to elaborate, she prompted: "More?"

"Andrew is smart and sweet and lovely, but in many ways, we are equal. I need someone bigger than me, stronger than me; someone I can rely on; someone who doesn't give in as easily as him; someone I can't wrap around my finger.

"He's like an open book, you know? Everything you need to know about Andrew you can tell after one conversation with him and that's nice – it's what attracted me to him in the first place – but I need something more."

Marianne nodded. "So you're okay about not being with him anymore."

Allegra threw the paper clip in the bin. "I hate that I am but, yes, I am." She stood and walked to the window behind Marianne's desk. The view over Westminster was beautiful. She watched hordes of people rushing around like they had the most important jobs in the world. She closed her eyes in the sunshine. It felt good against her face, against her headache. She could sense Marianne waiting, watching. She turned to face her, back pressed against the cold radiator.

Marianne chewed on a pen lid. "Hey," she said softly. "Can we talk about last week?"

Allegra straightened. She walked back to her chair and, after a moment's hesitation, sat back in it.

Marianne took it as an act of compliance. "You're not the talky type, I get that, but we *need* to talk about what happened. I need to know what you're thinking. We can't have you withdrawing into a nightmare. I know it sounds facile but if you talk about it, its power to haunt you will diminish – that I promise you."

Allegra sat stone still.

"When Michael asked you to meet Drake again after what happened the last time, how did you feel?"

Allegra swallowed. "I was reluctant, obviously, but I knew it had to be done."

"Reluctant? Not scared? Not angry?"

"There is no room for fright in this job. We are forced to watch every conceivable sick thing in desensitisation. It strips you of fear."

Marianne watched her cheeks flush red. "But anger – yes."

"Yes, I got angry at Michael, but so what? Anger is healthy."

"And how did he react to that anger?"

"The way he reacts to everything; calmly, methodically, pragmatically. I knew it had to be done. He just helped me see that."

"What about when you were with Drake? Did you feel angry with Michael then? Angry that he was watching?"

The fire in Allegra's cheeks spread to her neck, turning it a deep red. "It's his job."

"But how did it make you feel?"

"How is it meant to make me feel?" Allegra's voice rose. "Yes, it made me angry but that's his job – it's what he's meant to do."

Marianne waited a few seconds before speaking. "So you felt anger when you were with Drake. What else?"

Allegra shook her head. "What do you want from me, Marianne?"

"Hey, listen," she soothed. "Just listen. You don't need to talk, okay? You just need to help me figure out a few things."

Allegra tensely gripped the armrests of her chair.

"You don't need to put it into words. I'll do that for you, okay?" When she said nothing, Marianne continued. "When you were with Drake, you felt anger. Did you feel weak?"

Allegra met her eyes. "Yes," she said softly.

"Overwhelmed?"

"Yes."

"Hurt?"

Allegra bit her lip and said nothing.

"Okay. Did you feel exposed?"

Allegra nodded.

"Disgust?"

Another nod.

"Powerless?"

"Yes."

"Out of control?"

"Yes."

"Confused?"

"Yes."

"Did you feel pain?"

"Some."

"What about pleasure?"

Allegra's cheeks grew red. She shook her head. "I–"

"Hey," Marianne stopped her. "It's okay."

Allegra pressed an icy palm against her cheek to alleviate the burning.

"Allegra, have you ever heard of the Electra Complex?" Marianne placed the cap on her pen and set it down on her desk.

"Unless it's to do with that awful Jennifer Garner movie, no."

Marianne smiled faintly. "It's a stupid label given to what some say is a stupid theory." She paused. "There is a huge amount of research into female sexual development. Surprisingly – or unsurprisingly, depending on who you are – much of it links the sexual functions of a woman to her relationship with her father."

Allegra shifted in her chair. "I didn't have a father so I don't see how this affects me."

Marianne held up a hand. "Just hear me out. It has been theorised that turbulence or abuse in a girl's relationship with her father results in difficult and insecure relationships with all men in adulthood."

"Don't you get it? I didn't have a daddy to be abused by," scoffed Allegra.

Marianne shook her head. "Negligence and abandonment constitute turbulence and even abuse. Allegra, certain theories even speak of a daughter's libidinous fantasy of being raped as a result of the way her relationship with her father develops, concluding that the rape fantasy is normal and even universal."

Allegra felt inexplicably affronted. "Why are you telling me this?"

Marianne looked at her insistently. "To help you understand, Allegra, to stop you heading further down a destructive path. I'm not here as a useless sounding board. I'm here to help you understand."

"Understand what?" snapped Allegra.

"Understand your relationship with Andrew, with Michael, with Drake. To help you understand the very reason you said yes to this job and why you continually say yes to Michael even though he angers and hurts you."

"Because I miss my daddy?" asked Allegra bitterly.

"Because you miss protection, validation, discipline, authority."

Allegra stood up and slipped her shoes back on. "You're so off the mark, it's actually amusing. They give you a psychology degree for coming up with stuff like that, do they?"

Marianne held up her hands, palms out; a symbol of surrender.

"You don't need to do my figuring out for me, Marianne. I'm perfectly capable of processing my problems on my own." Allegra spun and stalked out of the office.

Michael sat with his head in his hands. His usually spotless desk was marred by a dark purple tie snaking its way across the oak surface.

"Everything okay?" asked Allegra. He looked up, eyes red-rimmed and weary. His top button was undone and his perfect hair was unusually dishevelled. It had an unnerving effect on Allegra.

He rubbed his forehead. "It's one of our agents," he said, subdued. "She was raped and beaten."

Allegra gulped. "Is she– is she alive?"

Michael nodded. "Only just. He beat her so hard, he gave her internal bleeding. She's in intensive care as we speak."

"Who is she?"

"She's a new recruit like yourself. Her name is Yasmine Ali."

Allegra's face paled.

Michael looked at her sorrowfully. "I'm told you were close to her."

Her face twisted with ugly anger. "How could you let this happen?"

Michael blinked. "Allegra, I'm not her special agent."

"I mean Vokoban! How could you let this happen to

her?" She couldn't believe what she was hearing.

"Her equipment failed. He took her into the shower. The equipment is usually one hundred percent waterproof but it failed and Rasel's team were cut off."

"But–" She shook her head in disbelief. "We have procedures in place for that kind of thing. They should have run interference. What happened?" Her voice grew shrill and hysterical.

Michael went to her side. He was scared for her but part of him was relieved to see anger and emotion in her eyes; at least she was feeling something. He placed two firm hands on her shoulders, anchoring her. "I'll take you down to see her, okay?"

She shook with anger, veins in her head pulsating with fury. "Which hospital is she in?" she demanded, heading towards the door.

Michael took a deep breath. "She's in the building."

Allegra stopped in her tracks. "In the building? But you said she was in intensive care."

"We have a fully equipped medical unit attached to the lab, along with special on-call doctors and surgeons. We can't divulge information about an operation to external healthcare professionals."

Allegra's eyes grew wide. "Why weren't we told about this? Do our agents get beaten up on a regular basis? My God, what happens if one of us gets killed? Do you just hide the body and pretend like it never existed?"

"Allegra, calm down."

"Calm down? First, tell me. What would have happened if Yasmine had been killed? Tell me!"

"Of course we would have told her family. We're not monsters."

She shook her head. "Told them *what*, Michael? Told them lies? Told them it was a street crime? A mugging? A random senseless murder?"

Michael grimaced. "No, Allegra–"

"Liar!" she shouted. "You're a liar." She shook her head. "I saw 'event of death' in one of the contracts you made me sign and I skipped over it – figured it was like any other company's policy – but it's not, is it Michael? You just cover it up, don't you?"

"Allegra, we haven't had any fatalities in Vokoban."

"That's not the point!" she shouted. "It's not the fucking point! The point is to have some honesty, some honour."

"Allegra, I promise you–"

"No! No more promises. No more commands. No more 'yes sir, no sir'. I'm done." Allegra's breathing was shallow and spidery. She looked up at Michael. "Take me to her."

"She–"

"Just take me to her!"

Michael nodded. In silence he led her down to the medical unit. It contained eight beds and four rooms with stark white walls and bright lights that hurt Allegra's eyes. She spotted Rasel sitting outside one of the rooms. He walked over and talked to Michael in heated whispers. Finally, he stood aside, letting them pass.

Hot tears sprang to her eyes as she took in Yasmine's face. Half of it was bloated and swollen, bruised into an ugly green colour. A bandage covered a gash above her left eye while a cast protected her broken right arm. *How could they let this happen?*

Allegra looked to the young nurse stationed in the corner of the room. "Can she hear us?"

The nurse shook her head, causing her small curls to bounce joyfully around her chubby face. It made Allegra want to reach forward and rip the ginger curls from their roots.

"She's sedated. It's going to be at least a good few days until she's conscious." The nurse left with a sympathetic look, silently followed by Michael.

Allegra pulled the vacated chair next to Yasmine's bed and sat down. She wanted to take her hand but was scared of hurting her.

"Hey Yas, it's Allegra. Or 'A Leg Rash' as some of my friends like to call me." A harsh laugh escaped her mouth. "Funny, we talk all the time but I never told you that. Guess we've been caught up in all this crap, huh?" She gestured out at the room. "I was busy getting fucked and you were busy getting killed." Another shrill laugh. "I'm sorry. It's not funny, is it?" Her voice wavered. "It's not worth it either, is it?" She tried to say more, wanted to say more. She wanted to tell Yasmine how sorry she was. She wanted to ask her what had happened and to tell her about Drake but the words caught in her throat. She couldn't speak so she sat in silence, softly stroking her friend's hair.

Three hours later when Michael returned, Allegra was sitting in the same position.

"Have you eaten?" he asked.

She nodded. "The nurse brought me something."

"Okay." He paused. "Listen, can you come up for a minute? We need to go through a few things before our meeting with Thomas tomorrow."

She shook her head. "I want to stay here."

"Allegra, you can't help her," he said softly.

"Michael," She tried to control the strain in her voice. "She has no family here. She has no mother or father and no friends to sit by her bedside so I am going to stay here."

He shook his head. "Allegra, we can't let you fall into deeper depression over this. Rasel will deal with Yasmine. We have our own cases to deal with."

She looked at him with blazing eyes. After a moment, she gestured towards the exit. Once inside Michael's office, she waited until he closed the door.

"How dare you?" she started softly.

"Excuse me?"

"How dare you!?" she screamed. "How dare you be so fucking insensitive? 'Rasel will deal with Yasmine'. She's his problem, right? Nothing to do with you or me. We don't have to give a fuck, right?"

"Allegra, calm down." Michael was taken aback by

her assault but, as before, also relieved – anger and frustration were healthy and normal.

"No, I will not calm down! Michael, you sit here in this polished little hole of yours, sheltered and warm, away from all the sickness we deal with. You see it, Michael, sure, and yes, that stuff hurts the same way desensitisation hurts but it's not the real thing. You don't feel any of it."

"Allegra, I'm sorry if I came across as insensitive but–"

She wasn't ready to let him talk. "Michael, I know you do good work. I know, but you can't imagine what it's like to be so exposed. Yasmine was relying on Vokoban, the same way I rely on you. She expected you to be there to get her out of trouble – trouble that you got her into. You should have all the bases covered!"

"Allegra, this doesn't happen often–"

"It doesn't matter how often it happens! It happens and that's enough. Michael, it's so hard." Her voice wavered. "It is so hard. Michael, I lay there with Drake as he cut away at my very humanity. I can't go to sleep at night because I feel him creeping all over me. I feel my hair standing on end and my skin crawling. I wake up soaked in sweat because I'm having nightmares about his body crushing mine. I lie awake and I can hear him breathing right next to me there on the pillow. I can feel him pushing his way inside me and–" Her face crumpled.

Michael felt a lump in his throat. He walked to her but she pushed him away with an angry cry.

"Do you think I want to be touched, Michael? Do you think I can be touched by you or any other man? I pushed away the one man who has ever treated me right because I couldn't fix my head up. Do you think I want you near me?" Anger and pain streamed down her face in hot tears.

Michael didn't know what to do. If his words or touch couldn't help, he didn't know what could. "Allegra, I'm going to send you home, okay?"

She shook her head. "I'm going to go to Yasmine."

He hesitated but, after a moment's consideration, said, "I'll take you down."

"You do that," she commanded through bleary eyes.

Once back upstairs, Michael paced back and forth in his office. He didn't know how to help Allegra. She was a good agent and apart from the one slip-up when she was recognised, she had carried the weight of the operation with skill. He couldn't afford to have her break down on him now. They needed to see this thing with Drake through to the end. Michael only wished that they could somehow find a link between Drake and Jemima Bradbury, the young girl that had been killed a year ago, but there was nothing connecting the two other than Michael's gut feeling; no DNA evidence, no witnesses, nothing. If their case ended in conviction, which it should, Drake would be put away for at least five years but if they managed to nail him for Jemima, that sentence would be multiplied.

Michael sighed and rubbed his eyes. Something was better than nothing and he couldn't complain after the effort Allegra had put into the operation. He sat down to review some notes from Thomas. They had submitted their documents to Ethan Frost. There wasn't much else to do but wait.

Downstairs, Allegra sat at Yasmine's bedside. The oppressive silence was all the more marked in the absence of Yasmine's lively talkativeness.

"Crazy, huh?" Allegra ran a fingertip across the seams in the blanket. "Who would have thought that things would unravel so fast?" She paused, regaining control of her shaky voice. "I'm just so mad, you know? I am so mad but I don't know who to be mad at. I don't know who to blame for this. Sometimes I blame Michael for bringing me into this world but then I start to question myself: what was so terrible about my life that I had to turn to this? Yes, I lost my job, but was my life so messed up that I had to choose this? I have a small but wonderful family, one that spends its days worrying about me now. I had a good man in my life, one that I've pushed away. I put such a strain on our relationship that it had to break. I had my intelligence and my ability. Why did I have to turn to this?" She looked at Yasmine, actually expecting an answer.

"How did we screw up our lives so badly that we ended up like this?" She sighed. "I try to keep in mind the good we're doing but..." her voice trailed off. "If I manage to get Drake off the streets, that's one less piece of scum roaming the world and if you–" She stopped and looked at Yasmine's swollen face. *Is it worth this?*

"I think I may leave," she said softly. After 10 minutes, she stood up and walked out of the room.

The neat white envelope was the only thing on Michael's desk that hadn't been there when he left last night. He checked the time: 7.50 a.m. Lyla wasn't in yet so this couldn't be the post. He picked up the envelope. On the front, in neat black letters, it said 'Michael Stallone'. He ripped it open and read the one-page document. When he finished, he screwed it up into a tight ball and threw it in the bin.

"Allegra, please sit," instructed Thomas.

With a sideways glance at Michael, she took the seat next to him. All remnants of guilt and concern over Yasmine had disappeared – here he was as fresh and perfect as ever, Allegra pale and broken in comparison. The past week had taken its toll – her olive skin had grown dull and tired while her glossy mane was withered and mousy.

"Ethan Frost has come back to us. He's obviously pushing for bail. As this is a Clause 160 case with an adult victim and because Drake is not a flight risk, we expect that bail will be granted."

Allegra nodded. She remembered all this from the

training seminar. Agents were given three options for the bail period: go into protective custody, commission 24-hour surveillance or do nothing. Targets were informed of the nature of their case and issued a gag order but the real identity of their field agent was not revealed until the case was in court. That, in itself, was a layer of protection so Allegra had chosen to do nothing.

Thomas leaned forward on the desk. "There is one thing that may cut out a whole mass of complications."

Allegra looked at his wizened nails on the table. *They need trimming.* She waited for him to continue but it was Michael who spoke.

"Allegra, we think that maybe if Amy Petronas confronted Joseph Drake – told him to tell the truth, told him that he could be helped – he might admit that he did all those things to you."

She stiffened in her chair. "But he knows I'm not Amy."

"All you have to do is talk to him as Amy – the way Amy does – and see how he reacts."

She shook her head. "Are you being serious? He's not an idiot, Michael. You know he's smarter than that."

"Yes, but he has a sickness – one he can't help. He was drawn to Amy – who's to say that has gone? Who's to say you can't walk in there with power over him?"

She couldn't believe they wanted to put her in the

same room as him. The power she had over him was born of a lie – one that transformed her into a fresh-faced 13-year-old virgin. Amy Petronas may have brought him to his knees but 26-year-old Allegra Ashe was more likely to bring forth a fit of violent anger.

"Hey," Michael said gently. "We'll be right there with you."

Allegra laughed derisively. "Isn't that what Rasel said to Yasmine? Isn't that what she thought when she was sent like a lamb to the slaughter?"

Michael frowned. "Allegra, if you go in there and get him to recognise his sickness then maybe he would come clean. If you hint that you would think more of him if he did the right thing, maybe he would do it. If he admits guilt he gets no bail, we streamline the conviction process and make life easier for everyone."

"Including me?" she asked rhetorically. After a beat, she looked at Thomas and asked, "Would Ethan Frost even allow that sort of exchange?"

"If Drake wants a private conversation with Amy – or you – without counsel, Frost can't do anything about it."

She sighed. "This will put him behind bars quicker?"

Thomas nodded. "If he admits his guilt, then yes."

The thought of facing Drake again terrified Allegra, but she wasn't going to let anyone see that. "I'll do it," she said quietly.

Michael sighed with relief. "Thank you."

Allegra watched gratitude spread over his features and thought of Marianne's words: *you miss protection, validation, discipline, authority.*

The lock on the metal door echoed across the room as it clicked to a close. Allegra took a few tentative steps inside. Her trainers made the same soft squeaking sounds as on Drake's gallery floor. She was dressed in the yellow T-shirt and denim cut-offs she had worn on the day of their last meeting. The chill in the darkened room caused her nipples to harden and protrude from her braless chest. She felt naked and exposed without the armour and fakery of Amy.

Drake's silhouette was hunched at one end of a long steel table. Dressed in dark overalls, he looked surprisingly unkempt. His face brightened when he saw Allegra's face.

"Angel," he cried. "You came."

She stiffened. Drake's demeanour and body language were different. Gone was the easy confidence and perfect diction. Instead, he seemed nervous and anxious. His gaze flitted over Allegra and across the room as if too frightened to settle in one place.

"Joseph?" she asked quietly.

He nodded nervously and offered her a slow smile. "They're watching us, aren't they Angel?" He pointed towards the two-way mirror.

She nodded. "Yes, Joseph. They are."

He smiled again. Leaning forward, he said, "Mr Frost

told me 'no private talkies' but I told him no – I have to see my Angel alone." He jabbed a finger towards the guard stationed at the front of the room. "Turn around!" he yelled. "You turn around!" When the guard ignored him, Drake shook his head rigorously and turned back to Allegra.

She cleared her throat. "Are you okay? Have they hurt you?" she gestured towards the mirror.

Drake smiled. "No, Angel. They gave me coffee."

She nodded. "Good," she said softly.

So much darkness hidden in so much light. I have so much to say to you, so much to do to you but angry men in mirrors – watching, unforgiving. I want to feel you, Angel. I want to feel your skin. I want to rip it open and ravage your soul. I want to rip you open and make you bleed, just as you make me bleed. I am bleeding, Angel. Watch me bleed.

Drake's eyes clouded over as he strained to control the desire building below the surface.

"Joseph," Allegra mentally mapped out what she needed to say. "I came to see you because I care about you." She watched his face brighten. "I think that you're a good person and that what happened between us was something that neither of us could control." She paused. "I think it happened because you couldn't control yourself. It was just an impulse. I think that together, we can battle it and help you."

242

Drake propped his elbows on the table and rested his chin in his hands. He stared at her lazily, taking in her body and the pertness of her small breasts. He smiled at her – a chilling, unnerving smile that was incongruous on his handsome face.

"Joseph, do you hear what I'm saying? I want to help you."

He sighed lazily. "I don't need help."

"Joseph, don't do this," she pleaded. "We shared something. Don't pretend that it didn't happen."

"It's beyond my control, Angel." He slipped a hand beneath the table.

"You need to tell the truth. We can get you the help you need."

Drake breathed jaggedly. He struggled to speak but when he did, he said, "It's beyond my control, Angel."

Allegra couldn't give up – not now. "Don't you understand, Joseph?" she pleaded. "If you tell the truth, you can get help and you can become a good man, a man that I could love."

His head snapped up in surprise. He started to speak but just then, a red-faced Ethan Frost burst through the door.

"You're done," he snarled at Allegra.

Drake sprang up. "No!"

"Leave the room," said Frost angrily.

Thomas walked in and helped Allegra out of her chair, dragging her out of the room. She heard Drake yell at Frost as Thomas shut the door behind her. In an instant, Michael was by her side. He held her and smoothed her hair. She didn't know why she was shaking so hard. The meeting hadn't been as bad as she had anticipated but she couldn't stop shaking.

"He– he's different," she whispered.

"Ssh, it's okay," Michael held her tight and tried to calm her. "You did a good job." He led her away from the room.

"What happened?" she asked. "I thought I was getting through to him."

"Frost wouldn't let it go any further. He said we were 'pulling dirty tricks'."

Thomas turned to Allegra. "You did a good job Agent but Frost thinks we overstepped the line. I don't think he'll let you anywhere near his client again."

Allegra looked at the two men. "So... what happens now?"

Twenty-four hours later, Joseph Drake was walking the streets.

CHAPTER EIGHT

"Are you sure you don't want security at your place?" asked Michael.

Allegra raised a brow, silently mocking the futility of surveillance.

His expression grew sombre. "Okay, but please be careful. Drake's trial is in three weeks so keep a low profile until then."

She nodded. "Aren't we going to talk about it?" she asked after a moment.

He looked up, green eyes as piercing as ever. "About what?"

"You know what, Michael. My letter."

"Letter?"

"Yes. My letter of resignation."

Michael heaved a sigh. "I've thrown it away," he said simply.

"Okay. Well, that doesn't change anything."

He shook his head. "Allegra, you can't leave. We

need you. You've proved to be a fantastic agent – look at how you've handled Drake. In a few weeks, he'll be in prison – something *you're* responsible for."

She nodded. "I know, Michael, and I'm proud of that – I am – but I can't do it anymore. This case has infected my life."

Michael frowned. "I know it's been tough on you but I promise it gets easier."

She shook her head. "I don't want it to get easier. What kind of person finds this easy? I don't want to be that person. I gave it a shot, Michael. You tried everything to get me to work for Vokoban and you didn't listen when I said no. This time, please listen. I can't do it anymore."

"Why don't you take some time off? Take some time to think things through. The first target is always hard. When you come back, I'll give you a repeat offender."

"I can't, Michael. I'm out."

He shook his head. "No. I can't let you go."

She smiled wistfully. "See, stuff like that is just the problem." She took a seat near his desk and gestured for him to do the same. She needed to close the chapter on Vokoban but couldn't without severing ties with Michael first. She picked up a pencil from his desk and used it to tie her hair in a bun.

Taking a deep breath, she began to speak. "The first time I saw you, I was struck. There was this raw magnetism, like nothing I had ever felt before. It wasn't just an attraction – it was something else, something I couldn't figure out.

"Anytime anyone has ever tried to push me, I push right back, Michael – that's just the way I am – but you," she paused, "I let you rip me into pieces and put me back together the way *you* wanted. And I couldn't figure it out but I think I see it now. I trusted you. I looked to you for validation. The force you had over me, I was captivated by it because I had never felt that type of control before. And then I felt the same thing with Drake – that's when I knew I had to stop. I can't carry on doing this because it's going to make me sick."

Michael frowned. "I don't understand what you mean."

She smiled. "You don't have to understand because *I* do," a pause, "I need time to figure things out, to get it together."

"I can help you," he insisted.

She shook her head. "No. I have to do this alone."

"It's my fault, isn't it?" he said sadly. "I shouldn't have let us get so close. I was warned against it – do you know that? Caitlin, she saw it right from the start. She's been working with me a long time and she saw the difference in me straight away; the effect you had on me. That's what we were arguing about when you saw us at that bar. She told me not to hurt you but I said it was none of her business, that everything was under control. She didn't know that it was already too late. I didn't do the right thing then but I'm going to do it now. I'm–" He took a deep breath. "I'm going to let you go."

Allegra swallowed the lump in her throat. She wanted nothing more than to be near Michael but their twisted relationship was damaging her – she needed to stop.

He reached forward and touched her chin. "You–" Pausing, he took another deep breath. "You don't even know how special you are." He tried to form the right words to say. He wanted to thank her for all she had done and tell her that she was amazing and strong and unique, that she was unlike anyone he had ever met. He wanted to tell her to stay, to be with him, to never leave. But he didn't say any of it – it was just their way.

Eventually, he leaned forward and unexpectedly planted a soft kiss on her cheek. She looked up at his eyes, harbouring darkness and light, and, in that moment, the beauty of him took her breath away.

"You're going to be okay, Agent," he whispered in her ear.

Allegra watched Yasmine struggle with the cup of water. She took a moment to compose herself and then walked into the room brightly, watching as Yasmine's wide smile turned her face into a bulbous mess.

"Hey!" Allegra used all her poise to stop herself from grimacing. She took the cup and lifted it to her friend's lips.

As Yasmine took a sip, tears formed in her eyes and spilled silently down her cheeks.

"Hey, c'mon, stop that." Allegra reached for a tissue and gently wiped Yasmine's bloated face.

"I'm sorry." A bout of laughter escaped her twisted lips. "It hurts to laugh. It even hurts to talk."

Allegra nodded sympathetically. "You're going to get better."

"I know." Through closed lips, she began to hum 'Eye of the Tiger'.

"You'll be dunking bread in the night before you know it."

Laughter spilled from Yasmine's lips followed by a groan of pain. She flexed her jaw and said, "It's okay, I can talk." She paused. "Lord knows I can do that."

Allegra smiled. "How are you doing? Did you sleep okay?"

Yasmine nodded. "I'm okay. I'm having nightmares but the doc said that's normal, that it's just my mind processing my fears. I'm just getting on with getting better now."

Allegra studied Yasmine's eyes. How was it that they still shone with spirit and verve?

"Dude, I know I look like the elephant man, but do you have to stare? I'm gonna have to start charging."

Allegra smiled faintly. "I'm just wondering how you manage to stay so positive. Stay... stay *you*."

A vein at the side of Yasmine's forehead quivered. "I'm–" She paused and took a deep breath. "I'm working through it, you know? Shit happens. Sometimes it happens to other people and you look and feel sorry for them and think, 'Thank God it was them and not me', but when it happens to you, it puts things into perspective. There's no point letting something like this beat you down because where will that leave you? I have to make a decision: am I going to let this guy ruin a few weeks of my life or am I going to let him ruin years of it? Maybe all of it? He's in custody now. He'll end up behind bars where he belongs and that will be that."

"But it's not that easy to stay afloat, to not let it get you down. Most people would be in pieces after what you went through." Allegra was shamed by her friend's resilience, but could not believe that anyone would escape such a violent experience unscathed.

Yasmine smiled weakly. "I'm not going to lie, Al, that man put the fear of God in me. He hurt me in ways I thought I could never hurt." She paused. "I'm no Virgin Mary but some of the stuff he did to me... I didn't even know it existed." Her lower lip trembled. "Do you know they have these devices to force your mouth open? He pulled my lips apart with these metal forceps and..." Tears welled in her eyes. "He kept pushing. I was screaming but he kept pushing and pushing and then I could taste him, could feel it, hot and slimy in my throat." She gagged, her body lurching forward with force.

Allegra rushed forward and held her shoulders. "Hey, hey – stop. It's okay. It's over."

Yasmine coughed and gulped some water. Rivers of tears snaked across her cheeks as her broken body shook with shame and disgust. Allegra gently wrapped her arms around her, allowing her to break down.

After a long while, when Yasmine's sobs had subsided, Allegra looked at her in earnest. "I'm leaving. I think you should too."

Yasmine's eyes grew wide, giving her face a gruesome effect. "Leaving?" With alarm, she listened to Allegra's reasons. As she processed the information, she realised that she didn't need to hear words or explanations – just looking at her friend was explanation enough. Allegra's face, eyes and skin had all changed, shadows of what they were.

"When?" asked Yasmine, hiding the sadness in her voice.

"It coincides with the end of my case, which means I can leave in two weeks. After that, I'll be paid pro rata for attending the hearing and taking part in the legalities." She paused. "You want to stay?"

Yasmine waved away the question. "Michael is okay with you leaving?"

Allegra leaned forward and kissed her cheek. "Michael Stallone does not have a say."

She placed the phone on the side table and curled on the sofa, stretching lazily as she basked in the warm Sunday twilight. She thought about what she would wear to the concert tomorrow. Reese had just called her, making her promise punctuality. As ever, Supermum Sienna had emailed her directions and a journey plan from Mudchute to Cadogan Hall. "No excuses. If you're late, they won't let you in," she had urged.

Allegra realised that she was really looking forward to it. It had been only two days since she had left Vokoban but already she felt re-energised. She stared out the window at the fading light and thought of Michael.

"It's not goodbye. It's see you later," she had said. She remembered the way he ran his fingers through his hair, trying to hide his distress; the way he held her hand and laced her fingers with his; the way he touched her cheek and breathed in her scent and said all the things she wanted to hear, only with actions – not words.

She remembered the way he had leaned forward and kissed her full on the mouth, the way his lips felt like warm, melted butter, the way it made her float and dissolve. "See you later," his whisper, warm on her neck.

Turning away from him and walking out that door had ripped away another layer of her skin, but she knew that it was necessary; she had to start anew.

A breeze wafted in from her bedroom, making her shiver pleasantly. Yawning, she rested her head on a cushion and lazily watched a re-run of 'Friends'. It was strange – she had no boyfriend, no job and no immediate prospects and yet she felt completely free.

"It's okay," she said to herself. *I have a wonderful family. And I did something good this year. Drake's trial starts in a week and then it will all be over. And I will have done something really good.*

Michael muted the DVD. Restless, he walked to the kitchen and looked in the fridge. He picked up a Granny Smith apple from his fruit bowl and bit into it absentmindedly. He sat back down and tried to relax. Why did he feel so on edge? After a long, hard battle, Drake was finally on his way down. Yes, there would be another, perhaps worse, version along soon but why couldn't he just enjoy this moment?

He thought of Allegra, her delicious hazel eyes, sad as they said goodbye. He had to let her go for both their sakes. Their attraction bordered on obsession and that was healthy for no one.

Frustrated, he stalked to his study and opened the top drawer. He took out a stack of cards and filed through them. "This'll do," he said with impatience. He pulled out his phone and punched in a set of numbers. "Yes," he said to the voice on the other side. "Account number 40105424." He waited. "Lara please." A pause. "Yes. Brunette, petite, hazel eyes." He nodded. "An hour? Great, thank you." A smile. "Oh, I plan to." He replaced the receiver, the smile widening on his lips.

Allegra bolted upright. The apartment was pitch black. The whistle of the wind outside was the only sound she could hear. What had startled her so badly? She blinked and felt around for the remote. She could swear the television had been on when she drifted off to sleep. Her fingers crawled along the edge of the table but found nothing. Something was wrong – she could feel it in her veins.

A low creak crept through the silence. She frowned. It sounded like it had come from the bedroom. She knelt on the floor and felt around for her phone. She didn't dare turn on the table lamp. *Just in case.* Another creak, closer this time, made her freeze with fear. Was she imagining it? A sharp, hollow sound rang out, like someone striking a tin pipe. Fear clawed at her heart. *This can't be happening.*

She crept up tentatively. *Don't,* said a voice in her head. She took a step towards her bedroom, breathing as quietly and slowly as possible. This time she heard footsteps. Confused, she turned to her front door. It sounded like they had come from outside. Panicked, she ducked back down. She tried to run through the self defence techniques she had been taught in WSN but her limbs felt heavy with fear. In silence, she headed towards the kitchen. *Phone. I need to find the phone.* She heard a rustling sound inches behind her. She spun, readying to scream, expecting to see a shape emerge from the darkness, but nothing – there was nothing. In silence, she counted to ten and then turned back to the kitchen.

Her feet made light pattering sounds on the tiles as she ran to the counter. Was that breathing she could hear? Shaking, she felt around for the phone. Every single blind was drawn, blocking out all sources of light. When had she drawn them?

As her fingers crept up the phone stand, she felt a sinking sensation in her stomach. The phone wasn't there. She wanted to scream with frustration. Moving across the kitchen, she opened a drawer and took out a butcher knife. She stood still. *Could it be him? Could it be?*

She had always thought that she would be calm in a situation like this but the blood pounded in her head, making her feel faint with fear. She didn't know if she should turn on the light or remain cloaked in darkness. After a moment's hesitation, she decided that she had to engage him. In a quiet whisper, she called out "Joseph?" Clearing her throat, she tried again, louder this time. "Joseph?" She heard a sharp snap in her bedroom, like a twig breaking.

"Allegra?" came the reply. The familiar voice sprang through the air, wrapped itself around her throat and squeezed.

Cold dread rooted her to the spot as she heard sudden heavy bangs pounding against her front door. She looked towards her bedroom then back at the front door, torn between the two separate sounds.

"Hey, Allegra, you in?"

Sudden realisation flooded her with relief. She ran to the door and flung it open. "Oh," she gasped. "Eric, thank God."

"Hey, are you okay?" Her neighbour, a 6'4" body builder, looked at the knife in her hands.

"I–" She breathed deeply, awash with relief. "I

thought there was someone in my apartment. When you said my name, I thought…" She shook her head. "I thought it was someone else."

He frowned. "Could it have something to do with these?" He pointed at a massive bunch of white orchids left by Allegra's front door. She half-gasped, half-laughed when she saw them. Scooping them up, she noticed that instead of a card, there was a post-it-note stuck on the side. She plucked it off and read it: *I miss you. Can we talk? A x*

She laughed out loud. "They're from Andrew. God, I am *such* a drama queen. I was freaking out. Thank God you stopped by."

"I just wanted to make sure you took these in. Listen, let me come in and take a look around, just in case, okay?"

She nodded. "Oh, thank you." She let Eric sweep the apartment while she found a vase for the stunning flowers. She thought of Andrew. He wanted to talk. Could they sort things out? Maybe once she worked through her issues, she and Andrew could be happy together. Maybe they could make it work.

Eric walked into the kitchen and assured her that the apartment was empty. "You should probably close your bedroom window though," he added as he left.

She walked to her room, shivering in the sudden chill. As she reached forward and closed the window, she failed to notice the pencil she had taken from Michael's office lying on the floor, broken and splintered.

Allegra scanned the milling crowd. She couldn't make out Sienna or Stephen anywhere. She had arrived at the concert hall 15 minutes early just to make sure that she didn't miss Reese's performance. As she looked around and absorbed the excitement, she couldn't help but feel positive. This time next week, Drake's trial would begin. Soon, he would be behind bars and she would move on with her life. Things were going to be okay.

She sent Sienna a text: *I'm here. Where are you? Left section or right section? What row?* A few seconds later, a dark-haired woman near the front row stood and turned. Allegra immediately spotted her sister. She looked radiantly happy. And why shouldn't she? Her wunderkind daughter had the only solo. Allegra waved and made her way to the front. She kissed Sienna, hugged Stephen, and sat down.

"You're looking good," said Sienna.

"Thank you. As do you, bella." In a figure-hugging black dress and three-inch high heels, Allegra looked and felt beautiful. She leaned back in her chair. This is what she needed: time with her family doing things she enjoyed. As she watched Stephen grip Sienna's hand, Allegra thought of Andrew. A warm smile spread on her lips. *Things are going to be okay.*

The curtains lifted to enthusiastic applause. Reese was to play the violin solo of Tartini's Devil's Trill Sonata after a short piece by the orchestra.

Allegra nudged Sienna and whispered, "I can't see Reese."

Sienna nodded. "She's going to come on for her solo. She's not a part of the ensemble piece."

The sweeping tones of the orchestra filled the room. The beauty of it gave Allegra goosebumps. The music reached a crescendo and then slowed to a lull, tapering into a quiet, understated finish. After a rush of applause, the auditorium fell quiet, electric with expectation. A long minute passed and a low whisper travelled through the audience. Finally, a teenage boy stepped forward and started to play a piece on the violin.

Allegra turned to Sienna in confusion. "Isn't that what Reese was practising when I was at your place?"

Sienna nodded, eyes fixated on the boy onstage.

"Isn't that meant to be the solo?"

She nodded.

"So...?"

She turned to Allegra, anger flashing in her eyes. "They must have bumped her off the list at the last minute. She's been practising that piece for months!" Someone behind them made a huffing sound so they quickly quietened. Sienna shook her head in anger. "How could they do this?" she whispered furiously. She tapped her foot impatiently and then stood up.

"Where are you going?"

Sienna either didn't hear or didn't care to answer. Allegra watched her storm to the end of the row and disappear through a side door, presumably to go and confront Reese's music teacher. She shrugged sheepishly at Stephen who shrugged back. They both turned to the stage and watched the piece. After it swept into a grand finish, applause ripped across the room and the audience began to stand up row by row. Allegra and Stephen stood too, clapping politely.

She leaned in towards him. "You think she's frying someone's balls right now?"

"Uh-huh. She'll probably be serving them up for dinner tonight."

Allegra wrinkled her nose. "We should probably find her before she does something really drastic, huh?"

"Yeah, we should," Stephen laughed. They edged their way out of the auditorium, but couldn't spot Sienna.

"She's probably backstage. Do you know your way around here?"

Stephen nodded and led her down the corridor and up a short set of stairs. They entered the backstage area and navigated to the main room in which the musicians congregated. They spotted Sienna but she wasn't chewing someone's ear off or carving up someone's testicles. She was standing there in silence, a stricken look on her face. When she spotted Stephen and Allegra, she cried out loudly – a strangled, pitiful sound.

"Reese is missing," she said in a small voice.

"What do you mean?" Stephen grabbed Sienna's hand.

"She was here. Right here. Mr Perkins said that he

saw her and she was all ready for her solo but when he went onstage, she never turned up. When he rushed backstage, Reese was gone. Stephen, she's a responsible child. She wouldn't just wander off somewhere. She's been practising for months." Her voice grew hysterical.

Reese's music teacher joined them. "I have scoured the entire building and the grounds outside. I have asked everyone if they have seen her but there's no sign."

Sienna moaned in anguish. "How could this happen? Something must have happened. She wouldn't just wander off."

Allegra touched Sienna's shoulder. "What about that guy she was dating? Johnny Savant? Do you think he could have snuck in and taken her away? Maybe she thought it was romantic?"

Sienna shook her head vehemently. "Allegra, you know Reese. She would never do something like that. No matter how crazy she was about a guy, she wouldn't let her class down like that. She wouldn't let herself down like that."

"I know, Sienna, but sometimes girls do stupid things for guys."

"No, something is wrong. I can feel it." She turned to Mr Perkins. "We need to call the police."

"They're already on their way," he replied, wringing his hands in despair.

Sienna's bottom lip quivered. She wriggled out from under Stephen's arm and began to pace the room.

"Someone must have seen her. How could she just disappear? Isn't there some kind of announcement that we can make?"

Mr Perkins nodded. "We have an intercom system. I can ask her to come to this room or ask if anyone has seen her." He rushed off to make the announcement.

Allegra felt her stomach sink. Sienna was right. Reese wouldn't just disappear like this. She was way too sensible to run away or go off with a boy. She had to be in trouble. Allegra thought of all the sick things she had seen in desensitisation; the evil, twisted men that tied up young girls and used everything they could find to torture them. *It can't be – she's okay. She has to be.* Allegra shook depraved images and thoughts from her head. Maybe this was karma's way of punishing her for leaving Vokoban and abandoning her duties. She swallowed, pushing fear back down her throat. *She's okay.*

Half an hour later, when the police still hadn't arrived, Sienna's concern turned into anger and then hysteria.

Stephen, debilitated by fear himself, didn't know how to help her. He looked to Allegra. "Thank God you're here."

"What can I do?" she asked helplessly. Sienna was the strong one, the organised one who always knew what to do.

"I'm just glad you're here."

When the police finally arrived, Sienna launched

into an angry tirade, quietened only by Stephen's firm hand on her arm.

Allegra jumped in. "Officers, please forgive us for being a bit edgy. You have to understand how difficult this is."

"Please, let's just all calm down. I'm PC Daly. This is PC Wildborne. Now what is the name of the missing person?"

"Reese Keaton."

"Age?"

"13." Allegra answered the officers' questions as calmly and methodically as possible, all the while keeping one eye on her sister. She watched in concern as Sienna took a seat and started to rock back and forth.

When an officer asked if Reese was a likely runaway, Sienna snapped up and re-launched her tirade. "You're wasting time with these questions!" she shouted. "You should be out there looking for her!"

Stephen pulled her away from the officers, letting Allegra paint a picture of sensible, mature Reese. Mr Perkins gave the police officers a programme, which contained a picture of Reese. After another half hour of questions, the family was told to go home and wait. Sienna was outraged – how could she possibly sit and wait when her child was missing?

The officers issued standard reassurances – 'we are doing the best we can', 'try not to worry', 'we will let you know as soon as we have an update' – and left.

Sienna sat, too stunned to talk. Stephen and Allegra coaxed her into the car and then took her home where the three of them sat in silence. A wordless Sienna stood and tearily stumbled up the stairs.

Allegra watched with concern. "You think it'll be okay if I stay over tonight?" she asked Stephen.

Gratitude flashed in his eyes. "Allegra, please do. Thank you. We really need you here."

She knew how lost and helpless Sienna was feeling. She didn't have confidence in the officers they had spoken to, but what could they do? She thought briefly about contacting Michael, but what good would that do? No, it was better for them to wait for the police to do their job.

She made some tea to calm their nerves. Handing Stephen a cup, she went upstairs to check on Sienna. She found her in Reese's room, sitting on the bed, staring out the window. Allegra handed her the tea and squeezed her shoulder.

"Sienna, she's going to be okay. She's going to be found. It's only been a few hours. She can't be very far."

"Reese was never afraid of the dark, not even as a child. You're too young to remember but I used to hate the dark. I used to beg mum to leave the night-light on."

Images of soft black hair and beautiful fair skin sprang to Allegra's mind. She could almost smell jasmine in the air.

"When a woman loses her parents she becomes an

orphan, when she loses her spouse she's a widow, but when a mother loses her child, what's the word for that? There's no word for that." Sienna looked up. "I can't lose her." Her voice broke with emotion.

Allegra hugged her tightly. "Don't you speak like that. Not you of all people. Reese needs your faith right now. She's going to be found and she's going to be okay."

Sienna wiped her tears. She stared out into the dark night with fright and doubt in her eyes. Allegra walked to the window and shut the curtains. As she turned to walk out of the room, she felt a sudden sense of dread – something wasn't quite right. She turned back to the room and surveyed it. Everything seemed okay. Why the sudden feeling of consternation? She swept the room with her eyes again and then slowly walked to the window. She reopened the curtains and looked out into the night. Nothing. As she moved to close the curtains again, a stab of fear pierced her chest. A strangled cry escaped her lips as icy fear wrapped itself around her heart and squeezed tight. There, on the windowsill, in a thin vase was a single pink rose. It was a day away from full bloom and its petals grew from a striking magenta to a pale pink.

An image flashed in her mind: Joseph Drake walking out of a bathroom, in his hands a beautiful flower, a single pink rose. *A beautiful flower for a beautiful woman.*

Sienna was at Allegra's side in a flash. "What? What's

wrong? Do you see her?" She searched the night outside. Hysterically, she reached for the lock and yanked open the window. "What do you see? What?" she cried.

Allegra was frantic. Words and images flooded her mind. Reese's voice on the phone: *He knows everything there is to know about music – did you know that Vivaldi had asthma?* Drake waving a hand over the Sarson paintings: 'Beautiful, aren't they? Like visual Prete Rosso arias, laid out for all to see'. *He's smart and sensitive... not like the boys in my year.*

"How did this happen?" Allegra's voice was shrill and her hands began to shake. "Sienna, Johnny Savant – did you ever meet him? Are you sure she wasn't seeing someone else?"

She shook her head. "No. I already told you – Reese is too sensible to go off with a boy."

Allegra shook her head. "Has she been spending time online? On social networking sites or using chatrooms?"

Sienna frowned. "No more than usual. Why?"

Allegra looked around frantically. "My phone. Where's my phone?"

"Allegra, what's going on? You're scaring me."

"Sienna, the phone!" she screamed. She ran down the stairs and into the living room. Rifling through her bag, she pulled out her phone.

"Allegra, what's happening?" Sienna's command fell on deaf ears. Stephen stood and found his way to

Sienna's side. They watched as Allegra frantically thumbed the buttons on her phone.

"Pickuppickuppickuppickup," she chanted. "Michael!" Her voice rose uncontrollably. Stephen and Sienna looked at each other in confusion. "Michael, you need to come. You need to come. Or we need to come to you." Allegra babbled into the phone.

"Allegra, calm down. What's wrong?"

She felt faint. She couldn't get a grip on her thoughts or on the words she needed to explain. "Michael. Are you still in the office?"

"I was on my way out but yes, I am."

"And David?"

"I think he's still here, yes. Why? What's happening?"

"Michael, please, you have to stay. Get David to stay. I'm coming over right now."

Michael was worried. Allegra didn't sound lucid. "What's happening?"

"My niece. Reese. He has her."

"What? Who has her?" Michael tried to make sense of her frantic words.

"Drake! Drake has her!" With that, the line went dead. Allegra turned to Stephen and Sienna. "We need a cab. Sienna, call a cab!"

She stared at Allegra. "Who did you call? Who was that? Who is Drake?"

"I can't explain right now. We have to go."

Stephen stepped in front of Sienna. "Allegra. You

266

need to tell us what is going on *right now.*"

She looked at them in despair, but then turned back to her phone. "Please. Let me at least call a cab first."

"Allegra!" shouted Sienna. "If you know where my daughter is, you tell me right now!" Her voice shook with fear or maybe anger.

Allegra held up her hands and backed away. "Sienna, please." She turned away and called a cab to the house. How was she to begin explaining the situation?

"Allegra," Sienna could barely control the anger in her voice. "What is happening?"

"Sienna, I–" she paused. "Please sit."

"I don't want to sit."

"Okay, okay. Listen. I think I know the man who has Reese. He–" another pause. "When I said I found a graphics job within the government, that wasn't entirely true. I– I was recruited as a field agent for a highly secretive organisation that targets paedophiles." Allegra paused to glean their reactions but they both remained silent. "Field Agents are put in contact with suspected paedophiles to see if they actually are paedophiles. I was put on the case of a guy called Joseph Drake. We targeted him and arrested him but he's out on bail."

"All you need to know is that I think he's taken Reese. I think he found out who I was a long time ago and that he befriended her. I think she used Johnny Savant – if he even exists – as an excuse for meeting Drake. I think he's taken her."

Sienna looked at her incredulously. "You mean you're a cop?"

Allegra shook her head. "No. Not quite." Seeing the confused looks on their faces, she said, "I guess you could call me that, yes, but a special kind working for a very secret organisation."

"So you work with dangerous men?" asked Sienna.

"Yes. Sometimes."

"Undercover?"

"Yes."

"And these men know your identity?"

"No, not during the operations but... there was this one incident when we ran into Jonathan from ImageBox and he used my real name. Drake may have figured it out from that."

"You think that's what happened?"

"Yes."

"And you didn't think to warn us about this?" Sienna's voice was cold and accusing.

"Sienna, this wasn't meant to happen—"

"You didn't think to warn us about this?" she repeated.

Allegra looked at Stephen helplessly but found no sympathy. "I— I couldn't say anything, Sienna. You have to understand. I'll probably get into trouble for telling you this much."

Sienna nodded. She then calmly walked over to Allegra, raised her right hand and slapped her across the face as hard as she possibly could. Allegra cried out in pain and surprise. She stared at Sienna in shock.

"You're working with paedophiles! Disgusting, dangerous men on a daily basis and you didn't think to warn us about it? I have a 13-year-old daughter. She's 13! A child! You didn't consider that one of these men could find out the truth about you and come after us? You didn't think to tell me the truth? What the hell has happened to you?"

"I'm sorry," cried Allegra, stung not only by physical pain.

"Get out of my house," said Sienna coldly.

"Sienna. You have to come with me." Allegra's voice shook. "Michael, he's the special agent I work with. He has access to resources you wouldn't believe. He can help us – more than the police can. The cab should be here any minute. It's going to take us straight to HQ."

"Screw you!" screamed Sienna.

Stephen stepped in and wrapped his arms around his wife. "We should listen to her."

"You want to listen to her? She's the one who got us here. My daughter could be killed because of her!"

Stephen shook his head calmly. "Her people will help us, Sienna, okay? They know what they're doing. They're experts."

The horn of the waiting cab punctured the air. Allegra, cheeks red with pain and guilt, gathered her belongings and staggered out of the house. Stephen and Sienna followed in silence.

As soon as they were in the car, Sienna started firing

questions, oblivious to the driver's presence. "Who is this Drake? What will he do to Reese? How do you know it's him? Where will we find them?" She buried her face in Stephen's chest, unable or unwilling to look at her sister as she whispered the answers.

When they reached Vokoban, Allegra stepped out of the car in relief. She needed Michael. She needed his calming presence. As they stepped into the building, she saw that he was waiting for them at the security bank. Sienna and Stephen watched as he pulled Allegra aside and exchanged heated words with her. After a while, his expression changed from anger to concern. He turned and walked to them, offering his hand.

"I am Agent Michael Stallone. Thank you for coming to us. Please come upstairs and I will explain everything."

Sienna was calmed by the authority in his voice. Allegra nodded at him to indicate her gratitude. He accepted it with a reassuring smile and led them to his office in which a group of agents had gathered.

One of the officers, introduced only as Agent Smith, asked a series of questions about Reese's last-known whereabouts and her relationship with Johnny Savant. He asked if she had exhibited any strange behaviour over the past few weeks and took details of the outfit she was wearing when she disappeared. After he was done, he and the other agents stood up. "I assure you, we will do everything we can to get your daughter back. Please try not to worry." He turned to Michael.

"When you're done," he gestured towards the door.

Michael nodded in response.

"We will also need to tap their phones in case he calls," said the agent.

Michael nodded again and then turned to Sienna and Stephen. "Mr and Mrs Keaton, I know this is extremely difficult for you but we *will* get Reese back. She will be absolutely fine."

Sienna nodded, the wildness in her eyes dissipating with every nod.

Is this the effect he has on me? Sprinkling magic stars, wondered Allegra.

Michael explained the inner workings of Vokoban, glossing over details as he did so. He explained every contact he or Allegra had made with Drake and took them all the way up to the moment he had been told about the pink rose. By the time he finished, Sienna's eyes were awash with tears. She stood and walked to her sister. Allegra stiffened, cheeks red with shame.

Sienna swallowed hard. "I'm sorry," she said quietly.

Allegra's lips trembled, her face threatening to crumple. "You don't care about the things I did?"

Sienna raised her chin. "I'm sorry I hit you."

Allegra moved forward to embrace her sister but Sienna turned towards Michael.

"Now find my daughter."

"I will," he promised, taking in Allegra's stricken face. With this last assurance, he slipped out of his office and joined the team in the hub. Among the assembled faces were David, Marianne, four special agents and two forensic psychologists.

"We've got Drake and the girl's computers," said Agent Smith. "We're inspecting them for communication between the two. All surveillance around Cadogan Hall is being pulled. We have teams at Drake's gallery and his home – no sign of him or the girl. His neighbours are being canvassed as we speak. His car is still in the driveway so we're thinking hired transport. We doubt he's stupid enough but we're pulling his Oystercard records just in case. We've pulled his phone records – landline and mobile – but there is no immediately obvious suspicious activity. We're putting a block on his credit cards and accounts. The media guys are on their way to make sure this thing stays under control." As he finished, Allegra walked into the room and took a seat.

Michael turned to the panel of psychologists. "Ideas?"

Marianne stood and walked to the front of the room. "Joseph Drake is a pathological paedophile. He identifies a potential female victim, builds a bond with her, gains her trust, and then grooms her for sexual contact. He is a 'nurturing' perpetrator rather than a sadistic one; he feels a genuine connection to his victims and cultivates what he thinks is a real relationship. He doesn't think he's hurting the victim, but that he is engaging in a special type of love that society fails to understand. He will treat his victim with

272

affection unless she acts against his will. If that happens, he will feel deeply betrayed and will punish her for violating his trust."

Allegra raised her hand. When Marianne paused, she asked, "What will he do to her?"

"It is difficult to say. Under normal circumstances, he treats his victims with care and attention – the way he would treat a lover – but on this occasion, he may deviate from his pattern. Usually logical and contained, he has acted out because he feels out of control. Prone to megalomania, he feels like a failure because he was outsmarted by Vokoban. This has caused him to break his usually rational train of thought and abduct Reese as a way of exacting revenge."

"Is he going to hurt her?" Allegra's voice shook with fear.

Marianne swallowed. "At this point, we can't say."

Allegra looked to Michael. "We have to find her." She stood and stepped towards him. "We have to find her *now.*"

Michael caught her as she teetered on weak legs. "I'm getting you out of here," he whispered in her ear. He held her arm and led her out of the room but instead of returning her to his office he led her down the corridor to a room she had never seen before. It was small and square, and had a number of blue chairs lined against three of the fours walls. In one corner was a water cooler with a tube of white plastic cups along one side of it. It looked like a waiting room of sorts.

Michael looked at her in earnest. "Are you okay?"

She was exhausted but nodded yes. "I'm okay but we have to find her, Michael. We have to find her."

"We will," he soothed. He tucked a stray hair behind her ear. "We will. I have some of the best agents working on this." He paused. "It's been a tough month for you, hasn't it?"

She nodded wearily.

"I want you to know that I'm always here for you. You can come to me any time you need to, okay?"

"Okay," Allegra said softly.

"You are a strong woman, Allegra. An amazing woman." He lifted her chin so that their eyes met. "I've never met anyone like you." He placed a warm hand on the back of her neck and drew her forward. Familiar feelings beat a path across her chest. He leaned closer and then slowly, gently, placed his warm lips on hers. She closed her eyes and let herself melt into him.

He wrapped his arms around her, a protective circle shielding her from the ugliness outside. His lips on hers grew hungry as his grip grew tighter. Allegra drew back to breathe but Michael's hand was on the back of her head, pushing her into him. His hands dropped to her hips and found their way up the side of her body, cupping the outer parts of her breasts.

"Michael," she said breathlessly. He silenced her with a rough, urgent kiss. "Michael," she cried as he pushed her against the wall. "Wait." His rough hands pulled at her dress. "Wait," she repeated, pushing him away.

He jerked her hands away and pressed his body hard against hers. Grabbing the hem of her dress, he pulled it up roughly.

"Michael, wait," Allegra urged. "I'm not–"

He held a hand to her mouth. "Don't talk."

She shook her head.

"Good." He kissed her neck, hand still pressed against her mouth.

She shook her head furiously and struggled in his grip. It was only when she clawed a gash into his hand that he jerked backwards and freed her.

She doubled up, hands on knees, and gasped in some air. Looking up with wild, angry eyes, she saw him step towards her – menacing, angry, unrepentant. In that moment, he seemed like a different person.

"Michael, stop." Allegra held out her hands, palms towards Michael – a helpless plea. "Please stop."

He blinked. "I'm sorry," he said, suddenly calm. He stretched out his arms, a reflection of Allegra's own stance. "I thought you wanted to, like before. I'm sorry."

She shook her head. "How– how could you think I would want to? Atatimelikethis?" The words twisted in her mouth, unbroken and incoherent.

"Allegra, I'm sorry."

She looked at him with disgust. Manoeuvring carefully around him, she turned and ran out of the room. He urged her to stop but she was already gone.

Bursting into the bathroom, she knelt next to the toilet bowl. The familiar taste of bile crept up her throat, making her retch. As she vomited into the bowl, her skin grew cold and shivery. She thought back to the nightmare she had had about Reese tied to a slab of rock. Soft, shaking words floated through her mind: *Did you know they have these devices to force your mouth open?* they asked. *He pulled my lips apart with these metal forceps and...* Allegra jerked forward as another wave of vomit rushed up her throat.

CHAPTER NINE

As darkness settled, Sienna faded with the light. She sat by Michael's desk, wild eyes turning weary. The slivers of grey in her hair suddenly seemed multiplied and the lines in her face deepened. Allegra watched as she pushed away the cup of stone-cold coffee and sank further into her chair. In the moonlight, she suddenly looked very much like their mother.

Allegra stood and paced across the room. It was nearing midnight – three hours since they had rushed into Vokoban HQ and almost five hours since Reese went missing. She glanced at the clock. *Five minutes to go.* She had been told to check in with the agents every half an hour – no more, no less. Impatiently, she left the room and walked to the hub, eyes instinctively finding Michael. She saw the plea in his eyes, begging for a chance to apologise. Tired of avoiding him, she nodded almost imperceptibly.

He stood and led her out of the room. "We have

him on CCTV at Westminster station, changing from the Jubilee to District line at 18.50."

She felt the blood rush to her head. "And?"

"And then he disappears. There's no activity on his Oystercard – he must have been using a paper ticket. We have pulled footage in and around Sloane Square but there's nothing so far."

Allegra sagged. "There must be something."

"We will find him. I promise." Michael reached out to touch her face but she flinched so hard, he retreated immediately. He took a deep breath. "Allegra, about before, I am so sorry. I should have been more intuitive. After everything you've been through and everything that is happening, I should have known. I should have been there for you." Genuine anguish clouded his green eyes.

Allegra felt a sudden rush of affection for him. Reaching out, she ran a finger over the small gash in his hand. "I'm sorry too," she said softly.

He touched her cheek lightly. "You know I care about you, don't you?"

She nodded and turned her head so that her lips lightly brushed his fingertips. He leaned closer and moved his hands to her waist, drawing her into him. As she stepped into his embrace, her phone began to ring, shattering the silence.

She grabbed it instinctively and answered "hello".

"Hello Angel," said a deep, warm drawl.

Allegra froze and felt her stomach clench. She turned to Michael wildly, gestured to the phone, and mouthed 'Drake'. Michael held out his hands, palms down, and pressed the air, gesturing for her to stay calm. He ran ahead to the hub and quietened the agents. Allegra walked in and watched them pull on headphones, all listening in on the conversation.

"Joseph?" she asked.

"And Bingo was his name-o!" Drake's loud laugh rattled through her bones. "How're you doing, Angel Face?"

She looked around the room. Michael held a thumb up to her. "I'm good, Joseph. I'm well."

"And how is your dear family?" He laughed again.

She breathed in deeply to control her anger. "They're fine."

"They *are* fine. Every single last one of them. Sienna is fine – beautiful and delicious, like a mature wine." Allegra's heart filled with icy fear. "Reese is most definitely fine." Another cackling laugh. "But you, Angel Face, are the finest of them all. The sweetest of them all. I have to say I'm not partial to a curvy form so I'm trying to work out how to carve her up to look more like you."

A strangled cry escaped her lips. "Joseph, please don't hurt her."

"I won't, Angel. I won't." He sounded surprisingly genuine. "I won't hurt one sweet little hair on her head. Or one sweet little hair on her pussy. Do you know that she has pussy hair? I was disgusted. I was hoping for a sweet, clean one like yours."

Allegra choked. With desperation, she looked to the

agent tracing the call. Fingers still flying over his keyboard, he looked up and shook his head.

"Joseph, please don't hurt her," she repeated, voice thick with fear.

"I told you I won't. But then again, honesty isn't exactly the foundation of our relationship, is it, Allegra?" *Allegeraah.* He drew out her name, injecting it with hate and poison.

"Joseph, what do you hope to gain from this? What do you want?"

"Isn't that obvious?" He laughed and waited for an answer.

She shook her head. "No, Joseph, it isn't."

"Tell me, Agent Ashe, how many of those cunt-fuckers are listening in?"

Allegra hesitated. "Not too many."

"Not too many." The smile was evident in his voice. "I'm not going to hurt her, Allegra. I'm just playing with you. Same way you played with me." With that, he hung up.

The dead ringtone made Allegra's head pound. She dropped the phone on the table and looked to the agents. "What now?"

The room sprang into activity as the agents started to duplicate and analyse the recording.

She turned to Michael. "Did you hear what he said? He's hurt her. God, he's probably killed her."

Michael shook his head. "Drake won't kill her. Allegra, he had sex with you but made no indication of violent behaviour. He won't hurt Reese."

"So it's okay to fuck her as long as he doesn't kill her?" she spat angrily.

Michael stood in silence, not knowing what to say to make it right.

"I have to tell Sienna what's going on."

"Allegra, be gentle," he urged.

"Can I be anything but?" she said bitterly as she walked away.

Outside, she straightened her dress and smoothed her hair before walking to Michael's office.

Sienna stood. Her hair was a knotted mess, her makeup smudged by a layer of shine. "What's happening?"

Allegra bit her lip. "Drake called."

Sienna's eyes grew wide. "What did he say? Does he have her?" A nod. She started to cry, crumbling into Stephen's waiting arms. "What did he say? Has he hurt her? Why didn't you call me? I want to talk to him," Sienna fired questions through her tears.

"He hasn't hurt her. He called me just to taunt us, to flaunt his victory in our faces."

"What did he say? What *exactly* did he say?"

"He just said that Reese was okay and that he has her."

Sienna started to sob. "Oh God, what has he done to her? What will he do? What does he want?"

Allegra shook her head. "Sienna, I asked him what he wants but he didn't say. He said that he's 'playing' with us. Michael said that Drake isn't a violent man, that he won't hurt her."

"Not violent? Allegra, he had sex with you and he thought you were 13! He likes children. What makes you think that he won't hurt her?" Sienna's voice became shrill and panicked. Stephen held her tight, face red with helplessness.

Allegra didn't know how to comfort them. Sienna's doubts were the same as hers but she couldn't admit that. She needed them to believe that Reese was okay. She couldn't have Sienna crack under all of this.

She took her sister's hand. "Sienna, Michael didn't tell me this, nor did any other agent or law enforcement officer or criminal analyst. This is coming from me: the reason Drake had sex with me is because he thought he loved me. He genuinely believed that there was something between us. Michael has put other agents on his tail before; agents that Drake could easily have taken advantage of but he didn't. He has very particular taste. He doesn't molest every girl that crosses his path. This makes me believe that he won't touch Reese. At the beginning of the operation, Michael set out a profile of the kind of girl Drake goes for. I fit that profile: small, boyish frame, dark hair, light eyes. Reese doesn't. He won't touch her. He's doing this for revenge."

"But what if he hurts her to get that revenge?"

"We will find him before he has a chance."

Sienna nodded, reassured to some extent. "They *will* find her, won't they?"

Allegra kissed her sister's cheek. "Yes, they will." She

paused. "I'm going to go back. Are you okay here? There's a cafeteria I can take you to?"

Sienna shook her head. "I can't eat."

Allegra left with one last reassuring nod. Back in the hub, she sat down next to Michael. "Anything?"

"Nothing. This bastard is cleverer than we thought. He used iSpeak and Freenet to call us. This changes his IP address every few seconds so we can never locate where he actually is. One minute he's in Oklahoma, the next he's in Tokyo. It's impossible."

Allegra straightened. "Listen, I know a guy who's a complete computer whiz. His name is Christian. Seriously, this guy can do anything. Do you want me to give him a call?"

Michael shook his head. "Drury's team has the best guys in the field. They have access to information that is classified to even you and me. They're working on it."

"And we're still getting nowhere." She propped an elbow on the table and rubbed her forehead.

"Allegra," Marianne pointed to a passage in Agent Smith's notes. "It says here that Reese has asthma."

She nodded. "Yes, since she was seven."

"Did she bring her inhaler to the concert? Do you know if she has it with her?"

Allegra's face grew tight with concern. "Why? Do you think she may be sick?"

Marianne shook her head. "I'm sure she's okay. I just think this could be important."

"I'll check with Sienna." Allegra stood and ran out of the room

Michael turned to Marianne. "What are you thinking?"

She frowned. "Stress can cause an asthma attack. If Reese doesn't have her inhaler, she may suffer from an attack."

"So basically we need to find her as soon as possible?"

"Yes, but also something else. As I said before, Drake is a nurturing character. His earlier phone call may have been particularly nasty but it was designed to make Allegra worry. I think, from his tone, that he's actually taking care of Reese – he's being good to her."

She continued: "It says in her records that Reese uses an aerosol inhaler with salbutamol. If she has an attack, I think Drake would try to help her."

Michael sat up in his chair. "He would try to get his hands on some?"

Marianne nodded. "Now, inhalers are not available over the counter – not as standard – but if he went to a walk-in centre, then it's likely he would have been given one."

Allegra walked back in. In her hands, she held a small blue and grey inhaler. "She doesn't have it with her. Sienna is freaking out. Guys, please tell me something."

"I'll talk to her." Michael glanced at his watch and turned to Agent Smith. "It's 00.30. Reese was taken at approximately 19.30, which gives Drake a five-hour lead to anywhere. Get Drury to run a cross-check on all NHS walk-in centres in a 200-mile, no make that 250-mile, radius stretching out from Cadogan Hall and check if anyone came in for an inhaler. Get on the phone to these guys – get descriptions. I want her to be found by morning." He turned and walked out of the room.

Allegra, on his tail, held his arm. "Michael, it's all well and good to tell Sienna about this lead but what if Reese doesn't have an attack? What if we're wasting our time?"

Michael studied her face. "You say Reese is a smart kid?"

"One of the smartest."

"Then maybe she'll fake an attack."

They headed upstairs to give Sienna her glimmer of hope.

It was 1 a.m. when Drake called again.

Michael grabbed Allegra's arm. "Get positive confirmation that he has Reese. Ask to speak to her."

She nodded and answered the phone.

"Hi Allegra," Drake said softly. He seemed tired this time, more subdued.

"Hi Joseph."

"I'm calling for an apology, Allegra. I want you to apologise for lying to me. I want to hear you say sorry for deceiving me."

"I'm sorry, Joseph," Allegra said emphatically. "I know you only shared what you did with me because you cared about me."

Drake snorted. "I didn't care for you. I cared for Amy. How bitter do you think it was for me to realise she doesn't even exist?"

Allegra grimaced. "I'm so sorry, Joseph. The truth is that I was afraid. You fell in love with Amy so I couldn't tell you the truth. I couldn't tell you that I was Allegra because you would stop loving me."

Michael nodded, indicating that she was doing well.

Drake laughed. "You're one dirty whore, Allegra. You pull some dirty, dirty tricks."

She swallowed her anguish. "See, Joseph? You hate me now. If I had told you that I was Allegra, you would have hated me just the same. I wanted you to care for me."

"Allegra, ssh," he said soothingly. "You may think I'm mad – hell, I probably am – but I'm not stupid."

She wondered if he was overusing her name on purpose. "Well, if you're a smart man, you should recognise that Reese had nothing to do with this. She's innocent. It was *my* doing."

"Yes, it was Allegra. Yours and that pretty boy Michael Stallone."

Allegra baulked and looked to Michael. He too seemed shocked at how much Drake had managed to uncover.

"Tell me, Allegra. Were you thinking of pretty boy Michael Stallone when I was fucking you?"

She flinched. Eyes downcast, she said nothing.

"I can't help but wonder if that's why you were so wet when I was fucking you. He does look like me, doesn't he, Allegra? Is that why your sweet, bare pussy was so wet when I fucked you?"

Allegra's face grew red with shame. She thought back to that day; of Drake's body on top of hers, his rough hands tearing at her clothes – hungry, desperate, insatiable. She swallowed. "It was for you." Michael held up his thumb but she refused to meet his eyes.

After a short pause, Drake began to laugh. "You're boring me, Allegra."

"Joseph," she said quickly. "Prove to us that you have Reese."

He laughed. "I think we all know that I have Reese."

"No. We *think* you have Reese. We don't know. Prove to us that she's alive and okay."

"Are you serious? What is this – some Hollywood B-movie? Sorry, Angel, but there will be no more cheeky tricks."

"Drake," Allegra tried to control her shaky voice. "You've got what you wanted. You got your revenge. I hate myself for what I did to you now please, please just let her go. Please Joseph. What else can you do with her? Just let her go."

"Bored now," he said in a singsong voice.

"Joseph, please tell me what you want."

"I already told you. I want to play." With that, he rang off.

Allegra screamed in frustration. "He's fucking with us!" She slammed the table with an open palm. "What has he done to her?"

Michael walked closer and held her shoulders. "Hey, it's going to be okay. We're still pulling the medical records – we're going to find him. Go and sit with Sienna for a while. Reassure her." He watched as an angry but wordless Allegra did as she was told.

Fifteen minutes later, he walked into his office. "We have two leads. We're gathering teams as we speak."

Sienna immediately started to cry. She turned to Stephen and buried her face in his chest. "Please, you have to find her," she said in muffled tones.

"What leads?" asked Allegra.

"We have identified two walk-in centres. One is in Newham, East London, and the other's near Edgware. Both have been made into 24-hour centres. Both prescribed inhalers at around 20.15. A staff member at Newham said they gave theirs to a man in his mid-thirties – that's the one I'm heading to."

Allegra stood. "I'm coming too."

"No," said Michael immediately. "I don't want you anywhere near him."

She glared at him coldly. "It's a little too late for that," she retorted bitterly. She couldn't help herself. One minute she wanted to be close to him, the next she wanted to lash out.

"I want to come too," Sienna said unevenly.

Michael shook his head. "I'm sorry but you can't.

You have to stay here."

Allegra thought of Reese – how would she react when a battery of men barged into the place? She turned to Sienna. "Listen, you stay here with Stephen. Let me deal with this, okay? I'm going to find her and I'm going to bring her back safely."

"But–" Sienna was silenced by Stephen's hand on her shoulder. He convinced her to stay – all news would be coming to HQ first which meant they had to stay there if they were to know what was happening.

Allegra gathered her things, exchanged hugs with Sienna and Stephen, and followed Michael out of the room.

He turned to her with weary eyes. "Allegra, I need you to stay here in case he calls again. We don't want him to have any indication that we're on the move."

She shook her head. "Save your bullshit, Michael. I'm coming." She pulled on her coat and stormed ahead.

He looked at the still, sleeping form crouched in the corner. The room smelled of ink and oil; of old books and yellowing paper. The ceiling paint was peeling and curling – it hadn't been touched in years. The thought brought a cold smile to Drake's lips. He looked to the window. *Always darkest before the dawn.* Were the drapes brown or had they just turned that colour from years of dirt? The carpet was red, patterned with dark brown paisley. A few patches had turned pink with age and wear. He walked over to one and measured his booted foot against it.

A small cry from the corner startled him. He turned to look at her. He could hardly bear it. All fat and white skin – it disgusted him. She moaned something unintelligible.

He walked to the corner, boots level with her face. "Are you ready?" he asked, voice full of scorn.

She moaned again. "Ngnuh guh."

He laughed at her feeble form. He stuck his boot underneath the thin mattress and kicked it up, making her roll back towards the wall. "Get up," he demanded. "Too fat to walk?" He crouched next to her. Reaching forward, he grabbed one of her breasts. "Look at this!" he said, disgusted. "You're nothing but flesh and fat. Mounds and mounds of it. As if I would touch a thing like *you*. It almost made me sick to be near you; to have you sidle up to me, feverish with gratitude, because I bothered to *look* at you." He smirked. Pausing, he took a few deep breaths and then crouched down next to her. "I'm ready." He pulled her up and pushed her towards the desk.

On shaky knees, Reese stumbled forward. Blurred words coated the floor of her mouth. "Noh-kay. Gonabee oh-kay." Drake pushed her from behind, making her wobble on unstable feet. "Skay," she said. "Skay. Have no fear, little one. Have no fear."

Drake laughed, his voice reverberating through the empty space. "No fear? But, my darling, this is where fear was born." His laughter echoed and multiplied as it bounced off the empty walls and high ceiling.

Reese shook her head manically as she tripped over the uneven surface of the floor. She jumped over the next dip. With a tiny laugh, she said, "Jump Jerry."

Drake stared at her as she teetered forwards. Had he given her too much? It should have worn off by now. He walked forward and grabbed her arm.

She turned and looked at him with vacant eyes. "Jump Jerry," she said with a dreamy smile. It made him want to dig his nails into her face and rip open her skin.

"The desolation of the wicked has cometh and it shall teach you to fear." He grabbed her hair, turned her around and pushed her down towards the desk.

Allegra switched stations yet again. Impatient, she drummed her fingers on the dashboard before switching to another station. She glanced at Michael. His eyes were completely focused on the road. Two tiny creases in his forehead were the only signs that he had something on his mind, something to worry about. Allegra opened her mouth to speak but then closed it again. What could she say? What needed to be said at a time like this?

As she sat back in the passenger seat, the final words of her favourite book echoed in her mind: *God's in his Heaven. All's right with the world.* She stared at the road, eerily quiet in the early hours of the morning.

The clock read 1.50 a.m. Reese had been missing for almost seven hours. *Where's God now?* Allegra reached out to change the station again, but Michael turned off the radio.

"Enough," he said quietly. After a few minutes, he slowed the car. "We're here." He parked expertly and got out. Walking round, he opened the door for her.

Allegra couldn't help but notice the small actions that proved him to be a gentleman. How could he be everything and nothing all at the same time?

He led her inside the walk-in centre and strode up to reception. Even at this hour, his piercing eyes and model looks drew every eye in the room. The young receptionist, melting in his gaze, greeted him with a seductive smile. She giggled when he explained why they were there.

"Oh, yes. Someone called earlier. They said they would be sending a few people down to talk to Doctor Lam." She punctuated the sentence with a giggle and a hair flick. Michael smiled at her warmly, dimples deep in his cheeks.

Allegra rolled her eyes. *She may as well stick her tongue out and pant like a dog.* "Well, can we see Dr Lam, please?" she asked impatiently.

The receptionist turned from Michael and looked at Allegra coldly. "I will let her know."

As the receptionist picked up the phone, Michael turned to Allegra. "Let me handle this, okay?"

She raised a brow. "Of course."

The receptionist directed them down a corridor leading to a large room with seven desks divided across it. Only two of the desks were occupied. A pretty young woman stood and walked to them. Offering her hand, she said, "I'm Doctor Lam. May I see some ID?" When satisfied, she led them to a table. "Please sit. I'm told that you're interested in one of the patients we treated this evening?"

Michael nodded. "Yes. He was given an inhaler at 20.17. We believe you're the one who spoke with him?"

The doctor nodded. "Yes. What would you like to know?"

"Can you describe him to me?"

She nodded. "Yes. Tall, about 5'11", slim but athletic, dark hair, green eyes, handsome." She smiled. "Actually, he looked a bit like you."

Michael smiled back. "Just less handsome, right?"

The doctor laughed but said nothing. Allegra bit her lip. He could really turn it on when he had to.

He pulled out a photograph. It was a still from Allegra's surveillance footage. It showed Drake in the gallery, face turned directly to camera. "Is this him?"

Doctor Lam looked it over and nodded. "Yes. Who is he?"

Michael waved away the question. "My team is pulling CCTV footage from the reception area and from outside the building. Do you not have CCTV in here?"

She shook her head. "No. We film customers coming in and out but not patients when they're talking to doctors."

Michael nodded. "Did he seem distressed to you? Suspicious or angry?"

"Well, yes. He was distressed – he needed his inhaler – but I wouldn't say he was acting suspiciously. He seemed pleasant."

Michael took a description of Drake's clothes, immediately typing it into his BlackBerry and sending the information to HQ. "Were there any security guards stationed outside that may have seen what he was driving?"

The doctor shook her head. "No one, especially at this hour. We only have a skeleton staff. Your best bet is CCTV."

Michael's phone rang just as they wrapped up the interview. "Michael Stallone," he answered in his ultra-efficient tone.

"It's Drury. We have him getting in a black Ford Focus at the north end of Belgrave Road."

Michael reigned in his relief. "Any sign of Reese?"

Allegra tiptoed so that her ear was level with Michael's phone.

"Not on the CCTV but, Michael, we have a partial on the number plate."

Allegra's hand flew to her mouth as she tried to contain her delight. Michael calmed her with a hand on the shoulder.

"Is the other team nearby?" asked Drury.

"Yes."

"Okay, get this. We picked him up on CCTV a few miles away on the A406 and then again driving past Cranbrook Road. We think we know where he's headed."

Michael shook his head. "Are you sure it's him? You've seen his file. Would he slip up this easily?"

Drury's voice was full of conviction. "Michael, it's him. The psychs agree. At this stage, he doesn't care. What are his options? Imprisonment or imprisonment. He wants revenge."

The weight of his words made Allegra fall back onto the soles of her feet. What would he do to Reese?

Drury continued: "He's going to go where he feels safe. He likes the outdoors and being close to water. Valentines Park is about six miles from you. It's a wide open space, quiet at this time – we believe he's taken her there. We've pinpointed two possibilities: the water or the mansions. The mansions are on Emerson Road, about half a mile from the water on the northwest side of the park. They're being restored so aren't open to the public. I think that's your best bet."

"Great job, Drury."

"Oh, we try." A pause. "Michael, leave Agent Ashe and go in with the other team, okay?"

He nodded. "Of course." He rang off and turned to Allegra. "Let's go."

Fear and anxiety made her youthful features look

even younger. He flashed onto hazel eyes, brunette hair and a tiny body beneath his. Her grating northern accent: *This Allegra woman must have worked you over real good, huh?* He thought of his anger and frustration grinding down into her. *That's it, daddy, give it to her hard. Give it to your little girl. I want it so bad.* He remembered her body, paler than the olive skin he craved, yet it hadn't stopped him from climaxing all over her with a single word exploding from his lips: *Allegra.*

He led her down the stairs, deeper into darkness. The wood creaked beneath his foot, making him freeze instinctively. He listened for sounds but there was nothing, no one – just the two of them. It was cold, so cold it made his hairs prickle his skin. He licked his lips to wet them and, after a moment's hesitation, stepped onto the floor of the basement. The enormity of the space seemed to swallow them; two solitary figures in a world of darkness. His heart beat hard as he led her further in. This is where it would all happen.

Sienna paced the room, glancing at her watch for the third time that minute.

"Do you think they're there yet? They should be there."

Stephen could only nod. Crippled with masked fear, he was exhausted from constantly reassuring his wife. What if they really didn't find Reese? How would they survive?

Sienna walked to the window and looked out as if the view was visible through the closed blinds. "Do you remember that time we lost her in Greenwich Park?" She paused. "It's stayed with me all these years; that feeling of utter panic and the disbelief that it was happening to us. But we found her, playing in the sandpit, and I remember being so relieved and thinking that I would never let her out of my sight again. I remember thinking that I would give anything, everything, to keep her safe. She is such a good kid, Stephen – how could this happen?" She turned to her husband, searching for answers.

"They will find her," he said, voice shaking with uncertainty.

Michael glared at Allegra. "Take those off," he said, pointing to her shoes. The high heels she had worn to the concert made loud clicking sounds on the floor. As she teetered on one foot, Michael reached out to steady her. "You should have stayed in the car," he said with clear irritation. "I *told* you to stay in the car."

Defiance flashed in her eyes but she said nothing. The chill of the concrete seeped through her tights, making her shiver. She slipped the shoes inside her bag and on tiptoe followed Michael into the darkness. They turned a corner, losing sight of the only window with its sliver of moonlight. Michael stopped and turned, making her crash into him in the darkness. He steadied her and then, leaning in close, whispered in her ear. "Use your night vision." As she reached towards her bag, he added, "*Quietly.*"

She pulled out the heavy goggles she had trained with in WSN. As they blinked to life, her world turned an eerie shade of green. She watched Michael slip on his goggles and gesture for her to follow him. Somehow, they seemed to obscure her hearing. The visual luminosity dulled all sounds, giving the place a dreamlike quality.

She watched Michael inch ahead, shoulder against a wall. She was filled with sudden gratitude towards him. All this time, she had raged about the fact that Special Agents sat in their comfortable offices while Field Agents did all the work, but here he was, fearless on the front line.

He stopped suddenly and held a hand out towards her. *Stop.* What had he heard? Her eyes widened as she watched him draw a Glock 17 from his holster. She had been trained with seven different guns in WSN but still wasn't comfortable around them. Michael aimed the gun ahead and took a step forward. Allegra followed him. *What if he shoots Reese?*

As she readied to voice her concern, a loud screeching sound echoed through the air, making her spring back in alarm. Michael crouched down and ran forward. Frozen by fear, Allegra failed to follow him. It had sounded like a chair scraping across the floor or maybe a bird screeching in pain or maybe...

With Michael a few metres ahead of her now,

Allegra ran forward to catch up. She didn't want to be in this place alone. She searched the space in front of Michael but there was nothing but green darkness. Again, the sound echoed out, louder and longer this time. She looked to Michael for reassurance but his gaze was fixed ahead. Quietly, he ran forward, moving away from the wall, towards the source of the sound. Allegra's heart slammed in her chest. *It's Drake – just Drake. A man you have seen and been with. It's okay,* she tried to calm herself. As she veered right, away from the wall, she felt suddenly exposed. She looked behind her and stumbled forward. Michael was forging ahead. She wanted to shout *don't leave me,* but knew she couldn't. Finding her feet, she ran faster to keep up with him.

They ran past wooden barrels that smelled of dry fish and vomit. It made her feel queasy. When the screeching sound rang out for a third time, Michael stopped and gestured for her to be still. They came to a vast area; a box dug into the floor of the basement. It was so wide, their goggled view failed to reach the other side. Michael silently jumped into the sunken area, gesturing to Allegra to do the same. She sat on the lip of the edge, turned around and lowered herself into the pit, landing with a soft thud.

Another screech, so close, rang out. Michael, pistol pointed straight ahead, advanced into the darkness. Allegra stepped forward. A loud grinding sound shattered the silence. The room flooded with sudden light, so bright it made her flinch. She ripped off her goggles and looked around in panic. Michael, a few feet away, swung his pistol in a full circle as he examined the pit. It was painted a dark blue colour and stretched into a 100-feet wide emptiness. He gestured for her to get against a wall. She followed his cue and crept closer to him, walking sideways with her back against the wall. Panting, she searched his face for answers. *What is happening?*

A quiet sensation vibrated against her chest. As it deepened, she realised it was her phone, secured into the strap of the bag. She took it out and showed Michael the display. *Private number.*

"Drake?" she mouthed.

He nodded. "Answer it on speaker."

With shaking hands she pressed 'Accept'. "Hello?"

A rustling sound on the phone was followed by a sudden screeching, the same as they had heard before. A slow laugh crept from the phone, wrapping itself like a cobweb around Allegra's fingers. Drake's voice: "Hi Angel. How are you?"

Her head buzzed with fear. With a deep breath, she said, "I'm okay."

Drake laughed again. "You're okay? You're not feeling... blue?"

She froze. The walls of the pit seemed to contort around her. "Where are you?"

"Did you really think it would be that easy? You're so fucking patronising. Did you stop to think for a minute that you're the ones who deserve to be patronised?" He laughed. "The oh-so-obvious clues – you ate it up like a piece of rotten meat thrown to a pack of dogs."

Allegra looked to Michael. His eyes clouded with anger and frustration as Drake's laughter rang out derisively. She sagged, exhausted by the swirl of thoughts and worries crowding her head. "Please, Joseph. Don't hurt her."

He snorted. "Do you think I *want* to touch her disgusting hairy pussy?"

Sudden anger surged in Allegra's veins. "Tell me, Joseph, do you ever feel guilty about the things you've done? Did you feel guilty about Jemima Bradbury?"

Drake was silent for a moment. He cleared his throat and said, "She loved it just the same as you." He laughed viciously. "That's the thing. These young girls love it. They do. Music videos and fashion magazines have been sexualising them for years. These girls are precocious beyond all that we've known. If anything, they should have changed the law to *lower* the legal age limit. Girls aged 13 are getting fucked by their little boyfriends all over the country. You don't think Reese has been fucking her little schoolboy friend? You don't think she was desperate to fuck me, even though I'm decades older than her?"

Allegra choked on his words. "She– she wouldn't." It was all she could manage.

Drake laughed. "Same way I wouldn't see through

your little act? Same way I would think nothing of your red-faced panic at the exhibition? Same way I wouldn't find out who you really are, *Allegra?*

"How blind are thee? If young Reese was innocent with no sexual feelings whatsoever, would she have been taken in by a smile and a wink? Would she have lied to her parents and pretended she was out with the schoolboy she used to fancy? Don't you think she would have walked away from me? Young girls are sexual beings, Allegra, armed with powers of seduction and riddled with lust."

She shook her head. "Just because they can act sexually mature, it doesn't mean that they are. Any young girl can imitate what she sees on TV or in a movie. It just means she has learnt to move her body in a certain way or speak in a certain way – it doesn't mean her mind is ready for that kind of experience."

"That's where you're wrong, Allegra. Do you really think there's much of a difference between a 13- and a 16-year-old? Does sexual maturity come 'Bam!' Just like that?"

Allegra shook her head, trying to untangle his twisted words. "Of course there's a difference. A girl of 13 hasn't even reached puberty yet. A girl of 16 has."

"Tell me this, Allegra. Did I groom you? When I met you, did I suggest that you should come back? Did I invite you into my bedroom? Did I touch you? I didn't. Same way I wouldn't with any girl. It's because you kept coming back that I did what I did; because I could see sexuality in your eyes. That sexuality exists in the eyes of all these young whores. You just have to look."

"No. You see what you want to see through your sick, twisted view of the world," spat Allegra. Michael placed his hands on her shoulders, urging her to stay calm.

"Think about what you are saying, Allegra. Really think about it. I am not sick or twisted. Those who enjoy five- or six-year-olds, *they're* disgusting but Amy and Reese, they're young women – not fully developed but developed."

Michael caught Allegra's attention. "Reese," he mouthed. "Speak to Reese."

She nodded. "What do you want, Joseph?"

"I want to play."

She swallowed. "Joseph, I will do whatever you want, but I want to talk to Reese. I want to make sure she's okay."

He laughed. "I told you – that's not possible."

"Then how do I know?" she shouted, unable to restrain her anger. "How do I know you haven't killed her? How do I know you're not just fucking with me?"

"You don't," said Drake coldly.

"Then I'm done." Allegra hung up.

Michael looked at her in shock. "*What* are you doing?" he asked angrily.

"He'll call back."

"And if he doesn't?" The aggression in Michael's

voice was strangely comforting in its authority. As Allegra began to respond, her phone rang again.

"You pull a trick like that again and I'll cut her like a fish!" said Drake's furious voice. He walked to Reese's limp figure and pulled her forward by the scruff of her neck. He jammed the phone next to her and barked, "Talk!"

Reese's eyes rolled lazily in her head. Snatches of words and phrases swam on her tongue. With a beatific smile, she said, "Have no fear, little one."

Allegra cried out, struck by both relief and anguish. "Reese! Reese, are you okay? Where are you?"

Reese blinked. "Jump Jerry." She rolled back lazily, her head hitting the filthy pillow with a soft thud.

"Reese? Where are you? What do you see? Tell me where you are."

"Uh uh uh," Drake's voice was back on the line. "Naughty naughty."

"Drake!" Allegra screamed angrily. "Tell me where she is!"

"All shall be revealed in time, Angel, but for now, you must be punished."

"Drake!" she screamed, but it was too late – he was gone. She cried out in fear and frustration. Michael touched her shoulder but she batted his hand away. "No!" she screamed. "Leave me alone." She turned towards the wall as angry tears streamed down her face. What were they going to do now?

Allegra balanced the three cups of coffee and pushed open the door to Michael's office. Placing them on the table, she looked at Sienna's haggard form. She wanted to reassure her, to tell her that they had something else, but the agents were getting nowhere. Drake had been meticulous in his planning, letting them see only what he wanted them to.

She blew on her hot coffee and took a sip, immediately scalding her tongue. Wearily, she placed the cup back on the table. She didn't know what to say. Sienna was always the one who knew what to do. She had always allowed Allegra to be the rebellious one, the free spirit without a care, while she took the parental role. Now, nothing made sense.

Sienna pushed a lock of dark hair off her face. With tear-stained eyes she looked at Allegra. "Tell me again. Tell me what she said."

Allegra bit her lip. "Sienna, it doesn't matter what she said. It just—"

"Tell me what she said!" Sienna's voice shook.

Allegra knew it would reconfirm Reese's drugged and disoriented state, but she did as she was asked: "She said, 'Have no fear, little one'."

Sienna nodded, struggling to control her sobs. "She didn't say she was okay?"

Allegra shook her head. It was the third time Sienna had asked the question. What else could she say?

"You know how they say when a person goes through a near-death experience, their whole life flashes before them? It's like that. I keep seeing her: the first time I held her in my arms, the first night at home, her first step, her first word, her first day at school – I can see it all. Everything up to now: her teasing her father about his greys, practising the violin, setting the table, getting frustrated when I fail to recognise the movie quotes *you* always manage to." Sienna shook her head. "I don't know what I'm going to do if we can't find her." She broke into quiet sobs.

Allegra watched Stephen comfort her sister. Memories of Reese snaked and splintered through her mind, filling her with melancholy. She could count the number of people she loved on one hand. She couldn't afford to lose one of them. Snatches of memories swam through her head. As she closed her eyes, a stray string of words ran through her mind: *Have no fear, little one.*

Sienna watched Allegra bolt upright.

"Oh, my God," she exclaimed. "How could I miss it? How could I miss it!?" She stood, wringing her hands with anxiousness. "Sienna, she was trying to tell me something and I– I didn't realise."

Sienna stood too. "What? What are you saying?"

"I need to talk to Michael. I think Reese was trying to tell me something. I think she was quoting films at me."

Sienna shook her head, confused. "But she didn't make sense."

Allegra's forehead creased. "Maybe I'm reading too much into this, but maybe I'm not. I'll be back. Let me talk to Michael." She dashed out of the office.

Michael was talking to the psychologists when Allegra ran in. She waved her hand to catch his attention and breathlessly began to speak.

"Reese – I think she was trying to tell me something. Her words – I think they meant something." No one spoke so she continued: "She said, 'Have no fear, little one'." Allegra grabbed a marker and wrote the words on the whiteboard. Underneath them, she wrote 'Jump Jerry'.

"This is what she said to me. They're movie quotes – or at least I think they are. The first one – have no fear, little one – is from 'The Omen'. I just realised. The second one I've never heard, but we should be able to find out. I think she may have been trying to tell us something." The room remained silent, a dozen faces eyeing her questioningly. Allegra held up her hands, palm outwards, asking for patience. "We play this game, Reese and I; this 'Movie Quote' game where we quote from a movie and challenge the other to name it. Like 'Keep your friends close but your enemies closer'."

"The Godfather," said Michael.

Allegra pointed at him. "Exactly! I think that's what she was trying to do."

Drury immediately started typing. After a few seconds, he said, "'Jump Jerry. Jump now'. Jerry Shaw from 'Eagle Eye'."

"Yes!" said Marianne. "I knew I knew that. I've seen 'Eagle Eye' – that's where it's from."

Allegra breathed in deeply. She wrote 'The Omen' beneath the first quote and 'Eagle Eye' beneath the second. She looked at the board blankly. "The Omen, Eagle Eye. I don't know what it means."

Marianne walked to the front and took the pen from Allegra. Next to the first quote, she wrote 'Young boy, devil, bible, priest, heaven, hell, God, religion'. Next to the second, she wrote, 'Military, computers, spies, cameras, big brother, birds, zoo?' After reviewing the list, she added 'church' to the first list.

"Drury, cross-check this stuff. Look for churches on military bases or near zoos, or those that have a bird's name in their title – anything that links these two lists," instructed Michael.

Drury, fingers flying over his keyboard, nodded. "I'm printing out a list of churches near or on military bases as we speak. You're going to be getting a list of churches in Eye, Peterborough, in one minute. I'm also running a search on churches or churchyards near the London Eye. Keep throwing ideas at me."

Marianne turned to Allegra. "Does any of this mean anything to you? We may end up with hundreds of possibilities. We need something else."

Allegra surveyed the lists. "Can I bring Sienna in? It may mean something to her." She looked to Michael for an answer but he was engrossed in a police file. His face was pale and drawn, and had deep worry lines across it as if aged by the past few hours.

He said nothing so Marianne responded: "Yes, but

Drake will have taken Reese to a place that means something to either him or to you so it's more likely that you'll be the one to figure it out. Keep looking at it – I'll get Sienna."

A few moments later, Sienna and Stephen were surveying the board with the same flummoxed expression as Allegra. Sienna shook her head. "We don't go to church." She stopped. "We went to Vatican City last year," her voice rose. "He couldn't have taken her abroad, could he?"

"No. Definitely not. Keep thinking," said Marianne.

"She's never even spoken to a priest. We have a bible but more for interest than faith. We've never been near a military base. We went to London Zoo a few years ago but I can't see how that would be related to any of this."

Allegra made a copy of the lists, handed it to Sienna and led her back to Michael's office. She didn't want her sister to sit through the chaos in the hub – she needed her to stay calm. With words of reassurance, she retreated from the office and rejoined the agents.

Taking a seat next to Marianne, she stared at the whiteboard blankly. How would this day end? What if they never found her? What if Drake disappeared? Would Sienna forgive her? Her head buzzed with words but she failed to string them into sentences. She willed herself to stay awake, to open her eyes, to stay focused but sleep and exhaustion clung to her eyelids, weighing them down. *When will this nightmare end?*

It was Michael, with three magical words, that ripped her from sleep: "I've got it."

Eyes snapping open, she saw him wave a file at them.

"It's in here. It was always in here. I can't believe I didn't see it before." Marianne looked at the file over Michael's shoulder but he snapped it shut and turned to Drury. "Get a team ready. I know where he's taken her. There's little time to explain but the only time Jemima Bradbury was ever left alone in public was at her local church – St. Mary's in Hampstead. I was sure that's where Drake met her so I went there to find witnesses but there were none. It was bought out by a construction company early last year but it's lain dormant since then. I think that's where he's taken Reese."

Drury shook his head. "But other than a physical likeness, there's no link between Reese and his past victim. Why would he take her there?"

It was Marianne who answered: "If Jemima was his first victim, the setting of their first meeting would hold a special meaning for Drake. It would conjure feelings of power and intensity. After being betrayed by Amy Petronas, it would be natural for him to revert to a place where he felt strong and powerful; a place that allowed him to exercise his compulsions and build a relationship where he held all the power. In that place, he feels like a God."

Drury's brow furrowed. "But what if that's a fluke? How can we be sure?"

"There's one more thing," Michael paused as the

room quietened. "There's a stained glass window that spans the entire north side of the church. Spread across it, is a sixteen-feet wide eagle."

Michael looked at Allegra's messy hair, her crumpled black dress and her shoeless feet. "Hey," he said gently. She turned and looked at him with sad eyes. "Listen, this time, I don't want any arguments. You're staying in the car."

She shook her head. "Michael, I've been trained for situations like this. I can handle myself."

He touched her arm lightly. "You followed me out of the car last time. This time, I'm not going to let you do that."

"What are you going to do, cuff me?"

"Don't tempt me." A faint smile spread across his lips. "Seriously though, the other team's stuck in traffic. We can't wait – Reese's been alone with him for long enough – but I can't put you in danger. You need to stay here."

"Please Michael," she started to protest.

He placed a finger across her lips, silencing her. "You need to stay here," he said firmly.

With a sigh, she relented. "Okay." As he left the car, she grabbed his arm. "Michael."

"Yeah?" he seemed breathless.

"Please find her."

He placed a hand over hers and nodded. Pulling back, he let her hand drop to the seat and closed the door with a soft thud.

CHAPTER TEN

The giant eagle loomed above him, deepening the pile of shadows that stretched across the room. Michael coughed in the thick air, feeling it coat his lungs with dirt, dust and secret confessions. His Gucci shoes squeaked on the floor as he crept towards the altar. Allegra's words rang in his ears, a single pitiful plea: please find her.

He was alone. Against all his instincts and all his procedures, he was here alone. It had to be this way – he alone had to find a way out. His eyes adjusted to the darkness as he searched the quarters in the back, creeping through the rooms like a thief in a temple. Thirty minutes into his search, he came to the final room at the east end of the building. Tentatively, he placed an ear against the thick wooden door. Instead of blazing in, gun drawn, he quietly turned the handle and pushed. The door's slow and extended creak cut at his nerves. With a deep breath, he stepped into the room. The familiar smell of old books, yellowing and curling at their aged corners, made him feel nauseous. He surveyed the large mahogany desk, majestic and forgotten on the faded red carpet. He looked behind the filthy curtains and inside the drawers, until finally, he found what he was looking for; a clue, an indication, an invitation.

Four lines were cut into the carpet beneath the desk, connected in a small but perfect square. He pulled up the fabric to reveal a trapdoor. Reaching forward to open it, he found that his hands were shaking. Unable to stop them, he straightened and walked to the window, taking quick, short breaths to calm himself. He was a professional, experienced in situations like this – why did he feel so nervous? He thought of Allegra and her pretty hazel eyes, entrusting him with everything she had. He needed to do this now. He had put it off for long enough.

He slid four fingers beneath the small handle of the trapdoor and pulled it hard. The door opened noiselessly, allowing him to survey the dark stairs beneath him. Beads of sweat crept down his face, defying the pre-dawn chill in the air. He wiped his forehead, gun in hand, and began to descend the stairs. His heart drummed in his chest, squeezed tight by a pervasive dread. Reaching the final step, he paused and listened for sound. With a ragged breath, he stepped onto the cold concrete floor, his heart thudding harder with each step forward.

The basement was shaped in a large, back-to-front 'L' with several massive pillars unevenly dotted around it. The walls and pillars seemed to be carved straight from stone. Layers of dust had settled everywhere. The dank smell made Michael's head swim. He could hear the quiet drip-drip drip-drip of water somewhere in the distance. He pulled at his tie, silently wishing he had discarded it in the car.

As he reached the joint of the 'L', he pressed his back against the wall. *He's here. He has to be here.* Heart racing, he took a deep breath and tore round the corner, gun aimed dead ahead. In the same instance, a blinding light shone into his eyes, making him shield them instinctively. Blinking, he regained his composure, gun still straight ahead. When his eyes readjusted to the dim light, his heart froze. There, unconcerned, unabashed, and undisturbed, stood Joseph Drake.

"Agent Stallone. Finally face to face. It is a pleasure," said Drake mockingly.

"Put your hands up," Michael's voice wavered just a touch.

Drake laughed a slow, leisurely laugh. He hooked his thumbs into the pockets of his jeans and took a few steps towards Michael. "Come on, there's no need for that," he said casually.

"Where's the girl?"

Drake smiled wistfully. "Always the serious one." His face turned suddenly solemn. "I do mean it. It's really good to see you, Mike."

Michael's lips stretched in a thin line. He kept the gun trained on Drake. "Where is she?"

"She's safe, I promise."

"Show me," he demanded.

"Hey, you know you can trust me," said Drake, voice loaded with sincerity.

Michael shook his head. "Tell me where she is or I'll blow out your kneecaps, I swear to God."

Drake smiled. "Come on, we both know you're too soft for that."

"Tell me where she is!" Michael's voice reverberated across the chamber.

"Reese is safe." He paused. "I would rather talk about Allegra." He stretched out her name, rolling it off his tongue. "I have to tell you, Mike, you sure did serve up a fine cut with her; a 100% pure and genuine slice of succulent Kobe beef." He laughed out loud. "For that, I must laud you." He clapped his hands loudly, each clap as loud as a bullet.

Michael swallowed hard and blinked away the pool of sweat on his lashes. "How did you find her?"

"Why would I need to find her when you gave her to me? A juicy little lamb sent right to the lion's den – you knew what you were doing."

"Joseph, you need help."

Drake snorted. "And you don't?"

Michael ignored the question. "How did you find Reese? How long were you grooming her?"

Drake laughed. "It was so fucking easy."

"Tell me where she is, Joe. Just tell me where she is and I'll talk to the people above me. We'll sort out a deal."

"I don't want a deal!" he shouted.

Michael looked at him pleadingly. "What do you want, Joe? There's no other way out now."

"I wasn't looking for a way out."

"What were you looking for?"

"Revenge. Absolution."

"Revenge and absolution? There will be no absolution for you. Not from me, not from the courts, not from Amy," said Michael bitterly.

Drake shook his head. "I was happy to admit what I did to Amy. If I had hurt her, I would have paid my dues but I cannot accept the stinging betrayal. Do you have any idea what I felt for her? Do you have any idea what it was like for me? Putting the sweetest thing in front of me and then ripping it away, telling me it didn't even exist in the first place. Do you have any idea?!" Drake thundered.

Michael pointed the gun directly at Drake's right knee and repeated, "Tell me where she is."

"Oh, you go ahead and shoot me, Agent Stallone." He held up a palm-sized box with two tiny red levers inserted on top. "All I have to do is pull this and it will snap her neck in half."

Michael shook his head. "You're bluffing."

"Oh, you want to test your theory? Come on!" shouted Drake, eyes bulging. "Come on, shoot me!"

Blood pounded in Michael's head. He had to do this the right way. "Okay," he said. "Okay, let's do it your way." He slowly bent down and placed the gun on the floor. "We're doing it your way, okay?"

Drake smiled. "I told you – too soft." He sat on the floor and gestured at Michael to do the same. "I'm impressed, Mike, and, if I'm honest, a little bit disappointed. I had planned another round of fun before this – your brain obviously works faster than I ever gave you credit for." He paused and smiled. "I remember everything, Mike. I remember coming second in that class test and, even though I resented it, from that moment, I knew I'd found you; the brother I never had. Even back then, we looked alike – people said it all the time, remember?"

Michael's face contorted in a disgusted snarl. "Brothers? You call us brothers?"

"Yes," Drake said without hesitation. "Brothers in arms watching out for each other, covering each other's backs, serving each other perfect slices of juicy steak." He paused. "I feel your pain, Mike. I've always felt your pain. You and I, we're connected irrevocably and infinitely."

Michael shook his head. "You need help."

"And so do you. That's why we're both here. I saw you, Mike. I saw how desperately you wanted your father's approval. I watched your heart break when he looked at you in that disgusted way. It almost made me glad I never had a father."

Michael shook his head. "Joe, just tell me where she is."

"Alessandro Stallone, big-deal multi-millionaire steel tycoon. It killed me to see him send you away – to send *us* away." Drake paused to steady his voice. "He should have helped us, Mike. He should have *helped* us." He looked around the vast space as if searching for something or someone. "Every night, Mike. We told your father about it and he did nothing – to save face, he did nothing!"

Michael shook his head. "Joe, please. Just– just stop."

"You remember our first Mass? Proud little choir boys, eager to serve and please? And then, down here, *every* night. First me, then you. You know I tried to satisfy him, Mike. You know I tried to keep him from you."

Michael felt something break inside him. He remembered the dogged eagerness in Joseph's eyes; the way he always went to Father Salvato first, full of contrived zeal, constructed from a twisted loyalty to Michael. Even as he felt his skin rip, he would keep quiet, masking pain with feigned pleasure. Whatever he tried though, Michael, who always fought, was Father Salvato's favourite. Michael, with his anger and vigour, proved to be far more satisfying.

As words and images flooded his mind, Michael held back tears even as his voice broke. "Every night," he whispered.

Drake watched him shake. Old loyalties made him want to hold his friend, to tell him that everything would be okay, but new divisions lay between then, holding them apart.

Michael remembered their year of terror – they had been a mere nine years old. He remembered how they finally built the courage to tell his father and the instant reaction; the shame and embarrassment. There was anger, sure, and calls for retribution, yes, but instead of understanding, there was disgust and instead of support, there was abandonment.

"The blood is gone," said Drake, watching Michael's eyes. "For an entire year, it was there. I know because I looked at it every night. Blood from your body dripping and splashing to the floor, drying, blackening, weaving the very fabric of this room. For a whole year, he left it there, a constant reminder of his power and our pain. It's gone, Mike. I looked for it. It's gone."

Michael said nothing.

"It's important for you to know that. I moved on in my own way but I know it still festers in you so you should know that it's gone. His power is gone."

Michael wiped away angry tears. "You didn't move on, Joe. Neither of us did. How could we?"

"Oh, but I did, Mike. I learnt to release my anger, remember?" Drake stood and took a few steps back. "I'm going to help you find that release. I'm going to serve you up a slice of juicy, delicious Kobe beef and let you eat it right up."

Michael stood on unstable legs, pushing away his memories. He didn't want to remember. He couldn't. "Joe, please. All I want is the girl." Drake moved a few steps to his right. As if on opposite ends of a giant circle, Michael too moved to his right.

Drake smiled. "I know you want her, Mike. I know exactly how much you want her. She's like nothing else, true? Her skin, so creamy and soft – irresistible. Her hair, like feathers, and those eyes!" He sighed deeply. "Well, you don't need me to tell you."

Michael shook his head angrily. "What have you done to her, Joe? She's 13! What makes you better than–" He stopped, words choking his throat.

Drake burst out laughing. "You're *over* it, Mike? All these years and you still can't say his name?" He took another step to the right.

"Please Joe, I just want the girl. She's innocent in all this."

Drake shook his head. "See, that's what I thought too but no – it was a mask weaved from deception and betrayal." He moved another few steps to the right, forcing Michael to do the same.

The view behind the pillar was suddenly visible, hitting Michael like an axe in the skull. There, strung to the ceiling, was Reese's naked, limp body covered by an intricate web of knots. A thick piece of rope was tied across her neck, with the other end secured to a ceiling beam. Her wrists were bound together by her groin. Three thinner lengths of ropes snaked across her body, from her shoulders down to her stomach and then between her legs. Like a horrific accident you just can't look away from, the scene captivated Michael. As if in a trance, he took a few steps closer.

"Wonderful, isn't it?" Drake beamed with pride. "Japanese rope bondage – genius in the way it utilises one's weight to cause pressure in the most... tender of places. See how she lies still, restricting her movement so the splintery rope doesn't cut her. See how she tiptoes to lift her cunt off the line?"

Michael, numbed with horror, was frozen to the spot.

"See the genius of these thinner ropes? See how they lie on each side of the labia; how they squeeze and tighten, forcing her juicy pussy to protrude between them?" Drake leaned down and licked one of her folds.

She jerked back, cries of pain bursting from her gagged mouth. Her head snapped up sharply.

Michael felt his heart seize. The girl – it wasn't Reese. *I told her to stay in the car. I told her to—*

Drake burst out laughing. "Oh, if you could only see your face!"

Michael stormed towards him.

"Uh-uh." Drake held up the box in his hand. "It's not Reese's pieces you'll get but your beloved Allegra's." He pulled one of the levers and a wooden plank, beneath the one Allegra was balanced on, snapped apart. "Guess which one's next?"

"Let her down." Michael couldn't think for the fury

321

coursing through his body. "You let her down you fucking sick bastard!"

Drake looked at him sympathetically. "But Mike, it's okay. She understands now. She knows why you made her do all those things she didn't want to. She knows you had your demons to fight."

Michael met Allegra's eyes. Rather than terror, he found a deep sadness; a strange wistfulness or perhaps even resignation. "Allegra, it's going to be okay. I'm going to get you out of here, okay?" he assured. Her head dropped again, exhausted, defeated.

"Of course you're going to get our little angel out of here. But she hasn't heard the full story yet, Mike. You want to tell it to her?"

Michael stepped back towards the gun. "Tell her what?"

Drake smiled. "You know what. Tell her about Winchester."

Michael took another step back. He had to do something. "Joe, please."

Drake held Allegra's left leg and pulled it, causing her to scream in excruciation as the splintery rope cut her between the legs.

Michael lunged forward. "Stop! Stop! Joe, please!"

"Then tell her!" he screamed, tugging her again. This time her face turned crimson with pain and muffled screams.

"Okay, please!" Michael held out his hands in a desperate plea.

Drake nodded. After a moment's silence, he gripped her leg again. "I'm waiting."

Michael took a deep breath. "Okay." He looked at Allegra. "Everything you've heard about what happened here is true. We–" he hesitated. How could he unfurl all the years of secrets and shame he had wound up tightly inside him?

Drake yanked Allegra's leg again. This time, she jerked up, one leg disconnecting from the plank of wood. Her body convulsed with panic and pain as her leg lashed to find footing. Her cries of anguish continued even after her toes found solidity. She looked at Michael with pitiful eyes. *Please,* they seemed to be saying. *Please make it stop.*

"Joe," Michael held out a hand. "Please. I'll do it." He watched Allegra's tiny, vulnerable frame strung up like a piece of meat. Her breasts were shiny with sweat. A bead collected between them and drizzled down slowly, leisurely. It was an eternity before it dissolved into her navel. With a deep, ragged breath, Michael began.

"We were nine years old the first time it happened. He– he asked me and Joe to help him carry some books to his office upstairs. Everyone wanted to please him – we all worshipped him as if he were God Himself. We came down here and I remember not feeling right. Even then, even before anything happened, I knew something was wrong." He paused. "He started to talk to us about brotherly love; about how God wanted us to be kind to each other; to love each other and pleasure each other. He told us that touching ourselves was wrong but that... if someone else did it, it was okay."

Michael's eyes flickered to the floor. He couldn't bear to look at Allegra. With a deep breath, he continued: "He told Joe to touch me... We were both terrified. When we didn't move, he took Joe's hand and... He said that if we didn't help each other, God would punish us; that if we didn't touch each other, we'd be compelled to touch ourselves. He made us do it." Michael paused. "Afterwards, Joe and I didn't talk to each other about it – we couldn't. I thought it had been a one time thing but the next time, he said that he would help us as long as we helped him and... it began." Michael watched Allegra shift on the plank, pain creasing her childlike features.

"It went on for a year. He began to get more and more violent. The things he made us do," Michael's voice wavered. "I couldn't sleep at night, haunted by visions of the two of us, kneeling in front of him, shaking and choking. He would... he would make us kneel, mouths touching while wide open so that he could slip himself into the hole in between. If we didn't use our tongues, he would dig his nails into our scalps and rip out whole handfuls of hair." Michael took a few short, sharp breaths.

"One night, Joe pulled me aside. He said we either had to kill him or kill ourselves. That's when I knew we had to tell someone." Michael coughed, shaking his voice free of splinters and cracks.

"My father, Alessandro Stallone, reacted so badly when he heard about what had happened. He was a well-known businessman, brought up as Catholic – things like this just weren't spoken of. When I told him, he– he was," Michael shook his head. "He couldn't even look at me. He sent me and Joseph to school in Hampshire. I barely saw him or spoke with him for five years. The holidays he allowed me to come home, he was always working. I told myself he did it so he wouldn't miss my mother but I knew the truth – he couldn't bear to be around me. He didn't know what to say to me and so it festered and festered and made everything worse."

Michael ran a hand through his hair. He couldn't believe he was speaking about this after so many years. "I got angrier and angrier. The only person that knew what was happening was Joe." He glanced at Drake, unable to reign in the flicker of gratitude. "It haunted me, Allegra. You have to understand how bad it was. I couldn't sleep, I couldn't eat. I dropped to eight stones. I had nightmares every single night."

Allegra's eyes were wet with sympathy. She finally understood why Michael was so dogged in his work, so passionate and so focused.

"Through years of school, I spiralled down," Michael continued. "I tried drink and drugs – nothing worked. Joe and I would go out together and women would come onto us but we'd be afraid – we were always afraid. But then one day," he paused, "we were walking in the New Forest National Park and... we saw this girl."

Allegra stiffened. She struggled to stay on her tiptoes, exhausted from her tussle with Drake.

"She was petite, dark-haired, beautiful. For a second, we actually thought it was Elina." He paused and met Allegra's eyes. "Elina was Salvato's daughter from before priesthood." The name 'Salvato' felt like a hot coal on his tongue. He felt it burn through the floor of his mouth, down his throat and into his stomach. There it burned with agony and unbridled fury.

"We–" Michael hesitated. "Elina was a few younger than us and when we saw this girl – about 14 or 15 – just walking alone in the park, we were... drawn to her."

Allegra shifted on the plank. *What did you do?* she wanted to ask. *Please God, what did they do?*

"Go on," urged Drake, taking a step closer to Allegra's body.

Michael nodded. "We were drawn to her – we couldn't help ourselves. She had always been this unreachable deity, walking around with this ethereal layer of protection. She was her father's princess – nothing could touch her or hurt her. When we saw her, we couldn't help ourselves."

Allegra started to shake. *What did you do?*

"We were calm at first, breathing in her scent, flirting with her. She was alone with two male strangers but she wasn't startled in the least – as if she too were beneath Elina's protective cloak. She enjoyed preening under our attention, playing us off each other – giving one a smile, the other a wink, a subtle hand on an arm. She knew we wanted her; she wanted us to. I touched her cheek – I couldn't help myself. She giggled and said my hands were soft, like a girl's. Joe grabbed her arms and said, 'What about this? Do I feel like a girl?'" Michael's eyes glazed over as his mind travelled to the past.

"She laughed, enjoying every second of it. She said, 'Not a girl, no, but not exactly a man'. Joe was insulted so he grabbed her hard, turned her around and pushed her against a tree. It was then that she realised we weren't kidding around. Joe held her against the tree by the back of her neck. She had on this tiny yellow vest with denim shorts. It didn't take long to undress her. Her breasts were unlike any we'd seen; soft and pert and delicious. Joe went first. When he offered her to me, I couldn't stop myself. I felt light-headed like in a dream."

Allegra twisted on the plank, crying out in anguish. "How could you?" The tape across her mouth turned her scream of accusation into an unintelligible moan. "How could you?!" she screamed again, her body convulsing with disgust.

Michael shook his head, as if caught in a trance. "She took away the years of anger and frustration. She helped us release it all." He glanced at Drake. "By the time we finished, she was a bloody mess. I didn't know what to do. I wanted to run away but I knew we couldn't." He caught the horror in Allegra's eyes and shook his head. "No, no, no – we didn't kill her." He looked to Drake for reassurance. "Joe, he– he *talked* to her, made her understand that if she told anyone, we would come back for her. We dragged her to the lake and doused her in water to clean her up. We dried her and dressed her and," he paused. "The kisses were amazing. Her lips – so soft – were quivering as we said goodbye. It was amazing."

He exhaled deeply and continued: "The relief didn't last for long. Afterwards, I felt sick with guilt but Joe was strong. Joe was calm and steadfast. He kept me under his wing and looked after me, but I couldn't get over it. I was haunted by that girl's face, by her pleas and cries for help. I knew I had to do something to make it right and so I started looking into law. I convinced myself that Joe was sick – that my way was the only way I could heal – but I look back and realise that, through all my years as a teen, that time with that girl was the only time I ever felt alive."

Michael looked at Allegra with strange, vacant eyes and took a subtle step towards Drake. She watched the exchange of smiles between them; smiles of solidarity and mutual understanding. In horror, she realised that Michael was switching allegiances.

Drake looked at him with affection. "This time, you can go first."

Michael smiled. "Come now, Joe. Let's not break

with tradition." He held out a magnanimous hand towards Allegra.

Drake shook his head. "I know how much you want her, Mike. From the moment you laid eyes on her, I could see lust weighing down your every movement. I won't make you wait a moment longer."

Michael shook his head too. "It wouldn't feel right, Joe. After everything you've done for me, I owe you this."

Drake's face was cold with conviction. "Mike, I want you to have her. I want to watch."

After a moment's hesitation, Michael nodded. A flicker of gratitude flitted across his face as he took a tentative step towards Allegra.

She shook her head, feeling the rope cut into her neck and shoulders, setting fire to her skin. Moans of horror curled forth from her bound mouth. "No!" she screamed. "Michael, no!"

"Enjoy her, Mike. Look at the way she quivers. Look at her breasts, the way they shine. Look at her juicy pussy lips, soaking wet. Taste her, Mike. Take her and fuck her, the way you want to."

Allegra shook her head, trembling with disgust and fear. How could he do this? After everything she had done for him? Had he been a monster all along? Hidden behind his mask of respectability and self-righteousness?

"Michael, please," she tried to say. "Please don't."

Her cries fell on deaf ears. Michael, eyes alight with

desire, reached out and slid a finger between her legs, touching her in long, gentle strokes. He looked up at her but she had her eyes closed, lids creased with anger and hatred. "Look at me, Allegra. I want you to look at me." When she didn't respond, he asked her again. "Allegra, please."

She shook her head as tears fell from unseeing eyes.

"Forget that," interrupted Drake. "Just do what you want, Mike. I know you're dying to taste her, the way you tasted Elina."

Michael trembled as he stepped forward. "I do, Joe. I want her so much." He traced the ropes tied between her legs and then leaned forward and started to lick her.

Allegra cried out in anger. They were going to kill her. How were they going to get away with this if they didn't kill her?

Michael's tongue grew hungrier. He dipped it inside her, flicking it in and out rapidly. She struggled to get away from him but it only made the ropes cut deeper. His tongue travelled over the lines of rope, licking every part of her. He reached up and placed his hands behind her, squeezing as he lapped her up.

"I want you," he murmured. "Allegra, I've wanted you from the moment I met you. I've dreamt about this again and again." He dipped his tongue in and out. "I watched you on camera with Joe but I wanted to feel you for myself. Having your pussy for the first time – it's making me crazy."

Allegra felt bile rise in her throat. She shook her head madly. She thought of vomit springing up her throat, only to find no way out, forcing her to swallow again. The thought itself made her retch.

Michael reached between his legs and started to touch himself as he licked her. His movements grew rapid as his breathing grew deeper.

"Fuck her, Mike. Fuck her brains out," said Drake.

Michael shook his head, lost in Allegra. "I just want to taste her. I just want to taste that juicy pussy of hers."

Drake laughed. "Come now, Mike. Let's not break with tradition. Remember how hard you fucked Elina? I know you want her, Mike. Do it."

He shook his head again. "I just want to–"

"The plank is strong enough to support your weight – I've tested it." Drake nodded in encouragement as Michael looked back at him. "Do it. I watch to watch."

Michael looked up at Allegra, still with her eyes closed. He grabbed the wooden frame and tested his weight on the plank. When it held steady, he launched himself onto it. He looked back at Drake. "Thank you," he mouthed. He undid his zip and held Allegra's hips.

Her eyes snapped open and she bucked against him. "No!" she screamed with anguish. "No!"

"Do it, Mike. Do it," said Drake.

"No!" screamed Allegra.

Michael grabbed her hair and plunged in, feeling her convulse around him. Tears streamed down her face as he balanced himself against her. He could smell her musky sweat and feel her juices coating him. It made him thrust harder and deeper as her muffled screams rang in his ears.

Allegra, lost in pain and humiliation, stepped outside herself. It was the only thing that would stop her from breaking. She closed her eyes as Michael grunted against her. All this time, she had trusted him. She had listened to him and followed him and relied on him and now... Now they would kill her. They would kill Reese and no one would ever know the truth.

Warm liquid splattered against her stomach, ripping her back to consciousness. Michael stepped off the plank and smiled at Drake beatifically. "Your turn."

Drake patted him on the back and walked to Allegra. He balanced the box on the plank and took off his shirt, revealing his toned body. He undid his zip and climbed up, wrapping his hand around Allegra's hair. He tugged it back, making her cry out in pain. "I was gentle with Amy because I loved her, but you – you I'm going to rip into pieces." He thrust into her with all his might, making her scream. As she struggled against him, he reached down and knocked her legs off the plank, making her body grind down onto his. She thrashed to find footing but Drake had raised her a few inches, making it impossible. As rope cut deep into her throat, she was forced to wrap her legs around him, using his body for support and balance. He held her tight and thrust deep, enjoying this new level of intimacy.

Michael felt nauseous with guilt. *I had to – I had no choice.* When he was sure that Drake wouldn't see, he rushed forward and grabbed the black box off the plank. Throwing it out of reach, he charged towards Drake and tore him off Allegra. Her legs hit the wood with a loud thwack, making her ankle twist sickeningly.

Michael was all over Drake in an instant, punching his face as hard as he could. Blood splattered across Michael's face as Drake spat at him. He smashed a fist into Drake's left ear, making him scream with rage. It was followed by another fist against his nose, already a pulpy mess.

Instead of fighting back, Drake lay there. He began to laugh as Michael smashed his face with fist after fist. "Soft hands!" he cried. "Like a girl's!" Angry knuckles shattered a cheekbone, but his words continued to pour. "I should have known! I should have fucking known! Even your dick was soft when you thumbed it in."

Michael stood and kicked him in the stomach. As Drake doubled up, Michael stamped on him, hearing ribs crunch apart.

Allegra, barely conscious, watched in horror as reams of blood patterned the grey floor. *It had been an act?* She heard Michael's plea in her ear – *Look at me, Allegra* – and suddenly understood his clue: *Having your pussy for the first time – it's making me crazy.* Why hadn't she understood? An initial rush of relief quickly gave way to pulsating anger. *How could he have done it? How?*

Michael was straddling Drake now. Pounding punch after punch into his face, neck and shoulders, he was lost in fury.

"Keep going, Mike. Keep going 'til you kill me."

The words pulled Michael out of his rage. If he didn't stop, he really was going to kill him. Leaning back, he steadied his breathing to calm himself. As he raised himself off Drake, bloodied and sweaty, he heard the sudden click of a gun's safety being switched off. He looked down to see a barrel pointed right up at him.

Drake laughed. "An ankle holster? Really, Mike? How quaintly clichéd." Another laugh made bubbles of blood drip down the side of his mouth. "I loved her, Mike. I really loved her."

Michael raised his hands and backed away slowly. "Joe—"

"Shut up!" screamed Drake. "Shut the fuck up! You betrayed me. You and Amy and her!" He pointed his gun at Allegra. "You all betrayed me. I can't— I won't take it anymore." He pulled himself up, slowly, painfully, and wiped his bloody face with a bare arm. "You have to understand that I loved her. I can't take it anymore." He turned to Michael. "You know what's it like, Mike – not being able to connect, only finding solace in the most harmless of women. What can I do if that makes me the harmful one? I can't do it anymore." With weariness in his eyes, Drake turned the gun around and pointed it against his own temple.

"No!" shouted Michael. "Joe, wait!"

"Save your concern!" he shouted. "The girl is here. I didn't touch her."

Allegra twisted her head round to the back of the room. "Reese!" she screamed. Her muffled cry barely reached the far wall. Tears of exhaustion streamed down her face as rope burns cut her everywhere.

"I couldn't touch her," said Drake. "I was going to string her up when your darling Allegra came tripping happily along, making everything far more interesting." He spat out a mouthful of blood. "I loved you," he said to Allegra. "I loved you – that's why I was with you but all I did was hurt you." He looked at Michael. "You too, Mike. I loved you too."

"Joe–" The air shattered as the bullet crashed into Drake's head, splitting it open with a sickening gush. After a motionless beat, he hit the floor with a slippery thud.

Michael watched the pool of blood spread across the floor, covering the stains and pains of years gone by. Exhausted, he turned to Allegra and stumbled forward. Using the in-built knife in his watch, he began to slowly, carefully cut her down. When she could finally speak, she coughed out only one syllable: "Reese."

Michael undid the three ropes cutting across Allegra's groin. "We'll go to her when you're free."

She shook her head.

"Do you really want her to see you like this?" he asked. "I'm going to radio the other team to find out where they are. I don't want anyone else to see you like this."

She nodded exhaustedly as the ropes fell away, freeing her from their torture. She crumpled forward into Michael's arms. "I tried, Michael. I tried to fight him. I tried everything I was taught but he was too strong."

"Hey, ssh, it's ok." Michael covered her with his jacket.

Clutching it tightly, she limped to the next room. As Drake had promised, Reese was there, gagged and bound, but largely untouched. With a cry, Allegra rushed to her niece and knelt by her side. Gently, she removed the tape from her mouth as Michael cut through the binding ropes.

Reese blinked as she came out of her daze. "Allegra?"

"It's me. It's me." She pulled Reese out of the chair and into her arms. "Oh, my God. Thank God you're alright. Thank God you're okay." Tears ran down her face as she looked at her niece's pale skin. She neatened a stray hair on her head and then kissed her cheek. "I love you," she said with a quiet sob.

Reese leaned back out of the embrace. "Ditto," she said quietly.

Allegra wiped her tears. "'Ghost'. Patrick Swayze to Demi Moore," she said, still sobbing.

Reese nodded with a weak smile.

Allegra enveloped her in a hug. "I'm going to get you out of here."

As they walked out of the church, the second Vokoban team pulled up with an ambulance in tow.

Allegra helped Reese into the back and began to climb in after her. As she did so, she felt Michael's hand on her arm, pulling her around towards him.

"Allegra, I–"

She drew back and, with all her might, slapped him across the face. "Don't you *ever* touch me again." She yanked her arm out of his grip, climbed into the ambulance, and slammed the door shut.

As she lay there, Reese thought back over the last 11 hours of her life. Everything was hazy and one memory melted into another. She remembered his voice on her phone, wishing her luck, begging to see her one last time before her solo. She remembered creeping out against her better judgement to see this dark, handsome stranger that had taken an interest in her. She remembered the door slamming shut and the feeling of sudden panic as the tyres squealed away. The drive had been long. They had stopped once to get food. He had given her water and shortbread biscuits. She had thought about her mother then and had cried. He had been sympathetic but then turned angry and told her that she "deserved it". *What did I do?* she remembered thinking.

He turned from nice to nasty in a split second and then back again. Everything after that was hazy. She tried to picture his body on top of hers. Could she feel his hands on her? No. It was okay. *I am okay.*

It was a gentle touch but it made Sienna bolt upright with a stifled cry.

"Allegra?" she breathed hard and blinked a few times. "Did you find her?"

Allegra smoothed her sister's dishevelled hair. "She's here," she said with a smile.

Sienna cried out in relief, rousing Stephen from exhausted sleep. "Where?" She stood on shaky legs.

"She's on her way up. The medical team have checked her over – she's okay."

The door opened and a nurse led Reese's small frame, shrouded in a hospital gown, into the office. Sienna felt her chest shake. A deep sob echoed across the room as she began to cry tears of relief. She rushed to her daughter and swept her up. "Reese, my beautiful Reese. Thank God." She felt Stephen's arms around them both as they wept in sorrow and relief. They had found her and she was safe. They were never going to let her go again.

Allegra watched them, clinging to each other for safety and support. *My family.* She limped over and wrapped her arms around them. Together, they wept in sadness and happiness.

Marianne watched Allegra reach for a paper clip. "Have you spoken to Michael about what happened yesterday?"

She shrugged. "There's nothing to talk about."

Marianne frowned. "I thought we were over this."

"Over what?"

"Over repressing emotions."

Allegra sighed. "I haven't spoken to him. I don't think I want to." She felt disgusted by the thought of talking to him.

"You don't want to or you're not ready to?"

"Either or," she said nonchalantly.

"Allegra," Marianne chided.

She closed her eyes for a long moment, stilling the emotion that shook in her chest. "I relied on him. I let him see the deepest, darkest, most pathetic parts of me and he hid everything from me like a fucking coward."

"He let you down."

"I don't know why I'm surprised – that's what happens," she said bitterly.

Marianne shook her head. "Don't do that. Don't slip back under that cover, no matter how comfortable it may feel. Allegra, you have been let down a lot in your life – I know that – but it's time to let it go. You have to stop fighting everyone and everything. You have to stop pushing people away just because you think they're going to leave eventually anyway."

Allegra glanced at the wall clock. "Our hour's up."

Marianne shook her head. "I don't have anything lined up. Stay. Talk to me."

Allegra stood. "Next week," she said softly before turning around and walking out.

Allegra sat on the sofa with a paper pad in her lap. She neatly wrote three names on three different lines:

Jonathan Malone, Luka Karev, Christian Taylor. She wanted her old life back and these were the people who would help her get it. With Jonathan's permission, and Luka and Christian's help, she planned to set up a new graphics design company similar to ImageBox. She had never been happier than when she was working there. Now that she had left Vokoban, she had a chance to start something of her own, something she could enjoy and love, something that would help her heal.

Sienna and Stephen insisted on investing money in the venture. Together, they would create something special, Sienna had said.

Allegra thought of her sister and the way grey hairs had begun to spring from her roots. The last week had taken its toll but her family was still there, intact and content. Reese had been to see a therapist. She was shaken from the ordeal but her scars would heal quickly. She was still the same sparky, sprightly young girl. The effect on Sienna had been more pronounced. New lines had appeared on her face overnight, her skin had lost its sheen and her eyes were heavy with disquiet. Allegra knew what it was like to live with a sense of unease; a sense that anytime, anywhere, someone could walk into your life and rip it to pieces. Maybe Sienna would heal if Allegra showed her that it was possible; that even when you've been defiled in unimaginable ways, there was still a way to be normal again.

A soft knock interrupted her thoughts. She placed

the paper pad on the coffee table and walked to the door, cracking it open after fastening the newly-fitted chain.

Despite everything – her anger and frustration and disgust – she felt her heart skip a beat when she saw him. His hair was freshly cut, just the way she liked it, and his green eyes seemed brighter than ever.

"Allegra, can I come in?" His voice was softer than before, giving him an air of humility and vulnerability.

She closed the door, undid the chain and then re-opened it. She wanted to turn him away but knew that they needed to talk if they were to get any sort of closure. He walked in, his confident stride replaced by a more subdued, self-conscious one.

"Would you like something to drink?" she asked.

"No thank you."

She smiled wryly. Only the British would be so polite in the face of so much tension. "Please sit." She waited for him to speak.

"How are you?"

She scoffed. "How do you think I am?" She watched his eyes fill with sorrow and shame, and remembered what Marianne had told her: *Don't slip back under that cover, no matter how comfortable it may feel.* She sighed and said, "I'm not okay but I think I'm going to get there in time. I'm–" She tried to find the words to describe how she felt. "All my life, I've swept things away – just brushed them under the carpet. 'Suck it up' I used to tell myself. All throughout my teens, that was my mantra. Anytime I felt tears in my eyes, I told myself to 'suck it up' and move on, and that's what I've always done. I've never handed anyone the power to hurt me – not Sienna or Reese or Rafael or even Andrew.

"I thought I could take this job at Vokoban because I was made of steel – how could it possibly hurt me? I wanted to help people, yes, but that wasn't even the real reason." She met Michael's eyes. "When I met you, it was like... something clicked into place. I wanted to please you, to make you approve, to make you happy. *You* were the driving force behind everything.

"When I heard what happened to you at that church, it broke my heart, not only because of the pain you went through, but because I realised that you weren't this all-powerful being I made you out to be; you were flawed and imperfect just like everyone else. And it just kept on going. The stuff about Elina and... what you did to me. I don't know if I will ever get over it."

"Allegra–" Michael started to speak but was silenced by her raised hand.

"But I will try. And that, just that, gives me hope because before, I wouldn't even try. Before, I would put it away in another box labelled 'pain' and let it lie. So while I can't forgive you just yet, I know that one day I will."

Michael's lower lip trembled. "Allegra, I'm sorry. I shouldn't have let it get so far. I shouldn't have let us get so close and I shouldn't have lied to you." He paused, a bitter smile on his lips. "I remember seeing you for the very first time when you were in the queue, trying to buy some wine. I remember researching you and then setting up that meeting. I was so caught up in my work, I didn't realise that what I really wanted was a date." He paused. "Instead, I pulled you into all this so I could be close to you. I didn't know I was leading you into a hell." He looked at her mournfully. "I am so sorry."

She shook her head. "I'm not the only one you need to apologise to, Michael. They know about Drake and Salvato. You need to tell them about the girl in the park. You need to come clean."

Michael's face twisted with anguish. "Allegra, I–"

She interrupted him again. "I'm not going to say anything to anyone, Michael. You are not a bad man – I can see that – but because of that very fact, you will never be at peace without absolution. You sit in your high office and play God with women's lives, and you think it's going to help you sleep better at night but it won't."

She stood up. "I'm going to call you someday in the future – maybe next week, maybe next year, maybe a few years after that, but I *will* call you. Until then, I don't want to hear from you again."

Michael stood and nodded sadly. He took a small step towards her. Shadows of conflict passed over her face but she stepped forward into his arms. They embraced for a long moment. He kissed her forehead and then softly said, "Goodbye."

She wistfully watched him leave, feeling something wither inside her. Closing the door, she turned back to her paper pad. She picked up her pen and wrote three more names beneath the existing three. The first was Andrew Crawford. She now knew she could not return to Andrew – they were not right for each other – but she had to apologise for the way she had treated him. The second name was Rafael Ashe. She was determined to draw her brother back into their family unit. The third name was Antonio Ashe. In brackets, with tiny letters, she added the word 'Daddy'.

Allegra lay awake, thinking back over the past few months. She thought of Michael and the special hold he had over her. She knew she had to stay away from him but she missed his presence every day. *In time,* she told herself, *I will think of him less and less.*

She only wished she could do the same with Drake. Sometimes, in quiet moments, she would remember him and what he had done to her; the scars he had burnt onto her flesh and her soul. When a breeze brushed her leg, she would flinch. When a stranger on the tube breathed in her ear, she would jump and cower away. In time, she hoped it would get better. She knew that darkness existed in the world and that human beings would always do horrific things to each other but she needed time away from that. She needed time to heal.

For now, she would focus on herself. She turned on her side and curled her knees to her chest. *God's in His Heaven. All's right with the world.*

ACKNOWLEDGEMENTS

Firstly, I would like to thank Colin Giles who taught me at Cayley. He somehow managed to look fifteen years into the future and was the first person to tell me that I would become a writer.

Thank you to Chris Talbot of Central Foundation who was so convinced of my ability, I had to believe in it myself.

Thank you to all of those who helped me research this novel: Nazir Afzal, Mark Freedman, Kelly Lam, David Veness and Charles Whitfield. (And, of course, Larry Page and Sergey Brin.)

Thank you to Amita and Gopal Mukerjee for taking a chance on a young writer who wanted to try something different (and for putting up with my occasional bouts of insanity).

Thank you to my friends Rabika, Rita, Rashanara and Siedah who understand every word I speak even when I speak them in silence.

Faraz, thank you for showing me that new friendships can be worth just as much as old ones.

Thank you, Zeeshan. For all that you are and all that you have been.

Thank you to my father. I miss you every day.

CHILD'S PLAY

Kia Abdullah is a 27-year-old author and journalist from London. She has previously published one novel: *Life, Love and Assimilation* (2006). She contributes to a variety of popular programmes, from BBC Radio 2's *Jeremy Vine Show* to Channel 4 News. She writes for numerous publications in her typically subversive style, and is one of the youngest journalists to write comment for the *Guardian* newspaper.

ALSO FROM REVENGE INK

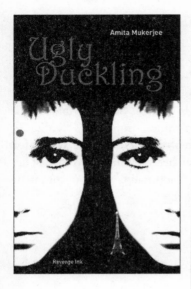

A tough-talking, funny book about being young, intelligent and out of sorts in your own life...

Naïve young Indian-American Mia Makarand is in Paris trying to start a career in translation and interpretation. But finding work is hard and she's feeling lonely and isolated. Worse yet, her dream of becoming a writer looks like it's dead in the water. But Mia is tougher than she thinks. And her sharp eye and caustic wit are helping her to see that success and happiness are important, but nowhere near as valuable as self-respect and that little thing called dignity.

ISBN 978-0-9558078-1-7

ALSO FROM REVENGE INK

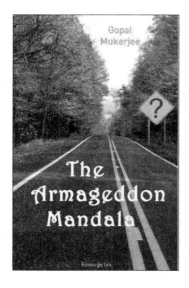

A raucously funny book about protecting nature, saving the world and recognizing your own inner hero...

Self-declared private eye Allen Ginsberg is a pleasure-loving slacker with 'nothing resembling drive or ambition'. But that's about to change. There's a stranger in town, a clownish and vaguely sinister Indian named Gyani, with a tantalizing PI gig on offer. The gig is just what the doctor ordered, except it isn't. Ginsberg soon finds himself trapped in a vortex of bizarre rituals and life-threatening ordeals that defy explanation. When all is finally revealed, Ginsberg must accept his new identity and prevent a planetary holocaust with the help of his cat Little Boy, a carrier pigeon named Kierkegaard and a 'wrasslin' alligator named Deklus Potreem.

ISBN 978-0-9558078-0-0

ALSO FROM REVENGE INK

A pretty boy's search for genuine happiness in a world of moneyed phoniness…

He's young, he's gorgeous, he's working in a perfect holiday club with all the perfect women he could want. But is Club Perfect for perfect suckers like him? Or is it for perfect vacationers cynically resigned to buying happiness? And what is happiness anyway? A sweet idealistic young man discovers it might not necessarily be found at the other end of a perfect credit card transaction. A story about sun, sea, sex and sand. And an innocent club stud who wants it all.

ISBN 978-0-9558078-3-1